Praise for Danielle Prescod

"A juicy story about the making of a dynasty and the hidden truth about to be exposed."

—Mindy Kaling

"With wit and the sharp eye of a woman who has lived through it, Prescod . . . takes the reader into the places and institutions of privilege where the idea of the Token Black Girl thrives . . . Both unsettlingly familiar and incendiary."

—Gabrielle Union

"Refreshing and brutally honest."

—*Glamour*

"Razor-sharp."

—theSkimm

"Trenchant, honest, and unique."

—*Kirkus Reviews* (starred review)

"Piercing."

—*Publishers Weekly*

"This is a book that doesn't only reflect our past but also our present, while giving us the tools to build a better future."

—Mateo Askaripour

The
RULES of
FORTUNE

OTHER TITLES BY DANIELLE PRESCOD

Token Black Girl

The
RULES of
FORTUNE

a novel

DANIELLE PRESCOD

MINDY'S BOOK STUDIO

Text copyright © 2025 by Danielle Prescod
All rights reserved.

Published by Mindy's Book Studio, New York

www.apub.com

Amazon, the Amazon logo, and Mindy's Book Studio are trademarks of Amazon.com, Inc., or its affiliates.

ISBN-13: 9781662520129 (hardcover)
ISBN-13: 9781662520143 (paperback)
ISBN-13: 9781662520136 (digital)

Cover design by Jarrod Taylor
Cover images: © NeoLeo / Getty; © David M. Schrader, © Larisa1,
© volkova natalia / Shutterstock

Printed in the United States of America

First edition

For Mommy and Daddy, who have given me everything.

Behind every fortune, there is a great crime.
—Honoré de Balzac

A NOTE FROM MINDY KALING

I'm a fan of juicy stories about secrets hiding in the (massive walk-in) closets of the wealthy. For readers who watched *Succession* with their breath held, or devoured books like *The Nest*, this fresh novel about a family in crisis won't disappoint.

Meet the Carter family. Technically new money, but I truly can't relate. They're first-generation billionaires whose level of image control rivals the royal family. They were helmed by a freshly deceased, unflinchingly calculated patriarch. He leaves behind his second-in-command, his wife, Jacqueline (my personal fave), a former beauty queen who runs the house, with an assist from some prescription helpers. Asher, their firstborn and rightful heir, is kind of a jerk and, let's face it, not the brightest crayon in the box. And finally, Kennedy, our idealistic, empathetic undergrad, blessed with talent and smarts—and she's about to find out some information that will put the whole family's reputation at risk.

Danielle Prescod weaves a tangled web of success and the lies that prop it up in *The Rules of Fortune*. Taking the reader from Martha's Vineyard to New York to Ghana, this is a story about the making of a dynasty, and the hidden truth that's just waiting to be exposed.

PART 1

<DATE>: February 17, 2015
<FROM>: T.Carter@gmail.com
<TO>: Ken.Carter@gmail.com

<SUBJECT>: PHOTO

Hey,

Found this Polaroid in a donation box given to the BSU when I was working on my thesis. It was just sitting there with some other old stuff donated after someone died. This is your dad, right? It says "William + Kofi, Ghana, 1969." Guess this is where it all began! Anyway, thought you might want it for the birthday thing. It's kinda cool!

xx, T

CHAPTER 1

William Carter Jr.

Watcha Cove, July 2015

A hurricane warning has been issued for Cape Cod, Martha's Vineyard, and Nantucket Island. We're expecting wind gusts of up to 110 mph and intense steady rainfall, which might lead to flooding. The governor of Massachusetts has issued a shelter in place advisory. Please remain indoors or find suitable shelter to wait out the storm.

William Carter Jr. mumbled at the television, the emergency broadcast interrupting his regular MSNBC programming.

The rain had started its assault on his Martha's Vineyard home hours ago. As an attempt at humility, the family referred to the estate as a cottage, but in actuality, the property was spread over twenty-six acres, with a private-access beach, a pool, a solarium, and three real guest cottages. The main house, an eight-bedroom monstrosity, allowed the family to be together while still maintaining individual solitude, an important quality in any Carter home. Every year, over the past two decades, the Carters would decamp to Watcha Cove. It had started as an annual two-month hiatus, where William could escape the pressurized canister of being a CEO and breathe. His two children, off from school and with limited supervision, would join a pack of rich vacationing

Northeasterners, becoming practically feral in the process. He enjoyed the feeling of the island, of the sea air and the sunshine, but over the last fifteen years, the size and scale of his growing company meant the idea of a vacation became a much more abstract concept.

Running the property required a full staff, deployed at least one week before the family would arrive to avoid last-minute scrambling. This was accomplished with a lengthy request form called a "pref sheet," ensuring that the chef and housekeeping staff were aware of everything from who liked to sleep with socks on, to who liked their bacon extra crispy.

For entertainment, Watcha Cove also included a tennis court, basketball court, and squash court, the latter housed in a separate building so that Asher Bennett Carter could practice his beloved sport in peace. There was a movie theater (more humbly known as the "screening room"), a garden where fresh fruits and vegetables were grown for a full "farm to table" experience, and a home gym and infrared sauna for "decompression" and "relaxation."

But most importantly, the property doubled as another Carter Corporation HQ, with dedicated office space and meeting rooms, making it a convenient tax write-off. So long as the C-suite staff showed up at least one workday out of the week, it was considered an essential asset.

At Watcha Cove, William Carter Jr. ensured everything functioned for his benefit, except for the weather, that is. He watched from a window as the team in charge of coordinating his birthday party scrambled to dismantle the tents and move accommodations indoors. A dozen workers in ponchos and raincoats were being blown back by the intense gusts.

William drew his attention back to the mirror. He was shaving himself, a rare occurrence and indulgence in that it gave him time to himself. He received a routine haircut and shave every other week from the comfort of his own home. It was important that he maintained uniformity in his appearance. Over the years, he'd discovered that as a leader, it was better to give people an image that they could count on, that they could trust: a traditional look from a traditional man.

When he was in his midfifties, genetic disadvantages had finally brought about typical male-pattern baldness. He'd carefully weighed the decision to shave his entire head, but his personal image team delivered research that said that bald Black men were more closely associated with fighting crime (e.g., Samuel L. Jackson as Shaft and Nick Fury) and comedy (e.g., Steve Harvey and Damon Wayans), rather than affluence and stability, so he opted to make peace with his receding hairline. The result—a peppering of gray on the sides and extremely sparse black hair on the top. Because he was dignified, he'd let his hair turn naturally gray.

His facial hair, also dotted in gray, more prominent now that he was coasting toward senescence, was shorn as close as he dared while still being present. When on the Vineyard, William used to relish the opportunity to break with the rigidity in his grooming standards, but those days felt far away now.

Holding his straight razor, he wanted to indulge in the solitude. In the early days of his company, the luxury was to be able to hire people to do everything for him, and now the luxury was being alone. Privacy was an illusion. He pulled the skin under his chin taut and was surprised at how far it had to stretch.

Just as he ran the razor under the water in the sink, his vision went blurry. He shook his head and blinked a few times. When he tried to catch his own reflection, he seemed to be moving out of sync with the man in the mirror.

The razor, a sterling silver Mühle, had been a Father's Day gift from his CFO, Jermaine Davis. It was simple, industrial, and weighty. When the razor slipped out of his right hand, it clanged loudly into the white porcelain basin of the sink.

William Carter Jr. tried to reach for it and discovered he could not, his arm now tingling with the familiar sensation of pins and needles and yet not responding to his brain's commands. Suddenly his right leg gave out from beneath him, sending his body careening to the floor. He made a motion to grab the sink with his other hand, but his response time was impossibly slow.

Lying on the ground, he tried to call for someone but couldn't remember any names. His thoughts rolled away from him like spilled marbles. He thought of his mother in his childhood home, sitting in a secondhand rattan chair reading *Ebony* magazine. He remembered his high school teacher, beaming with pride when he'd been accepted to Harvard. He heard the crash of his college roommate flinging a failed project model against their apartment wall. He saw his wife sitting across from him in a diner, demonstrating the accents she'd mastered. He saw himself working at his desk, working on a plane, working in a car, working at his son's soccer game, working before sunrise, working at dinner, working in the middle of the night, working at that very summer house. Numbers and documents and abbreviated correspondence flew around in his head until he saw nothing.

He was gone.

CHAPTER 2

Jacqueline Bennett Carter

Watcha Cove, July 2015

"Oh my God! William! William, can you hear me?" Jacqueline Bennett Carter cradled her husband's head in her arms.

Two housekeepers and William's first assistant rushed into the bathroom. "Call nine-one-one," Jacqueline instructed in a clipped tone, shaking her unresponsive husband.

For a moment, everyone simply stared, confused. Just fifteen minutes ago, William Carter Jr. had been barking orders into his iPhone and demanding that security be increased tenfold for his forthcoming milestone-birthday party, despite the coordination his team had already undergone with the Secret Service over the guest list.

Jacqueline stood. "He's not breathing. I need a phone," she said, extending her hand forward. "Now!"

The urgency in her voice knocked something loose, and William's assistant handed over his unlocked phone.

Jacqueline dialed 911 and waited for her call to connect. "Nine-one-one, what's your emergency?" the operator asked.

"It's my husband," Jacqueline replied. "I think—I think he's dead."

Everyone stared at William Carter Jr.'s motionless body. In her shock, Jacqueline simply expected him to spring up from the tasteful gray marble floor and demand to know the status of the tasks he'd assigned the staff. But the way he was lying there, a custom Turkish rug disheveled under his side, face half covered in shaving cream, clad in running clothes that were still damp with sweat . . . she knew he'd never let himself be seen this way.

Her husband was most certainly gone.

"Okay, ma'am, where are you located?" the operator asked calmly.

"We're in Edgartown at Watcha Cove," Jacqueline said. "We need an ambulance."

The operator paused.

"Yes, ma'am. Right now, with the storm, it's . . . taking our teams a bit longer to get to folks. Can I walk you through CPR?"

Jacqueline looked down at William's slack and frozen face. "Sure," she replied without much hope. She knew that 911 calls were recorded and that the recordings were often leaked to the press. She could do this. If there was one role she auditioned for and landed, it was doting wife.

"Tell me what to do," she said with more resolve, handing the phone back to her dead husband's assistant after switching the call to speaker.

After six rounds of desperate chest compressions, Jacqueline felt it was an appropriate time to announce defeat. "It's not working," the assistant said into the phone, finally finding his voice.

"Okay," replied the operator. "Help is on the way, but this storm— we can't promise that someone can get there soon. Is there somewhere you can move the body?"

The four living people in the room made uncomfortable eye contact. The assistant looked around the expansive primary bathroom. Jacqueline's eyes fell on the $40,000 tub they'd imported from Italy a few years before. A tub was not a tomb. She glanced at the ten-foot glass shower, complete with two showerheads and seventeen different jets and wondered momentarily if she'd ever turned on more than one.

"Not here," she said decisively, and the group parted so that she could stand and exit the bathroom.

The operator, still on the line, waited patiently. "Perhaps you want to place him on a bed?" the operator offered kindly into the silence. Jacqueline took slow steps into the bedroom and let her eyes roam. She shuddered almost imperceptibly, thinking about having to sleep next to a corpse, until it occurred to her it wouldn't be much different from sleeping next to an alive William Carter Jr.

"Yes, the bed, fine," she said finally. "I think we'll need help."

CHAPTER 3

Kennedy Carter

Watcha Cove, July 2015

A singular small curl formed at the base of Kennedy's skull as she started sweating. Though the air-conditioning at Watcha Cove was always set to an optimal temperature, her frayed nerves were making her hot. This was the way it always was when she was in this house. Some part of her was always trying to rebel, and right now, that meant her hair. She leaned back in the low upholstered empire chair—a French antique certainly not made for actually working at a desk but aggressively feminine and beautifully coordinated with the other aspects of the interiors in the room, just like her mother wanted. It wasn't comfortable or practical, but it looked great, similar to her silk press, which was coming undone.

Kennedy cracked her neck and tenderly touched the coil of her natural hair texture breaking through before reaching for a claw clip so that she could save the rest of her hair from a similar fate. She removed the headphones currently blasting her focus music as she chewed on her bottom lip and faced her computer screen. All morning Kennedy had been struggling to connect the dots of her edit. A year ago, her mother, juiced up with an impending seventieth birthday party to plan, had tasked Kennedy with assembling a tribute video that could be played at the milestone celebration. Kennedy had agreed, stunned she'd been given the job. There were several award-winning directors already on the confirmed guest list. Her mother rarely granted her an audience, let alone asked her for a favor, so Kennedy threw herself into producing the best thirteen-minute film that she could.

The project began conventionally. She contacted party guests whom her mother had placed on a specific list as "friends of the family," which included former presidents, Fortune 500 executives, and ex-classmates of her father. They all gave gushing testimonials, an undeniable sign that none of these people would be willing to tell the truth about William Carter Jr. Quickly Kennedy grew frustrated with the project, which was shaping up to be a banal PowerPoint presentation set to music, a glorified slideshow with sound bites about what a "tenacious" and "commandeering" man her father was—a corporate way of saying "cold" and "occasionally cruel." It's not that she was interested in uncovering some deep truth, exactly, but she wanted to share something unique about her father, something that could show what type of filmmaker she was going to be.

She envisioned the short film as one that would accurately chronicle the life of a modern titan, from his humble beginnings in Boston to his ascent to CEO of the Carter Corporation to his legacy of philanthropy and charity. But in sorting through his early life, Kennedy ran into roadblocks almost immediately, as if her father had no history. He was a ghost, leaving no footprints. Her grandparents were long dead, not that she'd had a close relationship with them when they were alive. Her father's only brother, older by a number of years, was in palliative care in Florida. And William Carter Jr. didn't have friends. He had associates, business partners, colleagues . . . and none of them were very forthcoming about anything that she hadn't already read in a *Forbes* article. So, like any good documentarian, she embarked on her own research.

Kennedy was good at research. It was a solitary activity, which meant that she was in total control of the outcome. If the choice ever came down to a group project or independent research at school, she knew which she would choose. It wasn't because she was antisocial. She worked hard at having relationships, at doing what people wanted, what her family wanted . . . mostly. She liked research because it was a journey. She would open a door that led to another door that led to another door and then finally to what she was looking for. It was exciting, requiring nothing of her but energy and time, both of which she usually had in abundance. Her notebook was open, several stacks of Post-it notes were haphazardly stuck to her wall for reminders, and about ninety browser windows were fighting for her attention on her computer.

For this project, she began with the facts she knew: Her father had started his company fresh out of business school and made his way to New York City, where he scraped and saved in order to accumulate the assets he needed to get approved for a loan so that he could begin building his domestic real estate portfolio. That portfolio was a counterpart to the international housing company that he founded in Ghana. Then he met Kennedy's mother and began his second lifelong pursuit of creating the "perfect" family, of which Kennedy was the youngest member. It was a neat narrative, totally without the drama she needed for the screen. Sure, there was grit, some struggle, but no conflict. It was hard to see her father as a hero with the material she had, and she'd decided it was her goal for guests to come away from her tribute thinking of William Carter Jr. as someone to admire.

That was, until her high school best friend, an unlikely source, sent her a scanned image over email. It was a Polaroid of her father as a young man, a year or two older than Kennedy was now. He was standing in a courtyard with his arm around someone she'd never seen—a tall, lanky, dark-skinned guy with a perfectly shaped Afro. Someone had written the word "Kofi" alongside her father's name under this image. Kofi was the mystery man's name, she presumed. Her father, similarly hued but shorter and softer, stood at the shoulder of this enigma with a self-satisfied grin. The two were radiating hope, it seemed.

It was unusual to see her typically stoic father so openly joyful. The photo became a guiding light for her film. She wanted to know *that* guy. She also wanted to know the guy who brought that out in her father. Maybe if she were actually working on a contracted gig, she could have just asked her subject or her client, "Hey, who's Kofi?" But since she was working in secret, and technically against the direction of her mother, she was working on figuring it out on her own. In her introductory film class at USC, she'd been instructed to follow the money when in doubt. In this case, a financial road map was not that helpful. And this photo, showing her father in an ill-fitting suit like he was playing dress-up, didn't quite fit with how she perceived him. And now that she knew what she knew from all her extra digging, guilt crept in about what she should do with the truth.

She had worked through the night on the video, hoping that something might spark her creativity based on what to do with the information that she had gathered so far, but nothing had come together. She couldn't actually let the video reveal the kind of man she thought her dad might be. Instead, in the early-morning hours, she'd watched clouds roll through the private bay outside the Watcha Cove window. Heavy sheets of rain soon obscured everything beyond the glass. Kennedy began to realize that perhaps the party wasn't going to move forward after all, that it might be okay that she had failed in making a tribute video worthy of being shown. Once again letting her family down.

Kennedy got up from her desk to source some necessary provisions, and on her way back from the kitchen, armed with enough snacks to get her through an afternoon of Final Cut, she ran into staff crying in the hallway. Her headphones still firmly over her ears, she heard their muffled, distressed voices breaking through the booming bass. Clearly something major had just happened. Seeing anyone outwardly express emotion, especially sadness, in *this* house was completely alien. "What's going on?" she asked two sobbing housekeepers.

"Miss Carter, we are so sorry," the one nearest to her said, fighting to gasp in air.

"Sorry for what?" Kennedy asked, looking around again for any clue that might tell her where this was headed.

"It's your father," the other housekeeper filled in. "He's . . ."

The unfinished statement remained suspended in the air until Kennedy demanded, more frantically now, "He's what?"

"Dead," the housekeeper finally whispered, wiping at her face with a tissue.

Dead.

The word didn't make sense. Her father had just been grumbling about the weather when he'd passed her room on his way to the private gym. Her father, who drank alkaline water specially delivered to him because he claimed he was sensitive to whatever came out of the tap. Her father, who punished himself by eating bran cereal for breakfast and vegan cookies for dessert for the sake of "health preservation." She knew he had a secret cigarette habit because she also had one, and they both were very bad at hiding it. She didn't know if he loved life, but she knew that he was actively pursuing not dying (aside from the smoking). Her father was, by all measures, a healthy man about to turn seventy in front of America's most glittering elite.

Her father was, apparently, dead.

Kennedy heard Asher's footsteps before she saw him running up behind her, and, like avoiding a stampede or a tsunami, she started to run in the same direction. Kennedy and Asher thundered down the hallway to the master suite. As kids, they'd been strongly discouraged from running inside, told to be careful of the priceless artwork that might be ruined. This rule was enforced after they had knocked into a pedestal and smashed an original Jeff Koons balloon dog statue bought at auction for $700,000 *before* it was insured.

But now Kennedy fell in behind Asher as his long legs glided down the hall. Asher threw open the door to his parents' bedroom and squeaked out, "Dad?" so distressed and pathetic that Kennedy's heart crumbled into a dry heap of dust inside her chest. She remained silent. Before she even realized what was happening, she was crying, tears cascading down her face. There was no one to answer. There was no Dad.

Their mother sat in a chair by a large bedroom window, watching the hurricane. Her feet were curled underneath her legs. She wore a gray cashmere tracksuit. The diamonds on her fingers, ears, and neck caught the light from the ceiling and did a twitchy waltz. She didn't turn to look at her children.

"He's gone," she said, her voice far away.

"No," Kennedy whispered as she spun around to see Asher standing by their father's bedside. The person she presumed to be William Carter Jr. lay motionless under a sheet.

Kennedy had hardly ever seen her father asleep. She was sure that he would hate anyone to see him asleep, even his children.

She had longed for intimacy with her father her whole life. They had never spent quality time together, not really, and the reality that they never would now was heavy in her heart. The video was the closest that she'd ever gotten to knowing who he really was. She had interviewed dozens of people, hoping for a clearer picture of him, but she never saw one. She wondered if that was due to the veneer he had begun to erect to keep everyone out decades before. She herself was guilty of upholding it. She'd filmed herself retelling her favorite story about her father, something not too private that painted him favorably.

When Kennedy was nine, her father had organized a private shopping day at FAO Schwarz, shutting the famed toy store down for just them. He told her she could get whatever she wanted, and she spent precious time debating what that would be, covering the shelves with her fingerprints, her light-up sneakers squeaking in the deserted aisles. She knew it was important for her to make the right selection, that her father wanted her to remember that day for some reason, and she did remember it, but the version of this story that she told on camera for William Carter Jr.'s birthday tribute wasn't entirely true. She'd watched the playback of it that morning. The footage showed Kennedy, bright-eyed, looking straight into the lens, fondly recalling the excursion.

"My father wanted to spoil me rotten. We were in there for hours, just the two of us, searching. The whole store was closed, and I tore through there because that was every kid's wildest dream. When we checked out, we had four people carrying the bags behind us. I think most of that stuff ended up donated, but it was the best day of my life." She'd even let a deceptive girlish giggle escape. She'd been telling that story for so many years, she almost believed it herself. It wasn't until she saw the cocreator of that story lying lifeless in his bed that the truth broke free in her mind.

When they'd gone to the register, William Carter Jr. looked down at the single toy Kennedy had selected. "That's *really* all you want?" he asked. Kennedy knew then that she'd made a mistake. She nodded dejectedly. Her father, now ready to do his part and pay, had been on the phone the whole time they were in the store. They certainly hadn't been there for hours. Her father would never have wasted so much time in a toy store, and he'd instructed her she had one hour to make her selection. He hadn't roamed around with her, helpfully look-ing for the toy that would speak to her. He'd barely made eye contact with her, her excitement and anticipation gradually giving way to panic as she watched his first assistant hover in the background, reminding Kennedy of an invisible countdown ticking by with every minute. In her mind, she was doing the calculations. They had eight minutes left. Two minutes left. She wanted to pick the right toy. She wanted to impress William Carter Jr. She had to.

Kennedy had ended up selecting a LEGO set, a simple house. She'd always been enchanted with the conventional, romanticizing how other people in happy, normal families might live. She always drew her family pictures in front of a house, a house modeled after that LEGO set. She hated that she'd lied for the film, but that was part of being a Carter.

Looking at her lifeless father, she remembered how the drawings didn't depict the penthouse that she had grown up in, and that artistic liberty had apparently concerned her mother enough that she sought out a professional opinion. "We have a *penthouse*, honey," her mother would say slowly and assertively as a reaction to her drawings, confused as to why Kennedy was not trying to capture the view from their sprawling duplex in crayon. Kennedy, she seemed to believe, was fetishizing poverty, a mental illness, surely. A child psychologist told her parents it was something that Kennedy would grow out of—that all kids had fantasies, and art is often simply an outlet for expression. Kennedy had pressed her ear to the door of her parents' bedroom suite the night after her first therapy session, feeling like something was wrong with her. "Why does she need a fantasy?" her dad asked. "Look at her life."

And now, yes, look at her life.

"How?" Kennedy said, her voice barely audible over the wind outside.

"What do you mean, how, Kennedy?" Asher said with the full strength of his voice, still staring down at the corpse of their father. "You know exactly what you did."

CHAPTER 4

Asher Bennett Carter

Watcha Cove, July 2015

Asher narrowed his eyes, hoping that Kennedy would feel the hate he was beaming toward her from his stare. He'd told her to back off, that sometimes things just don't make sense, and that was totally fine in the grand scheme of things, but nothing was ever good enough for Kennedy. Anyway, she'd only been working on a video that was going to be shown at a birthday party, not some prime-time feature. But she just had to keep asking questions.

The stormy daylight coming in through the many windows was soft, and he was horrified to find that tears had been gathering in his eyes. He turned quickly away from his mother and sister.

Asher was confused, embarrassed. He knew this kind of shriveling collapse was the exact opposite of the composed strength his father so often required of him. He turned and stared at his sister, letting himself be overcome by the most familiar of emotions . . . anger.

"You think your little project didn't do this?" he whispered to her.

Kennedy stumbled to find words. "It was—it couldn't have been. I didn't mean to . . . ," she said clumsily.

Jacqueline raised her hand lazily from where she sat. "Please," she said quietly. "Not now."

Asher and Kennedy's drag-out fights were household lore. They were never "allowed," technically speaking, to be physical with one another, but what's "allowed" is really limited to what you get caught doing. Asher had often violated that rule in their youth with shoves, kicks, and punches whenever he could seize the opportunity. He wasn't sadistic, just short tempered, and Kennedy worked his nerves nonstop. It was her goody-two-shoes, know-it-all attitude that grated at him. How she tried extra hard with everything. How she had such a big bleeding heart, and how much she wanted everyone to know it.

He snuck another glance over at his father, almost afraid to look. Kennedy, of course, was crying, her tears falling fast and free. Asher knew, or had suspected, that her so-called investigation was causing trouble. He knew that he was probably reaching, since their father was prepared and expecting this video and that he wouldn't have dropped dead from something as trivial as his daughter's curiosity. But still, it felt good to lay things at Kennedy's feet for the moment. To direct his anger toward something. Kennedy had come to Asher more than once about "inconsistencies" in their family history, fishing for more information. It was insane. He told her a million times that she should just make their dad a music video. Who wouldn't want that instead of some sad, serious feature that he suspected Kennedy was working on?

He hadn't been *jealous* that their mother had asked Kennedy to make the video instead of him, but his idea was obviously better. Their father, filmed behind his Financial District desk, a panoramic shot of the office, a close-up on his watch, a rapper commissioned to provide trap lyrics and beats. It would have been epic. In fact, Asher had worked out a rough draft of lyrics that included rhyming words like "set" and "jet," "boss" and "floss," "fly" and "guy," and "money" and "money." (The last couplet, he knew, still needed work, but it was an easier problem to tackle than trying to find a partner for the word "profit.")

As he reflected on all this, Asher felt his emotions going into hyper-drive. He'd tried to conceal from his parents that he was failing out of Harvard Business School. He had failed at that too. He couldn't help but think that perhaps maybe now he didn't need an MBA, since, well . . . he was about to be set for life. Well, as long as no one else knew what he had thought he overheard his mother and father discussing when he had been home in the late spring. The hushed voices of his parents were still echoing in his head, clawing to reach him through the fog from that night that was padded with beer and weed. Asher chewed the cuticle on his thumb and began pacing back and forth in his parents' bedroom, desperation for an outlet building up in his body.

His thoughts went to the only logical place they could go when you're the child of a billionaire: to his inheritance. It was his. It should be his. Because he was the first child and a boy, his father set out early to shape him into the CEO he'd hoped Asher would become. In that pursuit, William Carter Jr. attempted to inculcate the grave responsibil-ity into Asher of what it means to be "self-made." This was a confusing lesson for Asher, not only because he found most lessons confusing but also because he wasn't in the "self-made" club, as his father would never fail to remind him. Asher was not a self-made man but had to learn the struggles of how it felt to be one anyway. Struggles Asher found tedious.

He walked over to the intercom and buzzed down to the kitchen. "Can we have some bourbon? Three glasses." He slid his finger off the button. "Please," he added, forcefully jabbing the intercom again, feel-ing immediate guilt for not using his manners. Minutes later, the bour-bon arrived, and he tore at the top of the packaging with his teeth and set it down. He reached for the three glasses on the small coffee table in front of the fireplace with his left hand.

"You want?" he asked his sister while pouring for himself. Asher was annoyed with her, but she could still have a drink.

She came over to join him, eyeing him carefully, clearly guarded.

"To Dad," Asher said, knocking their glasses together before drain-ing his in one big gulp. He grimaced, afraid that it would come right back up, but he kept his eyes closed and willed the alcohol to start working. He poured again.

"The video was nice, you know," Kennedy said quietly to him, sipping her whiskey and trying not to make a face as the bitter drink spread over her taste buds and warmed her esophagus. "I pursued this because I wanted to know him. We don't know him at all, not really, and I really understood that when it seemed like the whole world had a better idea about his life than I did. I wanted to make him more real, and I thought I was the best person to do that." Kennedy raised her chin in the direction of their father. Asher's nostrils flared slightly.

"Well, were you?"

"Not really," Kennedy replied.

"Did you ever consider the possibility that he didn't want people to know him? I mean he obviously controlled the way we did everything for a reason," Asher said, a rare moment of clarity coming as a surprise to even him. He threw his head back and gulped down more bourbon, welcoming the wisdom the whiskey was providing him.

"There were just some things I wanted to know," Kennedy said.

"Like what?" Asher asked.

"I wanted to know if he was happy. If he felt proud, fulfilled. I just wanted to know something real."

Asher rolled his eyes dramatically and circled his neck around. He set his glass on the table. "Who. Cares. About. Any. Of. That?" he asked, punctuating each word with a clap in her face. This was exactly why he couldn't talk to his sister. She was always worried about the wrong thing. Their father wasn't happy, and he was pretty sure that Kennedy could figure that out too. The man radiated misery, but happiness had never been his objective. The day Asher got into Princeton was the only time he'd ever seen his father happy.

William Carter Jr. had made it explicitly clear that there were no more than eight acceptable universities for his children to attend as undergraduates. To achieve this goal, the Carters hired a consultant who polished Asher's résumé, including interests and academics that were most appealing to his top schools. But in the end, Asher was invited to bring his squash prowess to Princeton, and though it wasn't his alma mater, William Carter Jr. still found the school appealing.

When Asher announced his intentions for Princeton, every Carter had done their part. William contacted all his associates who were Princeton alums and invited them to his homes in Martha's Vineyard and New York. Asher then expressed his desire to attend Princeton, shaking hands and charming whomever was necessary.

Everything was fantastically coordinated by his father. There was the initial squash scouting overnight, a showcase where Asher would play demo matches for coaches with current students. There was also the matter of the tour and getting to know the current Princeton administration, which was what his mother handled. Jacqueline always asked pointed questions about what the school's needs were and offered assistance in finding a solution to any problems expressed.

As for Asher, like his mother, he was a professional when it came to putting on a performance. He said what he was supposed to say, looked how he was supposed to look, and at the close of his first trimester of his senior year of high school, he had applied early decision. Asher played the part of the perfect applicant, and Princeton bought it, especially after a donation for the restoration of a teacher's cottage to the tune of $200,000.

The next spring, Asher received his acceptance. He was surprised at the numbness he felt opening the letter.

"Well done, son!" William said, beaming with the purest form of pride and expression he could have offered. William wasn't a physically affectionate person, and had given his son a handshake for about ten seconds longer than a normal handshake would last. That night, William Carter Jr. took the whole family on an impromptu cruise on a yacht around the Long Island Sound. That was the happiest Asher had ever seen his father.

That his father was now dead and Asher was failing out of business school was humiliating. Worse still, his dad had asked him to keep his sister's little pet project under control and he had failed. He hated that the only thing he could finish perfectly was a squash match. After three drinks, he finally felt the alcohol settle nicely over him. He leaned his head back in the chair he was in, closed his eyes, and tried to slow down his breathing to let the thoughts go. He probably needed to text his girlfriend, but his thoughts were consumed by one thing, the only thing now.

The money.

CHAPTER 5

Jacqueline Bennett Carter

Watcha Cove, July 2015

When her children came rushing down the hall and burst into their—well, now *her*—bedroom, she didn't know what she was going to say. It hadn't even occurred to her to go get them.

Jacqueline was transfixed by the sight of her husband's dead body. She folded his arms tastefully across his chest before laying a white sheet over his five-foot-nine-inch frame. Then she second-guessed herself and pulled the sheet back to reveal his face, then opted for the first option again and put it back. It was hard to know what to do.

She let her body sink into a plush chair that she had designed expressly for this spot facing the window. She felt like her bones were collapsing underneath her skin. They seemed to be changing structure, liquifying into something soft and weak. She heard something slam into the house. A branch? An exclamation point to the hurricane ravaging the tiny Massachusetts island they were on. The storm keeping away interventions from the outside world.

She went into the bathroom where, an hour ago, she'd stumbled upon her husband (or was he her former husband now?) sprawled out in such an unbecoming fashion. Many times over the decades that they had been married, she'd flippantly wished that her husband would just hurry up and die, but the reality of his passing was so much more painful than she'd anticipated. Jacqueline always thought of him as a Jack Russell terrier, so small and smart and territorial, with such a sense of bravado that you really couldn't help but be convinced that following his scent was the only path forward. Mostly, she felt completely ill equipped to live life without him. William Carter Jr. was many things, but head of his own household and head of his own company were his two favorite identities.

The room still smelled like him, a mixture of his bodywash and shaving cream lingering in the air. In the bathroom, she tried to keep herself busy, coaching her body back into sync with her brain. She drained the remainder of William's beard hairs down the sink. She ran the silver razor under the water and felt the weight of it in her palm, the last bit of luxury that he'd held. She returned the razor to its stand behind the tall mirror on his side of the double vanity, then shut the door. She had the fleeting thought to complete his shave for him. She knew that he would prefer that it wasn't left unfinished.

She straightened the rug where he fell and used a plush white towel to mop up the shaving cream from the floor and counter. The Italian linens were custom designed for this property, stamped with the stenciled outline of Martha's Vineyard. She had thought it a unique touch. Before they moved William Carter Jr.'s body from the floor, a team of the domestic staff had helped her adjust his clothing and clean off his face. Then six people had maneuvered his body onto a sheet, lifted him up by holding the edges, and carried him as if he were already in a casket. They'd deposited him gently on one side of the king-size bed. Jacqueline would have to find somewhere else to sleep tonight.

She smiled slightly. Even in his death, William was able to dictate everything she did. Satisfied with the bathroom being returned to presentable, Jacqueline ventured over to her own vanity and opened up the mirror. Her children were bickering with one another in the other room. To officially transform into the grieving widow character, she would need some assistance.

A pristine arrangement of orange pill bottles was organized at her eye level. The pharmacy, as she liked to call it, was where she stored her prescription medications, of which there were many. She reached her right hand forward, surprised at how wrinkled it looked, confused as to whether her hands had always appeared so old or if it was something that had just happened in the last hour. The faint pink of her almond-shaped manicure was youthful compared to the lines and ridges on her brown skin. William Carter Jr. liked to say she was the same hue as the inside of a tree that had been cut open; the tawny undertones of her face were like a spotlight shining from within. He thought it was remarkable that she was both bright and brown at the same time.

She closed her hand around two different pill bottles and shut the mirror. Her reflection, which showed her deep smile lines, mocked her. She wasn't smiling. She was tempted to take a Klonopin and a Xanax but hesitated with the latter.

She ran the water in her sink, not bothering to reach for a glass. She flipped her hair to one side, dipped her whole head directly beneath the faucet, and filled her mouth up with lukewarm tap water. She opened her mouth again ever so slightly to let the tiny baby blue pill in and swallowed everything together. Though it was impossible for the medication to work that quickly, she swore she felt she was being gently rocked as it made its way down to her stomach. She considered adding the Xanax again, but she didn't want to mix too many sedatives. Not that anyone could really judge her—her husband just died, after all—but she suspected she should probably be more present than double-dipping in medications might allow. She had a second thought and popped a Xanax from the bottle anyway before she returned it to shelf, pocketing the pill for later.

Her phone, still in hand, started buzzing. Given the storm, she was somewhat surprised to have reliable cell phone service. She frowned at the caller ID. It was the Carter Corporation's CFO, Jermaine Davis.

Jacqueline considered him William's other wife. Jacqueline managed the home, his children, and social affairs, and Jermaine managed his money, sort of. Truthfully, there were several people whose job was to look over the Carter wealth, but Jermaine was definitely William's most trusted staff member. The Carters employed many people who tried to ingratiate themselves with William over the years, but Jacqueline had once found a discarded note from Jermaine in an office waste bin that read, "I aspire every day to make you proud. Your work ethic and what you have built remain a guiding light for me. You are a true beacon for the community, for your family, and for the world. I want you to know that you can always count on my loyalty and support."

The note was nauseating in its sincerity. It was clear to her that Jermaine wanted, more than anything, to be considered family by William, which was normal-ish, she supposed, for the amount of time they spent with one another. But over the twenty or so years that Jermaine worked for William, Jacqueline found his sycophancy desperate.

She began to answer cautiously, not really sure what she was going to tell him. "Hel—"

"Is it true?" Jermaine asked before she'd even finished her greeting.

Jacqueline, stunned into silence for the second time that day, didn't immediately respond.

"It's on the news," Jermaine said.

"No," Jacqueline whispered. "I mean, yes," she corrected herself. It was true that William had died, but she thought she might at least have one day before having to deal with William's death on a public stage. It had barely been an hour since William's passing. Everywhere had eyes and ears.

"Where was it broadcast?" Jacqueline asked. Someone in this house had to have leaked William's death, and now the world was aware that her husband's $18 billion in net worth was floating in the financial ether.

"Jacqueline, it's everywhere—CNN, the *Times*, *Wall Street Journal*, *Forbes*. Everyone is reporting on speculation. Obviously, there's been no official statement, but apparently there was a nine-one-one call?" Jermaine asked.

She put pressure on the bridge of her nose and inhaled. "Yes, there was. I think he had a stroke, but we have no idea. No one can get here because of the storm. His body's just lying on the bed."

"Okay, I'm down island, but I can probably get to you within an hour if I leave now."

"Jermaine, you can't. The storm. It'll be dangerous to drive, and who knows what the roads are like. Trees are probably down everywhere."

"We have an eighteen-billion-dollar problem. I'm on my way," he said before hanging up.

The Carter Corporation Memo

Date: May 7, 2015
Subject: Press

Please be advised that any and all press requests should be filtered through the company's official public relations department.

It is expected that there will be increased interest around the Carter Corporation and William Carter Jr. in preparation for his seventieth birthday, but no one is authorized to speak on behalf of the corporation or the family. All communication must go through the proper channels.

Coverage of the party will appear in the *New York Times*, *Essence*, *Black Enterprise*, *Town & Country*, *Vogue*, and several other pending opportunities. No other outlet has been authorized for coverage.

It has come to our attention that journalists are seeking information about the Carter Corporation and all members of the family. The universal messaging to be used if any questions are received is "No comment." If an interview has been scheduled, please refer to the preapproved talking points found in the email dated 4/30/15.

Please take extra caution in correspondence with one another and external parties.

CHAPTER 6

Kennedy Carter

Watcha Cove, July 2015

For many years, William Carter Jr. had been fond of sending memos—an effective way to communicate with his employees, and by extension, the family, who were usually so busy and scattered. Growing up, every weekday, each person in the Carter household would receive a personalized agenda with their schedule for the day, but if there was a change or something additional to look out for, it came in the form of a memo attached to the front page. Several people had a hand in creating the memos: a choreographed coordination of schedules helped keep everything in the Carter universe moving smoothly. Of course, there was no memo for William's death, but the memos leading up to it were forcefully insistent that the family go into lockdown and not communicate with outsiders. Kennedy had suspected that at least some of the secrecy had been in response to her attempt to uncover information for her video project.

Today, the absence of this document felt like a visible hole in a well-worn sweater. All three living Carters were in the same room when Jermaine Davis arrived on-site looking like he'd been through hell to get there. He had inched his black Range Rover over to Watcha Cove, perilously navigating the fallen trees and obscured visibility to arrive at the estate for this last-minute war council. He assembled everyone to instruct them on what to do next. The main office at Watcha Cove, where Kennedy, her mother, and her brother had gathered, was the room that felt it had the most, if not all, of her father's presence.

Jacqueline had ordered the staff to leave the family alone but firmly commanded that they not speak with any members of the press. Kennedy assessed the somber demeanor of the room and tried her best to stay present.

Jermaine spoke first, accustomed to hosting meetings. "So, what we're looking at in the immediate is a cancellation of the party. People will want to pay their respects, but we have to first flip the property to be able to receive guests, assuming you want to do that here and not in the city. There already are a lot of people in town for the birthday party, and you'd be surprised how *close* people become once someone dies," he said, glancing at Jacqueline.

"We should receive guests in the city," Jacqueline said definitively.

"Done. Next, we need to decide what statement to make to the press. So far, I don't think we know enough to say anything. William was a visibly healthy man about to celebrate his birthday. Of course, he was older, but people will want answers, so we should hold off on talking until we have them. This storm obviously complicates things."

The three living Carters nodded.

Jermaine stood up and went to the window. "There's another, more sensitive matter," he began.

"The money?" Asher interjected.

"Ah, no not exactly. Your father was famously meticulous about estate planning. Your trusts have been established since birth. You'll still get access to the majority of your cash funds when you turn thirty. The Carter Corporation's controlling shares will be split between the two of you, and as your mother is aware per her prenuptial agreement, what she inherits is up to your discretion. The homes and material assets are paid for, but there will be a legal team to advise you on how to proceed with tax payments and any other maintenance fees."

Kennedy stole a look at her brother, who gave her a frigid glare. She dropped her gaze.

"No, what I was referring to," Jermaine pressed on, "was that over the last few months, William had been receiving progressively concerning messages from his internal security team about someone who'd been investigating the origins of the company, particularly on certain activity in Ghana beginning in the late sixties and stretching into the eighties. I think your father managed to contain all information, but there are some things that might . . . come up now that he's gone."

Kennedy's heartbeat spiked at the mention of Ghana.

"Like what?" Asher demanded, jumping to his feet.

Jacqueline rested a hand on his forearm and sighed as she gently tugged him back to a seated position.

Kennedy squirmed. She wondered to what extent her probing was the reason that her father had been receiving security alerts. That was obviously what Asher thought. Kennedy hadn't exactly been forthcoming in sharing that she'd gone rogue with the assignment her mother had given her, and she'd only told Asher about it because she wanted to get him on camera for the video and felt that, ethically, she had to share with him what she was discovering.

At first, all her research had yielded ordinary results. She already knew most of everything, but as she dug into the more complex elements of her father's backstory, she was confused. Years ago, the international nature of a company might present a logistical obstacle to completing research, but the internet was worldwide. She had begun digging around on leftist forums, and she discovered a robust community of people online who harbored hateful, negative opinions about her family.

"He's proper evil, William Carter Jr. He's destroyed Ghana and he'll do it anywhere you let that company in."

"Heard he 'gets rid of' anyone in his way."

"Elitist scum who's betrayed his brothers and sisters . . ."

She knew that he wasn't everyone's favorite person, but these comments, though from random, unverified sources, made her feel ashamed. She knew if she asked him questions, her father would react defensively, as he always had to criticism, but there was something in those threads that she couldn't dismiss.

Over the years, she'd read things written about her online too, that she was a "brat," "spoiled," and "entitled." She wanted to numb herself to such judgments, like Asher seemed to have mastered long ago, but the words began to eat at her like bacteria infecting a host. Eventually she found herself shrinking from the critiques, trying to anticipate what actions of hers might be interpreted as "bratty," cultivating a way of being that was deferential and humble.

There were people, she knew, who harbored intense feelings about wealthy people, wealthy Black people especially, but her father had worked diligently on his image and asserted that there was no way to make everyone happy, especially when one was worth billions. But finding the forums felt sinister to Kennedy, like they needed further analysis. What part of her father was "evil"?

As part of her discovery, she'd found an invoice addressed to a woman in Ghana that felt like a lead. According to the timeline Kennedy was building, this woman had seemed to know her father back when he was a university student. Earlier in the spring, Kennedy had set up a time to talk to her, but the woman was old, and their Skype connection was unstable. Kennedy gathered that she had been on the Carter Corporation payroll for over twenty-five years, from what Kennedy could tell via company documents, as a consultant who was paid more than $5 million. Alone that wasn't too surprising, but on the video call, she'd said that her background was in housekeeping.

Before the call was disconnected, the woman's daughter, a lawyer in Ghana, said in accented English that her mother was potentially in violation of an NDA. "The person you need to look for is Kofi Asare." Kofi Asare, was the man who'd been smiling with her father in the Polaroid her friend had sent her. The video connection had continued to cut out in spurts, but that name again. With that, Kennedy was newly energized to uncover the mystery of Kofi Asare. When she did, what she had found left her with even more questions.

Kennedy tuned back into Jermaine's monologue and caught the tail end of him saying, "So don't give any statements to press. Your mother and I will handle everything, okay?"

He didn't know that she'd been digging. He couldn't. She'd only been trying to keep her project protected from any prying eyes, which was how she'd ended back up at Watcha Cove, head down and steadfastly working for two blissful weeks in solitude before the rest of her family had arrived.

In the coming days, she expected her father would be memorialized by his friends and in the media, but for now, the image she had of her father was as muddled as ever.

PART 2

<DATE>: March 12, 2015
<FROM>: admin@bostonmunicipalrecords.gov
<TO>: Ken.Carter@gmail.com

<SUBJECT>: Re: Housing Records

Dear Miss Carter,

Thank you for your inquiry. Please find the records for the home owned by Mr. and Mrs. William Carter Sr. purchased in 1958 at 740 Savin Street.

As you will see attached, the loan was granted by Family Savings Bank for a term of thirty years. It was refinanced in 1979. Before the conclusion of the new term, the payments were taken over by William Carter Jr. in 1990.

Shortly thereafter, the home was demolished.

We have no photographs available, but perhaps this map might be helpful for your research.

Best of luck,
Simon Wexler

CHAPTER 7

William Carter Jr.

Boston, November 1956

For several years, the Carter family had shuffled between residences in Boston's Roxbury neighborhood, where the Black population of the city was concentrated. William Carter Sr. was perpetually searching for a home that he could own, and his obsession meant that the family was pinching pennies for just as long. William Carter Jr.'s father's mantra was, "You never want to owe. You want to *own*," which actually wasn't bad financial advice for the time, but it was a philosophy based on emotion.

William Sr. wanted to own because owning felt like safety, and the rest of the Carter family would feel the burden of this owing-to-owning pipeline too. There was never any spare money because all the family's financial energy was directed toward accruing a down payment and saving for the eventual mortgage. "Can I have seventy-five cents for baseball cards?" from William Jr. was met with a frown from his mother and the words, "Sorry, baby, the house fund is low."

"We'll have everything once we have the house we want," his father would say as an apology. The family's frugality meant bland generic-brand foods, used books and toys, and sparse opportunities for escape or entertainment. When William Jr. reflected back on his upbringing, these elements actually made him glad, because without the incessant distractions of games or playtime, he really had limited options about what to do with his time. He decided that he would focus on his studies.

His circumstances also enabled his early fascination with money. Every Saturday morning, Walter Carter and William Carter Jr. would accompany their father on a single, very important errand. They would play the lotto. This anecdote was carefully crafted and rehearsed over time as to become central to the family myth, so ubiquitous that it would become something that Kennedy put in her tribute project.

Had the Carters been asked if they had an extra several hundred dollars a year to spend on anything, they would have said no with resolute certainty. Yet there was always money for the lottery. The conceit of the lottery was simple: You play, you could win. You don't play, you can't win. "You gotta be in it to win it!" William Carter Sr. would say, and every week he was in it. While they never won enough money to contribute significantly to a down payment, the Carters would win piecemeal sums that were exciting enough to keep them coming back: two hundred dollars here, fifty dollars there. It was always good to have money coming in that you didn't expect.

Getting a "winner" made everyone feel like one. William Carter Jr. retained distinct memories of what it felt like to hold a winning ticket, the way that his father was congratulated, and the way that endless possibilities of what to spend it on stretched out before them. William Carter Jr. wanted so badly to recapture the feeling around a winner that he began to make careful rituals around ensuring a positive lottery outcome.

He would regulate his actions down to the smallest minutiae. It mattered to him which foot touched the floor first the morning of the lottery (left). It mattered to him whom they might see before their pilgrimage across state lines (Mrs. Johnson, good; Mr. Wilson, bad). They had to drive to New Hampshire to play the legal lotto, which

William Sr. came to prefer more than dealing with the Irish mafia. It even mattered what clerk issued the ticket. (Winners only came from CJ Perkins.) This was all very elementary, and the rituals evolved as William Carter Jr. grew older. He was trying to make sense of the patterns that resulted in a win. His first instinct was to control his behavior and minimize external variables. But his second, wiser instinct was mathematics.

If he could estimate the number of entries and calculate the number of outcomes, he could ensure that his father would win the lottery, which he soon realized was a daunting task. But he wanted to win because it was one of the only times that he saw his father so openly express joy. William Carter Sr. was a working-class laborer without much free time, but these precious moments that were dedicated to playing the lottery exposed another side to him. He was full of gregarious predictions about how their lives would change once they hit the jackpot, a looming entity that morphed into this elaborate mythical creature that William Carter Jr. would see in his imagination. Sometimes it would look like a white rabbit dressed in a tuxedo, wielding a cane with a diamond handle. Other times it would just be a sack filled with cash. In the rarest of times the jackpot looked like the house his father wanted so badly to buy. It was a less glamorous apparition than the others, but this one was the most material.

Because William Carter Sr. worked nights, his circadian rhythm was usually out of sync with that of his family. When he would come home, the boys would be eating breakfast before running to catch the bus for school. This didn't make for the closest of relationships, but William Jr. loved Saturday mornings because he got to spend time with his dad.

One Saturday morning, William Sr. stepped over the threshold of the small second bedroom in the family apartment to see his youngest son, his namesake, flattened out on the floor surrounded by papers covered in equations and diagrams. "Son, I do think that there might be something missing from this math," he said in his booming voice, picking up a paper.

William Carter Jr.'s face registered panic. The suggestion that he might have missed a critical element in his assessment could really cost him.

"What's that?" he asked, anticipating the worst.

"Luck," his father said matter-of-factly.

"Luck," William Jr. repeated back, turning the word over in his mind.

"Son, luck is one of those things in life that you can't account for. It's not going to show up in an equation or on a chart. As you get older, you're going to see some people will get lucky and some people won't. That's what the lottery runs on."

William Jr. had to ponder this development.

"So when we win the lottery, it will be because of luck?" he asked, the skepticism very apparent in his voice.

His father sighed, clearly sorry that he had to bring this hammer of truth down. "Yes, you'll see. A lot of things in life aren't fair. Luck isn't fair either, but it really helps."

The Elkin Enquirer

May 5, 1972

LOCAL STUDENT HEADED TO STATE PAGEANT

Jacqueline Bennett, age 12, will represent Elkin at Miss Black Kentucky in a few short weeks after winning a local contest. She has won a record-breaking thirty pageants across the state and in neighboring Tennessee since she began competing. Her parents will be driving her and her four siblings to Kentucky's capital for the competition. The young beauty queen said, "I am honored to be competing in Miss Black Kentucky, and I hope that I can make Elkin proud." The local seventh grader will perform a monologue from the classic Broadway show *Porgy and Bess* while twirling a baton.

CHAPTER 8

Jacqueline Bennett Carter

Elkin, September 1978

Jacqueline Bennett had competed in 104 pageants over the course of her adolescence. As a beautiful child growing up in Kentucky, she was well suited to a life on display, her looks a source of power. Her delicate features, toasted-brown skin, and sweet speaking voice captivated judges all over the state. She won seventy-nine titles in total. (She didn't count the ones where she was first runner-up.) Initially, the pageants had helped her develop poise and grace, plus they gave her the opportunity to earn cash prizes. It was somewhat expected that Jacqueline might lose interest in the whole thing, but as it turned out, she loved the stage and was a natural.

Her proclivity for performing netted an unforeseen windfall. From ages four to ten, her parents pocketed her earnings, using the extra cash flow to support their family, but after age eleven, she directly received prize money and could use it at her own discretion. Her parents didn't object to this since her elder siblings began working and supporting themselves in their own ways. They opened a bank account for her at the local Black bank, and she deposited checks regularly, almost as if she were an adult with a full-time job. Like the husband she would marry later, she was self-made.

At first, the freedom she found from earning money was intoxicating. Unsurprisingly, she spent a lot of her cash on things like candy and toys. The excitement of spending on such frivolities eventually wore off, though, because how many Heath bars can one girl eat?

The Bennett family had been in Kentucky for several generations, first as enslaved people, then as sharecroppers, and then as independent farmers. By the time Jacqueline was born, there was still a lot of land but not much good farming left. Her father, Roy Bennett, sought out new work by graduating from wheat farming to working at a bourbon distillery plant. This required a ninety-minute commute each way daily. Her mother, Cecile Bennett, stayed home with their five children.

Of her four siblings, Jacqueline was the youngest, and therefore fighting for attention came quite naturally to her. Her mother enrolled her in pageants to give her daughter something to do and provide a proper outlet for her energy and theatrics.

As her career in pageants progressed, Jacqueline became more aware about the kinds of things that made a girl a beauty queen. Good posture was high on the list of traits that pageant girls had, as was the dismissal of pain of any kind. When the hair relaxer burned and the smell of lye made her shake, she just set her jaw. When she learned to walk in heels, her feet swelling with the pressure, she smiled through it. When the stage lights blinded her and made her sweat, she willed herself to be cool, which was why she was a winner.

She constantly observed older pageant winners, watching how brilliant the crystal crowns looked on top of their heads, a white-satin sash placed ceremoniously over a diaphanous gown. She wanted to siphon off their beauty and mannerisms for herself, and so she did—well, at least in her head. She rehearsed in the mirror constantly. She was self-possessed and careful. She spoke slowly, clearly. She trained herself out of her natural southern accent with diligent practice and kept her face and body blemish-free. She didn't run. She didn't jump. She didn't swear or make choices that would sabotage her looks. She sacrificed. She knew even at a young age that becoming Miss America was a long shot, but she still had goals.

Her biggest goal was to get the hell out of Kentucky. She imagined that her parents had given her such a long French name so that she could be destined for a life that required an elegant assembly of letters. When she first learned to write, she loved to put extra flourish on the *J* and the *q*, training for signing the autographs that she knew people would want from her eventually. She never went by Jackie. Her full name was the promise of what she would become.

At some point, she decided what she could become was an actress. The Bennett family could agree on a single splurge and that was a television set, an ideal investment of both time and money. Nothing could nullify the energy of five kids like a television. Thus, the Bennetts were TV people, not like the people *on* the TV but the people who watched it. The local channels in Kentucky were lacking, but the national channels had everything. The sitcom *Julia*, starring Diahann Carroll, became a sort of beacon for Jacqueline. Jacqueline, more than any of her siblings, was mesmerized by the women that she saw onscreen, fascinated to learn that it was all pretend. The people within the tiny box were *acting*. She did a variation of that on pageant stages almost every single weekend to an enraptured audience. Surely she could be one of those people one day.

Jacqueline had a single friend on the pageant circuit who was also a classmate, Helen Hudson, a chubby girl with family money who participated in pageant theater for status, a validation that her parents wanted. Helen wore her goodness as unashamedly as a baby takes a fall when learning to walk. Helen's father owned the Black funeral home in town and, well, death was good business, a reliable one. Helen never won any titles because congeniality does not make a queen. Helen was uncoordinated, undisciplined, spent too much time giggling with other contestants, and despite having everything needed to succeed at her disposal, she never learned to respond to the interview questions in the way that she was supposed to.

For example, during a regional competition, she was asked, "In what ways have philosophers like Confucius contributed to society?" To which Helen earnestly delivered the response, "Confucius invented confusion, and that probably made a lot of people happy because they felt confused before that but didn't know what it was."

Onstage that day, Jacqueline did not react while other eyes were still on her, but she did privately marvel at how her friend rambled like she had nothing to lose. Helen could play like she had nothing to lose because she didn't. She would not be changed by a win or a loss; she would still be the same person with the same position with or without a crown.

Jacqueline remained smiling, patiently waiting for her own question, which was, "Where would you like to travel in the world and why?" Jacqueline responded by saying, "I would love to experience as much of the world as I can. I think it is a beautiful thing to be able to learn from other cultures and to be able to exchange information and customs. I look forward to going to places in South America, Europe, Asia, and Africa. I probably don't want to go to Antarctica because it's very cold there."

"I just do this pageant stuff because it's fun," Helen said cheerfully backstage at the next pageant, unfazed by her poor performance while she flooded her orbit with a cloud of exhaust from a can of hairspray.

"Well, I'm doing it because it's good acting experience," Jacqueline replied in her best grown-up voice, fighting the urge to cough.

Her high school didn't have a theater offering. The Bennetts' church did, though, limiting Jacqueline's repertoire to religious texts. There were only so many years that she could exclaim "He has risen!" with a new inflection before it became stale. (According to her personal calculations, the limit was three.) She also joined the choir and developed the ability to float her voice above the others, demanding that she be heard.

Since she couldn't be in secular plays, she found a way to improve her acting abilities on her own, purchasing screenplays at the local used bookstore, with *Breakfast at Tiffany's* and *Cat on a Hot Tin Roof* becoming personal favorites. Even though she'd learned many of the songs from *Porgy and Bess* in elementary school, she got records and cassette tapes of other Broadway shows like *My Fair Lady* and *West Side Story* so that she could learn their lyrics and hear them with an orchestra. She closed her eyes and tried to envision what they would look like as real productions. She practiced crying and laughing on cue. Every chance she got, she found an opportunity to perform. She liked to experiment by giving new people a fake name when she met them just to see if they would believe her.

Helen hated to be a bystander when this was happening, feeling caught off guard when Jacqueline decided on a new outlandish narrative, like when she told people she was an orphan from Illinois, or that her father was a famous surgeon, or that she was concussed from being kicked in the head by a horse.

"You can't just lie to people," Helen would say after being forced to corroborate to a couple of strangers that Jacqueline was Helen's cousin visiting from out of state.

"Why not?" Jacqueline replied. "People lie every day. Look at Norma. You think she has a *real* headache every single PE class? No way. She just says that so she won't have to run around, and we all know it and don't say anything. At least my stories are interesting. And just so you know, I'm not *lying*. I'm acting."

"Well, it feels like the same thing, and I don't know what to do when it happens. I never know who you're going to be," Helen complained, her voice bordering on whiny.

"I'm always me," Jacqueline said. "Mostly."

Helen, who was more religious than Jacqueline, planned to marry immediately after high school, very certain that her future would start the day she became a mother. Jacqueline occasionally flirted with the idea of being more like Helen: moving closer to Louisville, finding a man to be with, raising kids of her own. It might be easier but the thought of being bored and isolated and with child made her want to jump through her skin. She knew her destiny was elsewhere.

Jacqueline's plan was to make it appear to her family that she was applying to junior colleges and endeavoring to pay the tuition with the money from her pageant wins. But the real plan was to use all the money to get to New York City however she could. She picked New York because it was geographically closer than Los Angeles, and therefore the bus fare would allow for her to still have funds left over to get a place to live and food to eat.

In New York, she would have to work, and it would be challenging, perhaps difficult. But from what she'd read, many actresses began their careers in the service industry. She was prepared to pay her dues to earn her place in a community where the action happened in the moment, where commitment to a character could happen unashamedly, nakedly, in front of a captivated audience. The dreams of what would be empowered her. Her imagination was powerful, but she hadn't quite imagined exactly what she would be giving up in order to have the life that she got.

The Galston School
45 Fox Trot Lane
Galston, Massachusetts

April 4, 1958

Dear Mr. Carter,

Congratulations! We are pleased to offer you acceptance to The Galston School in the class of 1963.

Attached to this letter is your admission packet in addition to the financial aid package we are able to offer.

Should you accept this offer, please reply by June 1 to begin registration and the dormitory assignment process.

We are looking forward to welcoming you on campus soon!

Best,

Francis D. Cooke

Head of School

CHAPTER 9

William Carter Sr.

Boston, March 1957

For years, William Carter Sr. toiled as an overnight janitor at a municipal building in City Hall Plaza. He began his shifts at 9:00 p.m., well after the offices had closed, since having a Black man scrubbing the floors would have been unseemly in the daylight. After two years, he was promoted and assigned to clean the mayor's office, also at night. The mayoral staff spent longer hours in the office than he'd initially anticipated, so occasionally there were moments of awkward interaction.

His goal was to remain as invisible as possible and pass through the night with minimal disturbance. He was aware that the more recognizable he became to these people, the greater the threat that he might say or do something that could be interpreted as offensive and might put him out of work. It wasn't uncommon for a Black civil service employee to disappear after complaints over behavior that included "too much chatter," or "takes breaks that are too long," or "general laziness," or "delayed responses to questions." He kept to silent, standard routines as much as possible to diminish his presence and therefore avoid conflict. This was a highly successful arrangement for William Sr., but one evening he was taken by surprise. The lights in an office were off, but someone remained seated at the desk.

When William Sr. went in to clean and change the trash, he flipped the light switch on and was jolted by the sight of a white man sitting perfectly still with closed eyes. John Sullivan, the deputy mayor.

"I'm sorry, sir. I didn't know anyone was in here," William Sr. said, his apology laced with fear.

"That's quite all right," the man said, rubbing his eyes. "I was in here just trying to pray on a solution to a problem. But please come in; I know you have to do your job. Don't mind me."

"Yes, sir," William Sr. replied from the doorway before slowly stepping inside the office. He tried to sound happy, hoped his ebullience was clear.

Over the next two months, John Sullivan continued to work late but left his light on so that it was clear he was in there. When William Sr. came to clean, John sought out conversations with him, which of course made him uneasy. William did his best to appear unrattled and relaxed, as if this were the most normal thing in the world for the white deputy mayor of Boston to befriend a Black janitor.

One evening, John Sullivan, smiling and appearing evermore curious about his nocturnal companion, asked William Sr. about his ambitions.

"Well," William Sr. said in a slow, drawn-out way to buy himself some time, "I'm fortunate to do this job right here." He nodded.

"But what if you could do something else?" John Sullivan pressed.

"I'm not sure what else I could do, sir. I've been doing this since I first started working."

"Okay, let me ask you this: Is there anything in life you want to accomplish?"

William fell quiet again and was unsure whether or not to reveal his aspiration to become a homeowner. He was sure John Sullivan, and all the Sullivans, for that matter, were already homeowners. He was reluctant to share something so personal and small with this person who had so much power.

"I'm looking to become a homeowner, sir," William Sr. finally said since he couldn't think of a believable lie.

"Is that so?" John smiled. "I hope you mean to do so here, in our fair city."

"Yes, sir," William Sr. replied and reached for the small trash can next to John Sullivan's desk to give his nervous energy a productive direction.

"My eldest son is a student at The Galston School. Do you know anything about Galston?" John asked.

"No, sir," William Sr. replied, scanning his knowledge for anything relating to a school named Galston. What he didn't know at the time was that Galston was one of the oldest boarding schools in the greater Boston area, counting among its graduates the thirty-second president of the United States, Franklin Delano Roosevelt. William Sr. also didn't know that in September 1951, three years before the landmark Supreme Court decision known as *Brown v. Board of Education* outlawed segregation in schools, Galston accepted its first Black male students. For some years, young Black men had been filtering through this elite boarding school, emerging ready to take on the top universities.

"They're currently in the process of hiring for a groundskeeper for the campus," John continued. "And because you have such an excellent work ethic, I thought you might be perfect for the position. It would be a much bigger job than you're doing now, and you'd have a much bigger salary. And I'm sure your sons could also attend the school for free."

William Sr. was surprised that John even remembered that he had sons based on their limited conversations. "That's very generous, sir," he said after a few seconds of stunned silence.

"I hope you'll consider it. I would love to have you meet with the school next week."

"Yes, sir," William Sr. said.

The following Wednesday, William Sr. made the forty-eight-mile drive to The Galston School for his interview and, upon leaving the campus, secured a new job as the head of the groundskeeping department, where he would oversee a staff of twelve landscapers who now reported to him. William Sr.'s pleasant demeanor and a recommendation from the deputy mayor were all that were needed for the headmaster to offer him the position. The interview, a mere formality. In an instant, the 385 acres of this historic institution were under his domain. The headmaster also confirmed that as staff, William Sr. could have his youngest son, William Jr., attend Galston with tuition completely waived. Even though his first son, Walter Carter, wouldn't be permitted to attend Galston because he was already midway through his high school education, William Sr. still felt especially energized about the opportunities that his namesake would have. He could never have predicted such a good fortune. Yes, it was as if he'd won the lottery. That smart, analytical boy of his, so damn *lucky*.

CHAPTER 10

William Carter Jr.

New York City, May 2015

William Carter Jr. had spent much of his life in meetings. There were always meetings on his calendar, color coordinated into blocks of hours, half hours, and tens of minutes. He hated looking at the crowded schedule, so he generally had one of his three assistants call out the time remaining during his meetings. It was an effective, wildly performative aspect of the job. This among many other quirks became one of his signatures, so that everyone around him would hear "hard stop in five" or "two minutes remaining" with regularity.

Even William tired of the callouts at times, but it was incredibly useful when it was time for him to do press because it helped him to gracefully exit potentially invasive lines of questioning. Limiting his time with journalists meant that he could only share so much. Today, he found himself locked in to a thirty-minute sit-down with a reporter from *Vanity Fair*. This very junior professional, whom William thought of as nothing more than a kid, was writing a feature on his seventieth birthday, his legacy as a Black billionaire, and what that meant. William had been as agreeable as he could stand to be for about nineteen minutes when the questions, in his opinion, took a turn.

"Your father worked at the school that you attended as a boy," the reporter said. "What was that like?"

"Ah, yes, my father was the head groundskeeper at The Galston School. He did that job until he retired, for about forty years. I didn't have the typical boarder experience or relationship, especially since I got to see him every day. He taught me a lot about hard work, about dedication and pursuing goals." William finished this statement while adjusting the watch on his wrist. Today he was wearing a simple yellow-gold Patek Philippe with a navy-blue face, the warmth of the metal complementing his complexion. He did this intending for the reporter to see and put this detail in the story that he was writing because the constant communication of wealth was just as important as the words he was saying.

"And how did you find the racial dynamics at Galston to be at that time?" he followed up.

"It was the sixties," he said, surprised by the question but remaining placid. "So it was tense in a lot of ways, but I actually found it to be navigable. I never felt stuck or held back. There were people who definitely had prejudicial opinions, but I think they respectfully kept their distance, and so did I. It did not have any bearing on the education I received," he said.

With that, William's third assistant made an appearance, knocking and then popping her head into the office. "Hard out in three, so last question," she said to the journalist.

William gave the reporter a closed-mouth smile. "Have everything?" he asked.

"Just one more thing," the reporter said, sliding his recording device closer to William. "You established the Carter Foundation Scholarship to help provide educational opportunities to young Black students who might not get them. Why was that an important thing for you to do?"

William cleared his throat. He knew there were many ways that he could answer this question. He went with the first thing that came to mind. "You know, some of the schools that I attended showed me that there was a whole world that I'd never even known existed, and in that world, people were making connections, solidifying their futures. But if you never get the opportunity to be in that world, your future is pretty certain. For me, it's about opening up possibilities. You never know who you're going to meet at school. It could be someone who could change your life."

The third assistant knocked twice on the door, and William rose to his feet and extended his hand. The reporter gathered his things and thanked him for his time before departing.

William was aware that there was going to be another meeting in a few minutes. There was always another meeting, but he stepped outside on the expansive terrace attached to his office to light a cigarette. He thought about his time at Galston, and though he told a version of what he wanted that reporter to know, most of it was actually true.

About a year after William Carter Jr. started at Galston, his father fulfilled a lifelong pursuit of his and became a homeowner. The new Carter house sat in the middle of a street peppered with multifamily units and a few simply designed properties, but it became a home that William Jr. barely knew. After he became a boarder, he spent only a single summer back in Roxbury, and while he studied hard and received top marks in his classes, his father's good fortune had set him on a divergent path. William Sr. thought that he'd gotten everything that he wanted, while William Jr. began to see everything that he lacked.

In late August 1958, he arrived on campus with his parents and a single duffel bag clutched in his damp right palm bearing all his worldly possessions. He watched the buzzing of move-in day with rapt attention. William had never seen so much green. He'd also never seen so many white boys. He found himself staring at how they dragged their trunks and luggage and books with so much self-assuredness and confidence, all seeming to know exactly where they were going. His parents had tried their best to prepare him for what his new school would look like. They'd begun a series of discussions with him leading up to his departure that detailed the other students that he should expect to meet and the ways that he had to behave. They informed him that a survey would be issued to the other Galston boys in his year asking if they would accept having a Negro roommate, and that some people would select *No*. They said that he should try to make friends but be cautious, that rules would be different for him, and that it was imperative that he remain out of trouble for the next few years he'd be living on campus. His parents also said that this was an Episcopal school, and that religious expression might be a little bit different from the Baptist church he was used to, but it was all the same God.

William Jr. received his dorm assignment, and the Carter family was greeted and directed by a friendly redheaded upperclassman, who led them into a brick building and up two flights of stairs to room 468. William was relieved to see his roommate was a tall Black boy with a teeny-weeny Afro and some faint facial hair breaking through his acne-riddled skin. The boy smiled big and easy and extended his hand to William.

"I'm Russell. Russell Johnson," the boy said.

"William Carter," William Jr. replied as the air became just a little easier to breathe.

"Well, I guess no one wanted to room with us since we're together," Russell deduced with a careless shrug. William's parents introduced themselves to Russell and asked about his family. Russell explained that he'd traveled here alone. He was from Newark, New Jersey, and his family didn't have a car to make the trip. He was recruited by Galston to play football, which he was excited to do. Russell asked if William Jr. played a sport as well, to which William shook his head no and Russell cocked his head confused.

"I work here," William Sr. said to close the loop on the mystery. Four pairs of brown eyes met to communicate the unspoken: We know we're not welcome here, so there has to be a reason for an invitation.

"I think there're at least five of us here, new, anyway," Russell said. "There's another Black guy on the football team—we've already been

here two weeks for preseason—and there's two more I've just seen today."

In their future "real world," William Carter Jr. and Russell Johnson would have such dissimilar interests and personalities that it was practically a conspiracy from the cosmos that they'd lived together for a time. Russell was charming, cool, good looking, and athletically talented. He could and would regularly "wing it," allowing his instincts and intuition to guide him along when interacting with others. William was introverted, bookish, and self-conscious about his size and stature. William thought about things very far in the future. He liked preparation and only trusted himself once he'd mastered a skill that he studied and practiced. Anywhere else in the world, they might have been too different to get along. But at Galston, they became highly dependent on one another.

William Jr. was changed in many ways by Galston, and while he noticed that sometimes Russell would roll his eyes at the overly ceremonial culture, William liked it. Within a few weeks of his enrollment, he began to crave structure and formality all the time. He liked the dress code, the rules, the expectations. The more his teachers encouraged him, the more he acted in ways he thought would impress them. He wanted very desperately to be somebody, to command respect—and maybe a little bit of fear. He wanted to be treated the opposite of how he saw his father treated by his classmates as the help, someone meant to serve them, and that became another issue entirely. This he couldn't say to anyone, which was why, after he'd amassed a significant fortune, he became famous for paying people in typically low-wage jobs triple the standard. This, like many things William Jr. would do, was motivated by guilt.

Though it was impractical for him to distance himself from his father, always on campus and with his same exact name (not to mention complexion), he still had to try. Everything was made just a bit weirder by the fact that his dad worked for his friends. He cringed when they would be doing laps in PE around the fields as his dad was happily mowing or painting lines on. His father would also know far more about his child's life than any other Galston parent simply because he was present. William Sr. often knew about assignments, grades, or interpersonal drama among students before William Jr. did. Any attempt to minimize their connection was quite futile, so William tried his best to remain indoors and away from the grounds.

The memories of his father and boarding school were drowning him now that they had just been brought up. Part of the motivation for never addressing his past was that he would never have to think about it.

By the time he was ready to return inside, he'd smoked two cigarettes. Back in the office, he reached for the cologne that he stored in his top-right desk drawer, a custom blend made for him in Florence, and sprayed himself. He also placed three mints in his mouth and breathed in as they dissolved into tiny grains on his tongue.

His next meeting was with his head of security, who wasted no time in telling him that someone was attempting to access information that he was less than forthcoming about.

"Was it that kid?" William asked, referring to the twentysomething *Vanity Fair* reporter who'd left not twenty minutes before.

"That guy? Definitely not. If anything, he's a fan. No, this is something else. We're not really sure why anyone's looking into your parents, but it's cause for concern."

"Can we kill it?" William asked.

"So far, sir, there's nothing to kill," he replied. "They seem to have accessed information that's already public. We'll keep an eye on it, but because someone accessed the housing record for your childhood home, we thought you should be aware. Also, there has been some interest in Kofi Asare."

At the mention of that name, William became immediately alert. Masking his reaction well, William simply told his head of security to keep an eye on things before dismissing him, his gaze falling on his desk. He wanted nothing more than to smoke another cigarette to squash down the anxiety rising in his chest, but meetings were on the immediate horizon. *It's nothing*, he told himself. *Nothing to worry about at all.*

William let this become his mantra for the rest of the day, relieved that the *Vanity Fair* reporter hadn't the slightest clue about the real story he should be chasing.

CHAPTER 11

Jacqueline Bennett Carter

New York City, May 2015

Uptown, Jacqueline was sitting at her dining table with her chief of staff, overseeing the plans for her husband's birthday party. The theme that she had settled on was "Zoo-phoria," and she'd been working for several weeks on securing permits to have endangered animals on the premises. She'd contacted the chef at one of William's favorite restaurants to work on a custom soul food–inspired menu. Guests would also dine on caviar, lobster, and oysters from both coasts, but the soul food would do the job of demonstrating to all in attendance that the Carters definitely had souls.

The entertainment was the hardest to manage. William Carter Jr. was widely known to detest music, but the guests would be expecting something magnificent in terms of entertainment when attending the birthday party of a billionaire. Some suggestions the team had put forth: a hologram performance from a digitally reincarnated Whitney Houston or Prince, or a huge critically acclaimed orchestra that would play twentieth-century jazz classics, giving the venue a big band feel. But Jacqueline knew that the only person who'd be acceptable to her husband would be Stevie Wonder, whose music William actually tolerated. But everyone had a price. As it turned out, someone asked Mr. Wonder's people what his price was and the response came back . . . $10 million, after taxes. "Book it," Jacqueline said. She would spare no expense on this party that was going to be attended by governing dignitaries, Academy Award–winning actors and directors, other CEOs, industry "thought leaders," and Mike Tyson for the tech crowd because he came with psychedelics.

This feat of hers was astonishing, especially when she considered her own humble beginnings. It was a miracle how far she had come and all she had learned to do just by being in this world over the last few decades. William had coached and molded her to the woman she was today, the woman who could be proudly on display as his partner. She'd been primed for a life of being seen, though it hadn't happened in the way she'd hoped.

Jacqueline had her own version of her autobiography, which she'd been working on for some time, and the way she told this story was second nature. She was good at saying other people's lines at this point, but she was the best at withholding information. As a child, Jacqueline Bennett was famous for keeping a secret. Jacqueline began cultivating her interior world quite early and nursed her need to conceal things from everyone. For her, like most things, this started out as an acting exercise, something that she learned in a book on craft that she checked out from the Elkin Public Library. But as she found it useful for her life, she kept her thoughts and aspirations confidential. They were unknown to her parents, siblings, or even to Helen. So when Jacqueline boarded a bus bound for New York upon her high school graduation, she told no one, not willing to risk any external influence potentially changing her mind. She left a note for her family that she would write and call upon her arrival, but there were no additional details since she had none to share.

Her bus pulled into the Port Authority Bus Terminal after nineteen hours of travel. After getting off, the first breath she took was a deep, slow inhale that felt like a culmination of every single pageant title she'd ever won. She thought of the bedroom she'd left behind, bursting with her spoils, and how much all that had once meant to her. But if the trade-off was feeling this free and full of possibility, she was fine with never setting her eyes on a crown or trophy ever again.

Jacqueline had discovered the Hitchings House Dormitory in the classified ads in the back of *Mojo*, a Harlem-based paper. It advertised itself to be a respectable home for Black girls who were residents of New York City, students, unmarried, and under thirty. To qualify for residence, one had to be accepted and follow the code of conduct put in place to deter potential conflicts. The rent was charged weekly—fifty dollars, pricey—but Jacqueline was armed with her plan. She'd arrived in New York with $7,000 in savings from pageant wins. She had enough to get by, at least for a little while.

Jacqueline interviewed with the Hitchings House mother, Miss Pat, a thin senior citizen with gray natural curls and a preponderance of gold jewelry. Miss Pat was clearly a chain-smoker and tended to gesture wildly with her hands, sprinkling ash over every nearby surface. She was a lifelong Harlemite who took her housemother duties extremely seriously.

"This ain't no brothel," she said, squinting her eyes at Jacqueline, who sat opposite her in one of two chairs facing a large oak desk. "This is a house for proper young ladies."

Jacqueline nodded and slipped into her pageant persona. She raised her voice one octave before replying, "Of course. Hitchings is so highly recommended, and I'd be *so* honored to have a place here." To really sell it, she flashed her winning smile.

This seemed to satisfy Miss Pat, who provided Jacqueline with an overview of the house rules. No male guests were permitted to stay overnight. All guests must sign in and out of the building. All residents had to check in before 11:00 p.m. on weeknights and midnight on weekends. No guests past 9:00 p.m. No drugs of any kind. No solicitation of any kind. No fighting. No stealing. No children. Chores were divided up evenly among residents and completed without complaint. Jacqueline was only half listening to the lecture, which was feeling like a revised version of the Ten Commandments.

Jacqueline handed over $400 to cover the first month of rent and security deposit as Miss Pat explained that their contract was on a month-to-month basis.

"Failure to comply with any of these policies will result in immediate eviction from the facility," Miss Pat wheezed out before dissolving into a coughing fit.

"I understand," Jacqueline said, eager to be let out of the small office, the air quite hazy from all the cigarette smoke.

"We have four openings right now, so I can show you the rooms, and you can select one as you like," Miss Pat said after another round of throat clearing.

"Please," Jacqueline said with a practiced smile, thinking it best for her to keep her words to a minimum. The less said, the better. It was easier to let people write their own story. Any good actress knew that the audience should be able to see themselves in her, that she was a mechanism for their own projection.

They walked together out of the office into the spacious foyer of the building. A onetime single residence, the dormitory had been converted to a home that could house up to twenty women at a time. The common spaces were downstairs as well as a large industrial kitchen.

Jacqueline decided then and there that she'd be playing the part of the sophisticated city girl, and like a snake shedding worn-out country skin, she worked to ditch everything about her old life. About two hours later, when the other girls returned home from their various engagements and obligations, the dorm surged with energy. Jacqueline was delighted to be among the sparkling young women of New York City. She met girls who were students at Hunter College and others who were dancers, or poets, or teachers, or secretaries trying to figure out what to do and where to go next. Each person she introduced herself to filled Jacqueline with eager anticipation. *I've really arrived,* she thought.

Jacqueline briefly considered calling home but thought that it might be better to wait until she had secured her first real role so that she might impress everyone in her family and inspire them to come see her in New York. So she decided to wait.

Even with the luck of getting a room at Hitchings, Jacqueline still needed to find steady work, something that would allow her to have income without impeding her ultimate goals. She decided to canvass the neighborhood to inquire about waitressing jobs. One of her dorm mates, a gorgeous secretary named Anita, discouraged this, saying, "The real money's Midtown. The tips ain't shit up here."

This is how Jacqueline found herself poring over a subway map to get herself to Midtown. The West Side was closer to Broadway, which increased her chances of potentially encountering a producer or a director who could give her a big break. When she got there, she was disheartened to find that she wasn't the first person with this idea, and after walking to seventeen different restaurants and cafés that had no openings, she turned her attention east. The East Side, from what she could tell, was extraordinarily corporate. Most people wore suits and seemed to be in a frantic rush. Thankfully, a diner on Forty-Eighth between Lexington and Third hired her on the spot for $3.50 an hour, with Marty the manager exclaiming, "Jeez, you look like a movie star!" (Jacqueline thought this a portentous sign she'd found the right spot to work.) The agreement was that she would submit her requests for time off when she received an audition or callback and make up any missed hours at another time. She shook her future boss's hand and was fitted for a uniform.

The servers at the diner, all women, wore crisp white dresses and short red aprons tied around their lower halves. On her first day at work, Jacqueline felt like a movie star indeed, her dress starched to perfection, her manner easygoing with customers, her spirits soaring. To be free and independent, already earning her own money in the greatest city in the world. But about two weeks into her job, Jacqueline's feet and legs were swelling with the stress of being on them for hours at a time, the inflammation wreaking havoc on her young body. Her roommate Jillian, a nursing student, volunteered to show her where she could find shoes that would support her new physical needs, admonishing her for wearing heels while waitressing.

Jacqueline was able to read and study scripts on her way to her job on the subway. She gradually became totally unfazed by the things she saw on the streets of 1970s New York that she walked every day, including, but not limited to, nudity, masturbatory acts, drug use, arguments, physical fights, and various stages of emotional distress. Her veins had turned icy, running a frigid stream right to her heart, which calcified against any tender feelings that might become a distraction.

After twelve months of big-city living, her funds almost depleted, Jacqueline needed to work overtime shifts. This also meant that while she was working so hard at the diner, she wasn't going out on auditions, which was fine with her because apparently the thing that she needed most was an agent. An agent could pitch her directly for roles and circumvent some of the industry red tape. Then she wouldn't have to deal with these open cattle call auditions, sometimes standing in line for hours with other women between the ages of eighteen and twenty-five (and some had been twenty-five for a while). The problem was that some agents weren't willing to represent Black girls, whom they considered too specialized, not in enough demand, and not guaranteed cash cows.

In her first few months of living in the city with no agent, Jacqueline went out for every role, but sometimes she would see in bold letters at the end of a casting document things like *blondes needed, slender brunette, feisty redhead* . . . and she knew that meant *not her*. Jacqueline wanted to rename the city "No York," since that's the most consistent phrase she heard.

Like any good apex predator, when she learned new information, she changed tactics, going after agents aggressively. She had to pay to have professional headshots done, which she did at a weird old man's apartment on the Upper West Side. He said that he would comp her session if she went topless and gave him the photos. She handed him thirty dollars instead. She enrolled in acting classes, another investment in herself that would require time and money, which were in short and dwindling supply.

The girls in the acting classes were the ones with all the tips. It was a mixed group, Black and white and Latina and Asian actresses alike. For the most part there was a resigned sisterhood that kept some of the inherent jealously neatly contained, even though it was always there. In acting class, Jacqueline was asked to do all kinds of exercises that had nothing to do with acting. She assumed that she would be learning how to do accents and stage fights. Instead, she was asked to do things like find an emotional anchor, exploring something that had happened in her life that might help her better connect to a character.

"Jacqueline, that delivery was stale," her teacher said after she did a scene from *The Crucible*. "I need you to dig deep. There's real pain in this monologue. Have you ever been hurt? Disappointed? Heartbroken? I need you to reach back in there and pull out what needs to come forth. The emotion in acting is never fake." *I am digging,* Jacqueline wanted to say, but she swallowed her comeback. Her teacher came over to touch the center of Jacqueline's chest, and she recoiled.

"Jacqueline, where's your anchor?" would be the question she would hear week after week. Her notes were to express vulnerability, to mine her own past for traumas and pain so that she could use it. It was uncomfortable realizing what she'd buried and shoved aside, the stony wall that she had built up to protect herself from countless rejections, the degradations she'd sometimes endured from customers at the diner, the way she'd become a walking mannequin with artificial emotions so she could win pageant after pageant. She'd placed so much importance on achieving this dream of getting onto a screen or the stage but really hadn't completely understood her motivations. An actress not having a clear sense of motivation, the most tragic of ironies.

As Jacqueline sat in that acting class feeling lost and unsure after hearing for the umpteenth time from her instructor that her

The Rules of Fortune

performance was flat, she wondered if she'd made a terrible mistake coming to the big city.

It had been years now, and she'd made her peace with her decision to press on, to stay. When she married William, she gave it all up anyway. Now she did not have the challenge of having to find emotional anchors to find the depth of a character. She was always playing one. Right now, she was a perfect party planner, and the idea was to have his seventieth birthday executed flawlessly. She hadn't prepared for all the replays of all the secrets she had been keeping for years for the sake of herself and William to come rushing to the surface.

71

April 25, 1960

Dear Mrs. Carter,

We would be delighted to host William for part of the summer in Martha's Vineyard. Everything will be taken care of. We're just so thrilled to see how close he's gotten to our boys.

We are sure he would love it. Please let me know if we have your permission to allow him to travel with us for a few weeks. I can be reached by letter or by telephone at 555-732-4413.

Looking forward to hearing from you.

God bless,

Mrytle Burke

CHAPTER 12

Kennedy Carter

San Francisco, April 2015

Kennedy let the windows down in her rental Audi SUV and felt the cool Bay Area air flow over her face and arms. With a few weeks to go until she had to be in Watcha Cove to hunker down on her video editing, she'd blown off her Friday classes at USC, flown to San Francisco, and rented a car for the drive to Marin County to interview one of her dad's high school friends. Kennedy was assembling the puzzle of her father's life, and a key piece of it was parsing out people who had authentic relationships with him. So far, the majority of people she'd talked to were either afraid of her father, or on his payroll, or a combination of both. There were a handful of people who'd known him for many years, and she hoped that their testimonies would add some humanity to her film.

The Burkes, a family that her mother had put on a list of preapproved participants for the tribute video, were all too eager to discuss her father. The twins had been his boarding school classmates, one now living in Boston and the other in San Francisco. She figured that she would fly to San Francisco to film in person and boarded a commercial flight since neither Carter child was ever allowed to fly in the jet alone.

Hours later, she waited for the gate to open to the estate of Philip Burke, the younger twin. Philip had made his money, like most of his Silicon Valley neighbors, by investing in a bunch of risky and seemingly insane ventures. A housekeeper answered the door and showed Kennedy to a cavernous living room complete with neutral, oversize furniture that appeared to have never been used. The space had strict, harsh lines and a punishing sterile energy, the type of home she'd been in many times before.

Kennedy had opted to do the filming for this project alone so that she could conduct interviews privately. The only person that she trusted to help her was her best friend, Tashia Carter. She slid her phone out to text her. Here at Philip Burke's place, she wrote. Hopefully will get something good, will let you know. xx

The two had met years ago when Tashia Carter had entered Dalton as a scholarship student in her ninth-grade year. She and Kennedy were forced into a bond by coincidence of having the same last name and constantly had to explain to the student body and faculty that they weren't sisters or cousins or even acquainted.

By ninth grade, the total number of Black students in Kennedy's class of ninety had capped out at six. There were three boys and three girls. The three boys, all Jack and Jill members, were longtime friends of the wealthier Carters, and two of them were Dalton lifers. Of the three girls, one was the biracial offspring of a white entertainment executive and her ex-actor boyfriend. She was a very beautiful but kind of clueless girl who, when pressed about her identity, almost always mentioned that she was both "white and Black." It only made sense when you processed that her Black father was a West Coast resident for the majority of the year, and she visited with him exclusively in the summer and even then, not the whole summer. The other two were Tashia and Kennedy Carter.

For Dalton, Tashia was considered radical. On appearance alone she rejected tradition and constantly challenged the dress code, many considering her Afrocentric jewelry and red-tipped locs to be a brazen statement. Tashia had eventually made peace with studying among the privileged, having decided that she had every right to access the type of resources through study and hard work that the wealthy took for granted. But she'd promised herself she would never change who she was. Kennedy loved that about her, had always yearned to have Tashia's strength. The two had managed to maintain a deep friendship over the years, with Tashia even venturing to help Kennedy out with research and editing on her dad's film.

When Philip Burke finally walked into his own living room, his approach was silent, his bare feet barely skimming his natural-stone floors. A lifelong friend of the family, Kennedy had an easy rapport with him as she explained the premise of her video and the types of questions she'd be asking. "So I was really hoping that maybe you could tell me something about my dad when you knew him at school, something no one else knows. I think getting some cool stuff about him in the video will make it really special," she said.

Philip Burke nodded and rubbed his clean-shaven chin, his round tortoiseshell glasses perched slightly down on his nose. His fair skin glistened in the light, giving him a slight glow.

"Well, I'll see what I can muster up. You know, this old memory isn't exactly like it used to be, and the Galston days . . . Well, that was a long time ago," he replied. "Okay, how about when we took your dad to Martha's Vineyard for the first time? That might be a good story."

Kennedy was practically salivating with enthusiasm. She'd basically grown up on the island, the Watcha Cove estate being a place of the happiest memories. This was going to be exactly what she needed.

"Now, like I said, this was a long time ago," Philip prefaced again.

"That's okay," Kennedy encouraged him. "Just tell me what you remember." With Philip's blessing, she had already set up her tripod and pressed record on her camera.

"I was a kid, so I guess that I remember my brother and me being very enamored with William. He was unusually studious for a high school boy. Not that we weren't, but there was something else inside him that was really pushing him toward something. We just liked having him around, so we asked our mother to see if he could come to the Vineyard over the summer break. If I'm not mistaken, your grandfather worked at the school, and his home phone number was listed in the directory, but our mother was formal so she both wrote and called. Your grandma . . . she was a bit shocked—maybe at the idea that children would spend entire summers as well as school years away from their parents. I think she said no at first."

Kennedy, who'd gone several weeks at a time without ever seeing her parents since she was born, wasn't fazed by this, though she could understand that this was a very mystifying request for the uninitiated.

"So as I understand it, on his next biweekly call home, William asked his mother if he could summer with us. He told her that 'summer' was a verb," Philip said with a laugh. "I can't imagine that went over too well. I think that your grandmother thought that school was changing him, and I think that maybe it was and it wasn't."

"But she said yes?" Kennedy interjected. She knew that the best interviews for screen were uninterrupted, and she didn't want to put too much of herself in the project, but she had to know.

Philip nodded. "She said yes, and the next time we saw William after school had let out was on the ferry to Martha's Vineyard," he said. "So listen to this, even though the ocean was right there and he'd never been on a boat, at least from what he admitted to us, William spent the entire time just looking at the people. I kept catching him staring at everyone. I never did figure out exactly what he was looking so intently at."

Kennedy was able to figure this part out on her own. Her father loved to talk about just how special he found Martha's Vineyard to be, how during his first trips there he was dazzled by the picturesque parade of Black families emerging from luxury vehicles, waiting to be transported to the island. So many people greeted each other with relaxed familiarity as everyone seemed to know each other. He could feel their delight and excitement over being reunited. This, one of the few joyous memories her stern, private father was ecstatic to share with his children.

Philip was laughing when he said, "I know you all call your property a cottage, but back then our house really was a cottage. It was a tiny three-bedroom on a five-acre lot." In the years since, the Burke brothers had leveled the original structure and erected a modern behemoth, filling it with late-twentieth-century art and cutting into the land for a private pool. But that was beside the point.

Kennedy looked at her camera's battery life. She'd been recording for twenty-eight minutes but still didn't feel like the story Philip shared was particularly unique since she'd heard it so many times before. And it wouldn't feel that special to her father's birthday guests either, she surmised. She decided to change course.

"Anything that you ever learned about in school that you think had a big impression on my dad?" she asked.

Philip fell silent. "Well, I guess, now that you mention it," he began, "there was a strange history lesson on blue bloods, which I think had an interesting effect on your father."

Kennedy waited for him to continue.

"So this was a schtick that one of our history teachers had been doing for years as a direct callout to the fact that at least eighty percent of the students at Galston considered themselves to be descended from aristocracy, and it was delivered like an elaborate inside joke."

Kennedy perked up. She'd never heard this.

"We're there, learning about European history, and at one point the Moors had begun to intermingle with white Spaniards, producing darker-skinned offspring, which was an undesirable result, to be sure, but ultimately a means of self-protection, right? Because if they can start to get the white people to look more like them, then they can't really be told that whiteness is such a virtue. So anyway, to avoid this fate, certain royals fled the impending wave of biological darkening and retreated to the mountains, where they remained indoors, letting their tanner subjects do the hard physical labor to keep the kingdom functional. The result for the ones who remained shuttered up inside was skin so pale that it made their veins look blue. Blue bloods."

"Is that true?" Kennedy asked.

"Probably somewhat," Philip said. "But what was interesting that day is that I think your father felt very lonely. I mean, for us, we're Black, but as you can see, I could easily pass for white in some circles." He continued with a shrug. "Your dad was the only visibly dark 'non–blue blood' in the room."

"Hm," Kennedy said in response. This wasn't the kind of anecdote she was expecting.

"I just remember the look on your father's face as the teacher spoke, as if he wanted to challenge him. Like he was being reminded that he didn't belong at Galston. I saw that look a few times on your father's face on campus. A mixture of anger and defiance, like he would show what he was capable of no matter how he was judged by his skin color. I always admired that about him, the vision he had for his life."

Kennedy ended the recording and thanked Philip, not at all sure what she could do with the footage she'd just recorded. Would her father want painful memories from the past to be showcased on his special day? She doubted it, but she did feel closer to him in a way, considering her own experiences at Dalton.

As she was getting in her rental car to leave, she shook a cigarette loose from her pack and put it between her lips for the ride. She wasn't supposed to smoke in the car, but they could charge her a fee. She texted Tashia: Leaving now, will upload later. I think my dad is obsessed with blue bloods? Call me.

CHAPTER 13

William Carter Jr.

New York City, May 2015

William wasn't a warm person, but at an early age he began to understand the need for good relationships or, at the very least, alliances. He first explored this back at boarding school, where he made two new friends in addition to Russell. Philip and Bradley Burke were twins. They were new to The Galston School and had come from Newport, Rhode Island, where they both were considered "gifted." The school had recruited them from another Massachusetts boarding school, overriding its own policy to keep out transfers after grade eight. They had identical schedules to William Carter Jr., so without much ceremony, they fell into a lazy camaraderie.

With his first year behind him, William found himself less intimidated by a friendship with two wealthy boys, even though they were Black, but barely. William thought he glimpsed it sometimes in the curl of their hair, but their skin was so fair, almost yellow, their noses so sharp and angled, their lips so thin and stretched that if he didn't know better, he wouldn't think of them as Black at all.

William didn't feel a connection to the brothers, not at first. But what was useful about their eventual friendship, which William was proud to retain to this day, was that William was able to bear witness to the Burkes' incredible and vast amount of resources.

In many ways, boarding school was an incredible equalizer. Galston provided all the basic necessities one would need to live: clothing, housing, and meals. In this way, you couldn't really tell what a student had by looking at them because they were all, in theory, supposed to look the same. William had learned to determine that other factors, ones that were invisible, indicated wealth, and the Burke brothers had them all. A black town car drove them to and from home visits to their parents. Their family had multiple homes all over the United States. Their parents didn't even spend the full summer in Newport, even though summer was why most people wanted to live there. Despite not having the kind of athletic ability that meant that they would excel in gym class, the twins were graceful skiers and traveled every year to the west coast of Canada to indulge. They could also sail, a niche sport and a kind of useless life skill that was only advantageous at boarding school.

Years later, when William knew that he wanted a family, he used the Burke brothers as his template, having an urgent desire to mold his own children into something like those two paragons of wealth.

Asher began at Dalton in kindergarten. Before the admissions process, William and Jacqueline had made him practice saying his colors in English, Spanish, and Mandarin. Asher had rehearsed his handshake as well as sitting still, and after the admissions evaluation was complete, he was taken on a rare outing with both parents for ice cream.

They each doted on him and congratulated themselves on a job well done. William and Jacqueline were excited because his acceptance into preschool put him in position to become a "lifer," the term given to students who remained at a single school for the duration of their education. So, pending no major scandals or disciplinary disasters, he would graduate from Dalton in thirteen years.

Aside from that initial interview, Jacqueline and William didn't make being at school with Asher a habit. At the beginning and end of each day, his Grenadian nanny would join the flock of Caribbean and

Eastern European caretakers snaking down Ninety-First Street. Some parents, years later, ashamed of how little parenting they did, described the complete delegation of childcare to someone else as "having a little help," but it was not something that the Carters felt any embarrassment about.

Asher would have mostly the same friends for his entire time at Dalton. William Carter Jr. had long abandoned the fable that an education was about learning. If his time at some of the best schools in America had taught him anything, it was who you knew, not what, that really made the difference in life outcomes. The wealthy conversed in a language known only to each other, one that he was determined Asher would be a native speaker in.

All Asher's friends, except for Teddy, had *A* names that ended in an *r*, evidently a popular impulse for boys born in the year 1990. So Alistair, Alexander, Asher (and Teddy) became known as the Triple A's and Teddy. Asher had never heard this directly, but this coincidence of names had pleased William, who found himself proud that his son's name was seamlessly synced with generational New York nobility.

There was just one issue: all these boys were white. That wouldn't have been a *problem*, per se, except when it was. William and Jacqueline had anticipated this scenario, of course. The Dalton school was 92 percent white. When they had toured the school along with many other families, it was noticeable that they were the only Black family present. This had become a frequent occurrence on the private school circuit as they searched for a place for Asher. Occasionally, a second Black family would be there or an Asian family, but always only one. The majority of the parents were white, a mix of WASP-y white and Jewish white. This was because Dalton was a nonreligious institution. In some ways, that did invite diversity because it meant education came without the added pressure of forced worship.

So the Carter family happily joined ranks with the school parents in hiring a severe island nanny to raise their firstborn child. Both adult Carters, neither of whom grew up with hired help, were unaware of the ubiquity of imprinting between children and their nannies. But, like his friends Alistair, Alexander, and Teddy, Asher developed a preference for fried plantains and, for years, would occasionally punctuate his sentences with "mon." He was dedicated to soca, calypso, and reggae music. It was less strange to have Asher consider oil down to be his favorite comfort food, since most people would just assume it was a cultural predilection, but when Alexander, Alistair, or Teddy might request roti or callaloo soup, it was cause for confusion. For all the boys, this was eventually a habit that they grew out of. Blue-blooded children developing attachments to their working-class caretakers' native foods was just another developmental stage, no big deal. Except to William Carter Jr., who was always running from his working-class past. He did not want his firstborn son carrying on with such a conspicuous fixation on an employee. He always tried to forget the way that it felt to observe his father fraternizing with his Galston classmates, making inside jokes with them and catering to their humor. It made him feel like his father was the joke, that a friendship between students and the school groundskeeper was so unlikely that the only thing it could be was funny.

William never discussed his rampant insecurities, not even with Jacqueline, who'd watched him grow his fortune. It was easier to simply dictate and demand and hope that no one questioned the origins of anything he said. For the most part, that's what happened, until his seventieth birthday was approaching. Jacqueline had wanted very badly to take the lead with party planning and William had let her. By now, she knew him and his expectations, but he still wanted to check in and make sure that all was going smoothly, just in case.

Two months before his party, late one night after dinner, he knocked softly on the door to Jacqueline's bathroom. She was sitting at her vanity in a champagne-colored silk caftan with a matching silk turban, applying copious amounts of La Mer moisturizer. When she turned to look at him, he entered. "Just want to give you an update that the Secret Service wants to do a sweep of Watcha so that they're set for the Obamas and Clintons. I had someone send an email to the team," he said.

"All right, that's reasonable," Jacqueline said evenly.

William lingered, locking eyes with her in the mirror.

"Yes? Is there something else?" she asked, returning the applicator to the tray in front of her and turning around to face him.

"Yes, actually. The security head shared that several of my former classmates have been contacted. The Burkes and Russell Johnson. Any idea what that's about?" William said.

"That's a bit strange, I guess. They are certainly on the guest list, but nothing unusual should be going on with them. Perhaps they are going to do a little performance for you or gathering some very embarrassing photos and someone is going to leak it," she said, teasing him.

William didn't return her smile. "Right," he said gruffly. "Well, please just make sure that everything runs smoothly. We can't afford any breaches or missteps. You know what's been popping up lately? Kofi."

Jacqueline's face turned somber. "Has he? Why? I can't imagine that anyone knows anything about Kofi. And trust me," she said, shifting the conversation, "this party is going to be everything you've ever wanted."

William walked over to pat her on the shoulder tenderly. He believed her.

CHAPTER 14

Asher Bennett Carter

Harvard, March 2015

"Bro, you'll never guess who I saw last week," Asher's friend Viraj told him on the phone. "He was working at a coffee shop near Columbia. Made my Americano and everything."

"Who?" Asher asked, refusing to attempt a guess.

"Ernest Morris," Viraj answered, pausing for a reaction.

A thing that was widely known, even to Asher Bennett Carter, was that he wasn't very smart. He also had a fairly terrible memory. Aside from these two little things, he was an asset to his family in every way. He was handsome, charming, athletic, and most importantly, didn't ask that many questions, especially compared to his irritating sister. He didn't question himself, his place in the world, or anything else that might cause him to have to consider subjects beyond two categories of thought: squash and money.

"I have no idea who that is, man," Asher said finally.

"Bro! Yes, you do. He got his ass beat outside of Ivy. Come on, you have to remember that. He was like in a coma or something," Viraj said.

"Oh yeah, that guy," Asher replied. "Guess he's awake."

Viraj chuckled on the other end. "He's just as weird as ever and still such a try hard. I bet you he interns at NPR or something. What a tool." Viraj changed the subject to the upcoming summer and asked Asher if he wanted to join his family in the Mediterranean.

Asher said he'd get back to him on dates, with his attendance at his dad's seventieth birthday party mandatory for obvious reasons. They hung up, and Asher went back to staring at an email that he was planning on writing to his nicest professor to see just how he could salvage at least one of his failing grades. Year by year, school had increasingly become a nightmare.

As much as the Carters were eager to give Asher access to the greatest networking opportunities a kindergartener could have, there were certain unavoidable consequences to putting your Black child into an elite white environment. In grade school, Asher had the Triple A's and Teddy, and that friendship thrived as much as it could but ultimately had limitations. As they matured, they began to compete, really compete, for everything—sexual partners, admission into more elite schools, sports, careers—and there were ugly holes that began to puncture an otherwise peaceful picture. With stakes so high and competition so steep, a very slight, very steady stream of resentment would flow toward anyone who had any kind of perceived advantage, and for Asher, that could mean either his money or his Blackness.

The question of how any below-average student who happens to be exceptional at a sport ends up at the best school in the country is a pointless one to ask, doubly so if said student's last name is set to become part of the American dynastic canon. This was Asher's general assumption before he got to Princeton, but when he arrived, it became clear that the question would be asked of him over and over again. His world had expanded to include a new campus and new people, and those new people had questions.

Even though he didn't want to admit at first that he remembered him, one of these new people was Ernest Morris. Ernest liked to go by the name Earn, since he said he had to "earn everything" he had. Ernest Morris, a boy so thin that his elbows and knees could be considered registered weapons, hailed from a small town outside of Atlanta, Georgia. Occasionally when he would speak, a drawl would slip through and drape a syrupy sedation over his words. He was the class valedictorian at his public high school, which would have been more impressive had it not been a statistic for most of the incoming freshman class at Princeton. Ernest wore his hair in a flattop fade, a living tribute to one of his idols, Spike Lee. There was something vaguely '80s about the way that he presented himself, his classmates unsure if it was a purposeful stylistic choice or a sign of a profound lack of style. All this to say that Ernest stood out, and he liked it.

Asher and Ernest had in fact met before Princeton. Ernest was the recipient of the Carter Foundation Scholarship, a fund that William Carter Jr. personally oversaw to ensure that some of the best and brightest young Black minds would be able to attend college debt-free. Every year, twenty students from around the country were offered these scholarships, and in a big, flashy, well-photographed ceremony, William would present them with a check. He would give a short speech about how "these young minds would make a difference" and how he was happy to be a small part of their story.

During his senior year at Dalton, Asher happened to have a squash tournament in Florida. If he wanted to get a ride on the jet, he had to first stop in Atlanta with his father, which was where he and Ernest met for the first time at the scholarship ceremony.

He'd made polite small talk with several of the kids, including Ernest, the two boys mostly discussing what they knew about Princeton once they'd figured out they'd be attending the same school. Even though Asher had never really experienced a person like Ernest, after their brief interaction, he counted on forgetting him immediately.

"So I'll see you on campus?" Asher said distractedly as he was leaving and offered Ernest a closed fist.

Ernest, slightly frazzled, returned his own shaking fist forward before stuttering out, "Ye-yes, see you there."

Asher first ran into Ernest in his American film seminar. Ernest made it a habit to sit front and center for every class. He greeted Asher enthusiastically every time. He desired to be both seen and heard. He engaged constantly with the material, but he was also very outspoken about his opinions, which he himself described as "rooted in Black liberation."

Asher liked to sit in the back of the class with whatever other athletes were present. Sometimes he had a squash friend, but he would also settle for companionship from someone on the tennis, crew, football, basketball, or lacrosse teams. In the class that he shared with Ernest, he had two squash team friends. One was an Indian immigrant, Viraj, who was the descendant of diamond dealers and spoke four languages fluently. The other was a sandy-haired Californian named Canon, who was a competitive surfer until he went to a Silicon Valley private school where he discovered that squash was more than just a vegetable. The three boys were a trifecta of collegiate youth and attractiveness, looking like a GAP ad but sounding like the wrong side of a Reddit thread.

One day, midway through their first semester, Ernest cornered Asher before class. Ernest slapped down a flyer printed on blue paper that looked to Asher to be a homemade imitation of something that might announce a band performance.

"What's this?" Canon asked, making a motion to pick up the flyer.

Ernest slid the flyer just out of his reach. "This is a private invitation," he said, spectacled eyes still on Asher's as he moved the piece of paper closer to him.

Asher lifted it to read while Viraj and Canon framed him and read over each of his shoulders.

POWER TO THE PEOPLE

THE BLACK STUDENT UNION AT PRINCETON IS PLEASED TO WELCOME YOU TO THE INAUGURAL MEETING OF POWER TO THE PEOPLE, A NEW INITIATIVE FORMED BY ERNEST MORRIS FOR LEADERSHIP, COMMUNITY, AND ACTIVISM.

THURSDAY, OCTOBER 9, 2008

After he was finished reading, he looked up at Ernest. "We hope you'll join us," Ernest said.

"Oh yeah? What about me?" Canon asked, a tone of mock hurt in his voice.

"Like I said," Ernest replied with a small smile, "it's a private invitation."

"Uh, thanks man. I'll have to check my schedule and let you know," Asher said. "I have squash pretty much daily, you know? Takes up a lot of time."

"Hope to see you there, brother" is all Ernest said with a nod before turning to make his exit.

"Poindexter-looking ass," Canon mumbled before grabbing the flyer, crumpling it up, and tossing it in the trash.

From then on, Asher made it a habit to avoid interactions with Ernest, but it felt like Ernest spent a strange amount of time seeking out opportunities to be near Asher. Asher found a minimal reprieve sophomore year when it was time to bicker for an eating club. He chose Ivy Club, or rather, it chose him because out of all the eating clubs on campus, it was the only one that made sense for a student like him.

Historically, Ivy was the most formal of the eating clubs, where children of mostly Northeastern families opted out of the pedestrian dining hall and into a social club-cum-cafeteria where everyone was thought of as "Ivy material." Years later, when these students were sitting in front of co-op boards and joining other rarified institutions like country clubs or advisory committees, the experiences they had with Ivy would have laid the blueprint. Their muscle memory would kick in, and they would sail on to the next step, bypassing the anxieties that people more unfamiliar with such a process would ordinarily feel.

It wasn't as if Ivy was only about money, but it was one of the most expensive eating clubs, and that did tend to deter applicants who might not be able to afford the fees. There were other things that were important to members when they thought about curation for the club, like having the right "look" or being freakishly talented in something quite unique. Someone poor but hot might just get lucky. For the most part, Ivy was extremely white, as was all of Princeton, but particularly Ivy.

Asher did weigh all his dining options, and he thought it might be controversial that he was going to bicker for Ivy, given its history, but given his own history and as a member of the squash team, it was already where most of his friends were. His freshman year, it didn't matter because the students were sorted into residential colleges where they ate and lived, but after that, it was imperative for the preservation of the social experience that he find an eating club. The most persistent problem that he could find with joining Ivy was that there were few to no other Black student members. Ordinarily, he expected this just based on where he lived and went to school before college, but in this case, he would be intentionally selecting to place himself in an environment where he was, once again, the only one.

Plus, he'd begun dating Tatum Bamford, a bombshell knockout from Connecticut. And yes, she was white. Asher didn't consider himself the girlfriend type, but Tatum had a magnetism and authoritative presence that made resisting her pointless. They met by random chance, lined up on the same side of a flip cup game. Neither she nor Asher missed once, draining their cups in a speedy chug and then balancing the red plastic on the edge of the table to flip them upside down. Tatum was a blond pacifist heir to a weapons fortune who'd spent her high school years at Taft and invested in African charities, including raising money for Darfur. She was familiar with the Carter Corporation and all their positive work in Ghana, which Asher was barely conscious of, but he wasn't above using it as a means to an end, which in this case was a hookup. It turned out, after the good sex, that he actually enjoyed spending time with Tatum. She was sweet, uncomplicated, and very into him. Tatum had an older brother in Ivy, and so she knew before she even set foot on campus that was where she would bicker. She more or less convinced Asher to do the same, though the push came with the force of a feather because really, he'd already decided that's where he'd be.

So yes, when prompted, he did remember Ernest Morris getting his ass beat outside of Ivy and all the other things that happened while he was at Princeton. And still, Ernest wasn't really on his radar because he had bigger problems. He felt sad about how complicated everything in his life felt now. The rare spark of ambition that he felt after his gap year working with his father had led him here, but this wasn't the life for him. He'd never wanted to be at Harvard Business School, and he should have never had to enroll, all of this crystal clear in his head especially now that he was in danger of failing out. He had to come up with a great story for his professor before his parents were alerted to just how messy the perfect life they thought they'd given him had become.

January 18, 1962,

Dear Dean Weismann,

I am writing to endorse an extraordinary Galston student for acceptance into Harvard. William Carter Jr. has been with us for the last four years on a faculty scholarship. Hailing from the inner city of Boston, he has overcome the odds to demonstrate prolific intellectual capacity, tenacity, and leadership. He is set to be the salutatorian of the class of 1963 and is a pleasure to have on campus.

William Carter Jr. is beloved among the faculty for his conscientious approach to learning, his curious nature, and his meticulous character. We are so proud of the young man that he has become, and we think that he is an example of the rewards of integration, of what achievements are possible.

His exemplary disciplinary record along with his strong academics tell me that he has a bright future ahead. He would be an asset to the incoming Harvard class. I would be happy to discuss him on the phone if you would like to know more.

Best,

Dr. James Perry

Dean of Students

CHAPTER 15

William Carter Jr.

Harvard, October 1963

If you asked William Carter Jr., he might say that his life began at Harvard. The day that he'd slipped into the customary white pants and blue blazer that signified the last frontier for departing Galston seniors was his farewell to boarding school. The ensemble had been completed by a straw boater hat accessorized with a red, white, and blue ribbon around the middle that matched the same decorative accessory each boy wore on his lapel. William had felt ridiculous, but Russell's healthy Afro meant that the boater hat sat directly on top of his head, perilously balanced like a halo.

"They love to try to keep a good brother down," Russell had joked, patting the sides of his head. William, who wore his hair shorn close to the scalp, loved that Russell was so comfortable with his nonconformity. He imagined his athletic talent yielded a lot of confidence, something he would miss when he had to start all over again making friends and building a community at Harvard. Russell was off to Penn in the fall, ready to continue playing football on a new field. And for the first time in their lives, the Burke brothers were taking separate paths, one going to Stanford and the other, Edinburgh. William's friendship group, going their separate ways.

In a last-minute offer, an alumnus at Galston had secured William a campus library job at Harvard for the summer, so he went there early. He'd felt both ready and not. He had submitted all his paperwork, filled out all the forms, checked off that he would accept a roommate of color just like he had for Galston. But unlike when he started at that school five years ago, he now had a better idea of what to expect, and this had intimidated him. At Harvard, everything would be magnified. He would have female classmates for the first time. He would be closer to home. He'd worried about adjusting to the changes. Still, moving in early meant that he would avoid at least some of the confusion of the general move-in day, and fewer people would see him fumbling around with his parents. Image was everything.

In the end, William Jr. had let William Sr. and Evelyn have their full send-off experience, with his mother in particular far more emotional about his starting college than she had been when he began boarding school. His parents strangely hadn't seemed as out of place on Harvard's campus as he'd assumed they would, and he regretted not wanting them there. His dorm assignment was Matthews Hall North, and his room on the third floor was so small that the fact he was a de facto minimalist was an asset. When he'd turned the door handle, he had been startled to see someone was already inside, and that was the first time that William Carter Jr. encountered Kofi Asare. Kofi, his new roommate, hailed from Accra, Ghana, which had confused William at first because he had a very ostentatious British accent. Without knowing anything about him, he'd branded him stuck up and immediately put up walls that he'd never had with Russell.

In October of his freshman year, having had a highly successful academic season so far, William arrived back at his dormitory to find a crimson envelope bearing his name on the floor. He looked around, even though the hallway and his room were both empty. He shut the door, dropped his belongings, and stepped out of his shoes all while tearing at the sealed envelope. He thought it might be an invitation of some kind to a party, and in some ways he was right.

> Dear William Carter Jr.,
>
> Your presence is requested at a gentleman's meeting to welcome a select group of Harvard freshman. Please keep this invitation confidential. The meeting will be hosted at the home of Professor Raymond Hill on Saturday evening, October 19, at 5:00 p.m.
>
> Proper attire required.
>
> The Hill residence is at 38 Banks Street. There is no need to RSVP. Kindly burn this letter after reading. We are looking forward to welcoming you to campus.

William read the letter again, surer with every reread that this letter was a prank. He went to his student facebook, cracked the spine to get to *H*, and looked up the professor who would be hosting this alleged meeting. Raymond Hill was right there between Professor Stephen Hayes and Kevin Howard. To burn the letter felt unnecessarily dramatic, so he tucked it inconspicuously beneath some books in his middle desk drawer. If this were a prank, it was a very elaborate one, but if anyone could pull off an elaborate prank, it would be a Harvard student. He weighed the decision to go or not, but at over a week away, he still had some time to do some more research to find out just how real this was. There was no letter for Kofi, and he didn't know whether or not he would ask him about one. When Kofi returned back to the dorm, William carried on as usual and didn't disclose that he'd been asked to attend a secret meeting at the house of a professor who wasn't his professor . . . on a weekend. It just seemed too bizarre to explain.

When October 19 arrived, William found himself placing an ill-fitting blue sport coat over a white polo and khaki slacks. He didn't yet have a coat that would be right for this combination, so though the temperature dipped to a chill, he had to endure without the added layer of protection. He didn't fully understand the nuanced instruction on dress code suggested in the invitation, but he'd learned a thing or two at Galston beyond the books and figured that "proper attire" meant no sneakers or sweatpants.

William Carter Jr. left his dorm at 4:15 p.m., which was an excessive amount of time to leave to walk to a residence less than a mile away, but William liked to account for every potential scenario, and he also liked to be on time. He arrived with plenty of time to spare and was let into Professor Hill's home by a similarly dressed Black upperclassman. His shoulders settled into relaxation for having made two right assessments, the first being that this meeting wasn't a prank, and the second being the correct assumption about what to wear. When William was shown inside, he was also delighted to discover that he wasn't the first person there. Five other Black freshmen sat awkwardly on the open seats between the living and dining areas sipping water and what looked like red wine. Two boys made room for William on the sofa and he sat, giving a closed-mouth smile to everyone else in the silent room. Suddenly, the upperclassman who answered the door appeared again and asked William what he'd prefer to drink. William hesitated, not knowing what to say at first because he didn't drink alcohol yet, and then he replied, "A glass of red, thank you." Keep it simple, he figured.

He looked around. From what William could tell, the home was decorated in varying shades of red and featured a very worldly collection of antiques. The paintings on the wall were a combination of pastoral landscapes and what William's limited artistic knowledge could decipher as Black American folk art. More boys filtered into the house until it was filled with twenty-seven students, almost the entirety of the male Black students in his class. He'd seen them all since they were hard to miss on campus, but he did not know all of them. The boys, all transmitting unspoken anxiety for various reasons, kept their chatter to hushed whispers and short sentences. No one wanted to draw attention to their conversations, but most of them couldn't bear the silence.

At 5:01 p.m. exactly, Professor Raymond Hill appeared and clapped his hands one time with a single reverberating snap that made William jump. Professor Hill was a man of average height looking to be in his midfifties. He had close-shaved salt-and-pepper facial hair and a slightly crooked incisor that some would say gave his smile character. He wore a navy suit with a blue-and-white patterned oxford underneath, an especially decorous decision for someone who was already home. "Welcome!" he exclaimed. "Welcome to my home and a belated welcome to Harvard. I'm so glad to have all of you here."

The crowd of boys murmured their appreciation.

"So you're likely all wondering what you're doing here, and I'm eager to tell you. But first I have some questions for you," Professor Hill said.

William joined his fellow freshman in adjusting their posture. This was a pop quiz of sorts. They'd do their best to excel.

"Why don't we get to know each other by introducing yourselves, saying where you come from, and telling us what you're studying here," Professor Hill offered.

As far as questions went, this was a relatively easy thing to tackle. Professor Hill gestured to the first student on his left, a dark-skinned boy with deep brown eyes and absurdly long eyelashes.

The boy cleared his throat twice before saying, "Um, hi, I'm Chris Vernon, and I'm from Virginia. I'm studying medicine."

"That's wonderful, Chris," Professor Hill said encouragingly. "Welcome."

This went on for the remaining twenty-six people in the room. There were boys from Florida and New Jersey and South Carolina and Missouri and Michigan and Illinois. They were studying to be engineers and doctors and lawyers and economists. By the time it was William's turn, somewhere in the middle, he'd already taken several generous gulps of his red wine, and although the taste was bitter, he appreciated the calming effect that it had on him. He spoke clearly: "William Carter Jr. I'm from Boston, actually, and I'm studying business." William truthfully had no idea what he was studying just yet. It was barely six weeks into the semester, but so far he'd deduced that the best professional track for him to be on was either law or business. In this moment, he picked business.

Professor Hill maintained an uncomfortable amount of eye contact with him and said, "A hometown hero. Welcome William Carter Jr.," before letting the rest of the room complete their introductions. After every boy had gone, Professor Hill spoke again.

"Now, what do you notice about this room?" he said. The boys all looked at one another and tried to avoid catching a gaze for too long. None of them had a real answer aside from the obvious.

"Okay, don't hurt yourselves," Professor Hill said. "I'll tell you. You might be thinking this is a Negro convention, and you're right. At least that's what we called it when I was a student here. I started teaching at Harvard in 1951, and by the time that freshman class had graduated, it was becoming out of favor to refer to us as 'Negros.' We had graduated to being Black, but the sentiment surrounding the fact that we didn't quite belong at Harvard remained.

"It's now many years later, but you might be feeling the same way that I once did about walking onto this historical campus and not knowing exactly where you fit. This room is to affirm for you, for all of you, for now and for the future that you belong here. There will be a lot of talk in your lives about excellence. You *are* excellent. There will be a lot of people who say things about you like 'He thinks he's special.' Let me be clear to you right now: you *are* special. There will be professors here who will treat you with open contempt. These people do not want you here and they will not pretend otherwise. There will be other students that do the same. There's also an aspect of this education that many of the other students here are getting outside of the classroom, in their homes, in their fraternities and clubs and teams that you will not be allowed into. So in this room, we will be giving you that education. You will learn all of the things that you need to know in here to compete with them. But let me tell you something, you don't win a race by tying your opponents' legs together. You win a race by running faster, and you will have to run faster, and be stronger, better, smarter, and more dedicated than your white peers. And that's forever."

William Carter Jr. swallowed hard. This man's command over the room was a marvel to witness.

"So, first things first: your appearance," Professor Hill said. "You all might have noticed that I added a dress code to this invitation even though it is on campus and on a Saturday, and that's because one of our first lessons is to learn how to command respect. Some people will tell you that this doesn't matter, that the clothes do not make the man, and in some cases that's true. But it will not be true for you in the world that you inhabit. Casual dress is a privilege for those given the benefit of the doubt. It is for people who will be accepted without question, and that's not you. It might be one day, but right now, that's not you. I don't want to have to tell you that you'll have to negotiate for your humanity, but it would be a lie to say that you don't, and one thing that we will never do in this room is lie to one another. If any of the things I've said so far aren't things you want to hear, please know that you're free to leave. This is an elective club, one that I hope many of you will see as an opportunity." Professor Hill paused and looked slowly around the room. None of the boys moved to leave, and so he continued.

"Aside from knowing how to dress, in this room, you'll also learn the quiddities of the elite. We'll talk about wine and art and music. We'll refine your tastes so that you'll be prepared to inhabit the world with knowledge and power."

William found himself enraptured. He'd been navigating this world since he was thirteen with limited guidance. Unlike some of the other boys in the room, whose fathers had also attended Harvard, William was gripped with the fear that his ignorance of this world would lead to his downfall. Some of these boys looked incredibly comfortable, their body language indicating that they'd heard speeches like this before. But William sat up and leaned in. This was the first time that anyone had even bothered to concede that this school was overrun with invisible obstacles and populated by many who were very determined to exclude the people in this room from accessing the spoils that came with a Harvard degree.

"With your excellence, you make white people feel uncomfortable because you threaten their illusion that life is a meritocracy," Professor Hill continued. "They believe that they've worked hard to get here and that because you're Black, you've cheated. So I'm going to say this again: You actually are excellent. You are better than them, but here, you still have to play their game, with their rules, on their field. Luckily, I know how to do that, and by the time you graduate, you will too. This club has fostered many students and set them free in the world, and they will also help you. You are not alone, and now that you're here, you won't be again. In return, all we ask for is loyalty and discretion. As the invitation mentioned, we do not discuss this club. We do not invite anyone else to be a part of it, so welcome to the future of Black America. The invitation was personal and nontransferable, and I hope that all of you can respect that."

After this sermon, the room became more comfortable, safer somehow. William met the other boys who were to become members of this unofficial fraternity. These relationships would come to define William's opinions on Blackness, what the responsibilities were, what the obligations were, the rules and specificities.

At boarding school, he had learned the term "in loco parentis," which essentially provided a way for adults who were part of a school administration to act as parents in a situation where there were no parents. Seeing as his own father was present for the five days of the school week when he was at Galston, he thought the concept of in loco parentis didn't apply to him. But now, he felt energized by the surrogate father role that Professor Hill embodied.

William listened to Professor Hill continue his lecture for almost another half hour, hypnotized by the man's voice, realizing that being in the room was the ceremony where he would be getting the keys to having the life he was meant to live—the rules of fortune.

CHAPTER 16

Kennedy Carter

Los Angeles, April 2015

A flight attendant placed a flute of what Kennedy assumed was champagne (but could have been prosecco) on the glossy surface that mimicked wood in front of her. Next to her, Asher was already a single bourbon deep, and the plane had just taken off.

Kennedy hated the Gulfstream G280, the smallest jet in the Carter Corporation fleet that shuttled the family back and forth to Martha's Vineyard. She found it cramped, suffocating. She flattened her palm and drummed her rings on the shiny fake-wood table.

Her parents sat directly in eyesight on the sofas that took up the long wall of the cabin, completely disinterested in their children not forty feet away. She watched them, distantly remembering how at one time in her life, the ride to the Vineyard was the epitome of fun. Either they were anticipating an amazing summer, buoyed by the temporary suspension of work and school in place of lobster rolls and lawn games, or they were contentedly returning to so-called real life, wrung out with exhaustion from overindulgences and sunshine. They hadn't had a summer like that in years. The Vineyard was once a source of joy but had since become another extension of the family business, an office with a better view. Even now, in transit, both her parents appeared to be animated models in a Norman Rockwell painting about Black people in corporate America.

Her mother was furiously scrolling on her iPad, glasses balanced on the tip of her slender nose, her blown-out, light-brown hair elegantly held in a claw clip at the nape of her neck. She was doing work, which in this case was loosely defined as party planning for her husband's seventieth birthday. Her father was dialed into a conference call and was simultaneously texting his first assistant that his second assistant should be terminated. In the terminal before the flight, Kennedy had snuck a peek at his phone screen as he typed expletives full of errors at a snail's pace. The assistant had failed to expose the source of escalating security alerts that were not only a nuisance to him personally but also alarming in general for a corporation with a reputation to protect.

No one in the family had made eye contact with each other in quite some time. Since they were comfortably at cruising altitude, Kennedy tried to get her brother's attention by rising from her seat and waving her hand in front of his face. He removed his left headphone. "What, Ken?" he asked, clearly irritated at having been disturbed.

"Can I ask you a question?" she whispered.

He shifted his head downward and his gaze upward and opened his palms as an invitation to speed things along. The Carter children, from birth, had been schooled in the notion that time was a precious resource. Not many kids understand what a "hard out" is before they're hitting certain developmental milestones. But that's why Kennedy initiated this conversation: for at least the next thirty-eight minutes, Asher had nowhere else to be.

Kennedy leaned over the table and dropped her voice to an even lower whisper. Asher did not mirror her closeness. "I'm working on something," she said. Her brother remained impassive.

"What's the question?" he deadpanned, signaling even further that he had no desire to engage with her as a coconspirator.

"Well, do you know, how—" She paused and instantly regretted not coming up with a more rehearsed question. She really should have practiced something. She didn't even know what she was trying to achieve with asking Asher. He knew just as little as she did, although at this point, she was betting she knew just a little bit more. "—how Dad started the company? Like, what's the story of it?"

"Kennedy . . . what?" Asher looked vaguely disgusted. "Why are you even whispering about this? You *know* how Dad started the company."

"I don't think we do," Kennedy responded, still whispering and trying to telepathically communicate to her physically close but psychically distant sibling.

"Ken, we do. It's very well documented and publicized, okay? The story has been told a million different times." Asher began to put back on his headphones.

"Wait!" Kennedy whispered to him, really trying to convey urgency. "What I'm trying to say is . . . I've been working on something, and some weird stuff has come up, and I think there's something else going on. I don't think we know the full story."

"'Working on something.'" Asher contorted his face and put air quotations around his sister's words. "You're 'working on something' that investigates our family? Are you crazy, Kennedy? After everything they've done for us, you'd do that?"

Kennedy shrank back. "It's just—"

"No, cut it out, Ken. You're being a fucking baby. You're trying to punish everyone else for your mistakes."

"I'm not!"

"You are," he said reaching across the table to slide the glass of still-untouched champagne directly in front of her. "Less think. More drink."

Asher raised his empty glass to gesture to the stewardess that he wanted a refill. She immediately reappeared with a bottle of Weller's Antique Reserve. He set his glass on the table, and the small jet lurched.

The stewardess expertly steadied herself by placing her free hand on the side of the plane, balancing the bottle in her other hand.

Kennedy's heart rate quickened, but no one else seemed flustered by the turbulence. In fact, no one else moved. The stewardess returned to her task of refilling Asher's bourbon, which he downed in a smooth, steady swallow, then dropped the glass onto the table for another. The plane suddenly and unexpectedly dipped to the left side. Kennedy gasped from the shock and frantically looked again at her parents, both of whom remained unbelievably committed to their devices. The plane once again righted itself after a few seconds.

Kennedy hated this small, stupid plane and the treacherous fog-filled flight pattern to and from the Vineyard. She cursed under her breath as she watched the stewardess fill her brother's glass a third time. He defiantly stared back at her with dull, glazed eyes and put his sunglasses on when he felt he'd sufficiently intimidated her into silence.

And the plane made a terrifying drop. This time, it didn't immediately rebound into place. It kept falling, picking up speed. Her breath caught in her throat but no sound came out. Asher's head arced upward as it followed the liquid flying out of his glass. The stewardess was brought to her knees by the sheer force of the decline.

Her parents' eyes remained locked on their devices as the plane plummeted, as Kennedy closed her eyes and gripped her armrests and shrieked and shrieked . . .

"What the fuck, Ken?"

Kennedy jerked awake at the sudden flood of light in her eyes. As she tried to focus her vision, she immediately saw the slippered feet of her roommate, Brianna Glen, who stood in the doorway with her hand on the light switch, wearing a confused expression and an oversize silk bonnet.

"You're *screaming*, in your *sleep*," Brianna said, willing Kennedy to understand what was happening.

"I'm . . . I'm sorry." Kennedy panted. "I was having a bad dream. I just—it was so real, I—"

"Yeah, it was so real for me too," Brianna interrupted. "Look, it's four a.m., Ken. Can't you just take a Klonopin like a normal person and relax?"

"Yeah, I'm really sorry, Bri."

"You said that," Brianna replied, angrily turning the light back off and closing the door as she made her exit.

Kennedy shook herself further awake and settled back into bed, realizing that she hadn't actually been talking to Asher. He had been dodging her calls for several weeks. This wasn't unusual. She figured that she was going to have to go to Boston and see him in person to get his interview done. That was fine since she planned on being at Watcha Cove to finish her film before the party.

She strained her eyes in the dark. She was back in California in the downtown high-rise that she shared with Brianna, the daughter of an actor and comedian. As one of the stipulations of her West Coast relocation, she needed to find someone to live with, a partner to help navigate the transition, but even whom she chose was met with her father's disapproval. He had always looked down on Black people who had made their money from entertainment, considering it cheap and demeaning. He also felt it was a fickle industry, but who else was she going to live with in Los Angeles if not the descendants of entertainers? It wasn't exactly a hotbed for the "right kind" of professional aspirations.

Kennedy patted the top of her hair to check if she'd sweated out her silk press with the intensity of that nightmare. She'd wrapped her hair before bed and secured it with a scarf, but the scarf was on the floor. She hadn't worn her hair like this since she graduated high school. The sleek look was the preference of her mother and her father, and at this point, she wasn't even sure why she still did it.

Most of the time, while alone and free in California, she'd worn goddess braids, a natural style that her mother coined "ragamuffin chic," which suited Kennedy fine. But now, with the school year wrapping up, Kennedy would be heading back east for the summer, and that meant she needed to look exactly how her parents wanted her to look. Relieved that her hair was fine, she reached over to her nightstand to retrieve her laptop.

The screen read 4:25 a.m. She groaned. She wanted to smoke but was too tired to go outside. Instead, she opened her emails. Not that many people were sending correspondence at 4:00 a.m., but she just wanted to see if she'd gotten any responses to the dozens of probes she sent out recently trying to get in touch with her father's former roommate from college. She first contacted Harvard, then Kofi's family, who owned a hotel in Accra, and lastly hired a private investigator, who, for a flat fee of $12,000, would actually go to the hotel and see what he could find. As suspected, nothing on that front, but there was an email from Russell Johnson (sent 7:04 p.m. EST).

Subject: Meeting

Kennedy, would love to participate in your father's tribute. Let me know when you'll be coming to my place. We'll coordinate schedules.

Best, RJ

Kennedy opened a folder labeled *CC DOC*, which housed all the research that she'd done so far on the Carter Corporation and her father. After Kennedy's trip to Northern California, Tashia had texted, **Heard there was a secret society at Harvard for Black men when your dad was there. People say it kind of disappeared. Maybe one of them knows something about Kofi?** But it wasn't as if she could just google "Secret Black Society/Harvard," because she had tried that and gotten nowhere.

In a week, she would be flying back to the East Coast to finish her film project, so she could stop at Russell's Connecticut house on her way up to Watcha Cove. At least this interview might hold some promise. Russell was the second of her father's high school classmates to be included in the film, but she'd yet to find anyone from college willing to talk. On her laptop, she once again brought up the photo of the Polaroid of Kofi, which she'd saved so that it was part of her files.

"Who are you?" she whispered in the dark, moving her eyes close to the screen, enraptured by this mysterious figure who she thought held the key to her father's past.

CHAPTER 17

Jacqueline Bennett Carter

New York City, May 2015

Jacqueline Bennett Carter gently patted her hair. Back when she couldn't afford to dye her hair, it was dark brown, almost black. Now, it was an auburn brown with red highlights. She had made this change years ago, a subtle stab at the fountain of youth, which turned out to be a successful gamble. "Darling, show me the screen, please. I need to check my frame," she instructed Kennedy, who flipped the screen out from the back of her camera and reversed it to face Jacqueline. Jacqueline was seated in her study, and she reclined lazily against the armrest of her bouclé couch. She reached behind her for her glasses and pulled them out to look at the screen. When she was satisfied, she placed pillows behind her back, pushing herself upright and toward the edge of the couch as she sat at attention before her daughter.

It had been several weeks since she touched base with Kennedy on the project, but she had full faith that it was being executed as expected. Kennedy had flown back east, claiming that she needed to go up to the Vineyard house to get some B-roll, but before that she wanted to film Jacqueline's testimonials for the video. Jacqueline had rolled her eyes when Kennedy had emailed the house manager asking for her room to be made up.

B-roll for a nine-minute movie was so unnecessary, but she agreed to let it all happen. She supposed Kennedy had been conditioned to overachieve, though, and, thanks to Jacqueline's influence, had always loved anything to do with film. As a girl, Kennedy, in her desperate little way, would watch movies with Jacqueline from the doorway of her mother's bedroom, waiting to be invited in. If and when Jacqueline noticed her daughter, she would allow the girl to join her and provide her with an education on cameras and angles, on narrative and on technique. Asher wasn't interested in connecting in this way over art and craftsmanship, but Kennedy was, so Jacqueline taught.

"Okay, Mom, so we're almost ready. Are you?" Kennedy asked her, finger hovering over the record button.

Jacqueline took a dramatic look around, craning her neck for emphasis. "Who is *we*, pumpkin?" she asked, highlighting that they were, in fact, alone.

Kennedy averted her gaze, embarrassed, and fumbled with the notes on her lap. She was such a timorous girl, which was why Jacqueline was more naturally tolerant of Asher. She didn't like who he was either, but she had always made the most of her lot in life. Though her son was a simpleton, he performed so much better under pressure.

Kennedy cleared her throat. "Mom, can you tell me when and how you met Dad?" she asked.

Jacqueline tossed her hair behind her shoulders and checked her posture. She paused for a moment, remembering which version of the story to tell.

The real story couldn't be recorded on camera. She knew that, but a different, better version had been invented, and that's what she would share. That version didn't include Jacqueline's being a waitress. It also didn't include her being an escort.

The real story was that early on in her New York experience, a girl from her acting class, a curly-haired blonde from Virginia named

Donna (which was definitely not her real name), told Jacqueline that she could make some extra cash by going out on dates with older men.

Jacqueline walked up to a conversation before class had started one day, where Donna was balancing a slim cigarette between her lips, waiting for a light. She paused to look at whom Donna was speaking with and recognized two other young women, one actively doing modeling work and another who was gunning for a role on Broadway.

"Do you know how many dumb rich men live in the city?" Donna asked, oozing nonchalance.

The shorter girl, the Broadway actress, sighed. "Well, sure, but what happens when we get famous?"

Donna shrugged. "It's not like they know who you really are. You make something up." She inhaled and looked at Jacqueline. "You interested? Guys love variety," she said, raising her eyebrows.

Jacqueline flushed uncomfortably. "So what are we talking about exactly?" she asked, wanting Donna to clarify.

"It works like this: These guys, they just want some company. They're looking for a little relief from their stressful lives or wives and whatnot. They do a little coke, or maybe weed . . . they really just want to talk, mostly, and you just sit there and listen. You build a little client base and you're basically an entrepreneur. The money, it helps."

Money was indeed getting tight, but Jacqueline felt like she knew how this story ended and politely declined. She made an excuse to go inside to class, but she remained distracted through the whole thing as she tallied the way that her expenses were piling up against the nonexistent opportunities. She approached Donna after class to learn more.

Donna smiled a wry little smile and put her arm in Jacqueline's as they strolled down Fortieth Street together. "I'm sure you're going to be great at this. You're so good in class. It's basically an acting exercise. You build a character, or a few if that's your thing, and that's who these guys meet." Donna paused to look at Jacqueline. "No offense, but if you want to do this, you're probably going to need to get some new clothes," she said.

Jacqueline smoothed out the pleats of her mid-length skirt and looked down at the printed silk blouse she was wearing. "Why?"

"Oh, come on, all productions need costumes," Donna said, grinning. "Look, part of what you're selling is an experience, a fantasy. If you dress the part, it'll be easier."

Jacqueline nodded. So she needed more money then. Of course. Jacqueline, still a virgin but at least aware of the mechanics of what she was being asked to do, asked Donna if she would be expected to "spend the entire night" with these men.

Donna laughed. "You're such a Pollyanna! You only have to do what you want to do. We mostly just hang out with them at parties, sit on their laps, and let them buy us things. If you want, you can sell those things for cash. And they might leave a little 'tip' at the end of the night. They're probably married but just want the company of a young woman who'll listen to them and tell them they're smart and funny. We're not doing anything beyond that, unless you want to."

Jacqueline was hesitant, but since she was also broke and needed a way off an ever-spinning hamster wheel, a relentless cycle of hard work, she agreed to accompany Donna on an outing. Jacqueline's new chosen name was Wanda, short and to the point, sounding enough like Donna that she thought it might be a good fake name. Wanda was from Philadelphia, the city of brotherly love, a place Jacqueline had never visited. Wanda was twenty years old and smoked Virginia Slims cigarettes so she always had something to do with her hands. Wanda wore her hair feathered and sported fluffy, fanned-out false eyelashes. It was, indeed, just like an acting experiment.

At the end of the night, Wanda had received seventy-five dollars from a stout, balding man who'd taken a liking to her, and also a promise to be invited to the next party. She decided this was something that she could do, so she reduced her overtime at the diner, left work in enough time to regularly attend her acting classes, and did nights with Donna as Wanda or Camille or Marlene, all personas that she liked to try on for size.

Remarkably, this new revenue stream helped to keep Jacqueline's dreams afloat, at least temporarily. And she grew to like it. This kind of work, not unlike acting, had an expiration date. Once you were no longer young and beautiful, the party was over, but since she was both at the moment, she decided that she would have fun. She got a safety-deposit box at the bank so that she could store her cash. She also opened a bank account but only kept enough money in there so that she could write small checks. She was learning fast about city life.

Just over ten years later, she was on the cusp of thirty. By the time that Jacqueline first encountered William Carter Jr., she'd been struggling in New York City for a decade and she hadn't booked a single acting job. But she was still doing escort work with Donna and had shed the small-town stench she once feared she'd never be rid of. In fact, instead of becoming famous, she had become worse than ordinary, scraping together tips for a pack of cigarettes and on the verge of aging out of Hitchings House if she didn't figure something out. And fast.

Approaching "too old" for a women's dormitory, though, was less of a concern when she knew that her youth was still a currency that she could use outside of those walls. She was charming, sexy, and mysterious, even when she found herself almost perpetually exhausted. On top of all that, the years she spent at the University of Life in New York City had made her very smart, and she knew a good mark when she saw one.

He always came into the diner alone, armed with the *Wall Street Journal* under his arm and a frown on his face. She resented that she knew who was a regular and who was not at the diner. It meant she was a regular too, that the venue had really become her place of full-time employment. When she observed William Carter Jr., she saw that he didn't engage with another soul in the diner and barely engaged with her, always leaving the minimum amount of tip required. She'd noticed early on that he didn't wear a wedding ring, so she assumed that he was either concealing a relationship or simply single. He looked to be at an age, though, where a man should be in want of a wife. Usually with regulars, there was some sort of rapport, but with this one, there was only formality. On some level, she thought this was a comfort, especially since he was such a cheapskate with his tips. This kind of guy wouldn't be asking her when her shift ended, hinting that they should spend her nonworking hours together. The patron she would eventually come to know as William Carter Jr., bland but respectable.

One Thursday evening, well after the dinner rush, William entered the diner. There were only a few other people eating at the time, including a family with two loud, young children. Two older white ladies were in the process of spiking their coffee with Baileys. Since it was later and slow, Jacqueline was handling the place herself, which she preferred most days. William ordered his typical eggs and a coffee, which he ate day or night, and unfolded his newspaper without so much as a glance at Jacqueline. Nearby, the children played a rowdy game with their action figures while their parents ignored them, deep in their own conversation. Jacqueline spent time casually surveying the customers, on call if they needed her but not wanting to hover. She snuck glances at a script that she was reading, trying to do some at-home learning now that she could no longer afford to attend regular acting classes.

The children soon began mock sword fighting with their silverware. They got up from the table and made use of the empty space. William looked over at them as if to will the brats to sit back down and be quiet, an unsuccessful, feeble attempt at mind control.

The children crashed around the diner, knocking and banging on anything that made a noise, a spirited rebellion against the rules of the adult world. Around 11:30 p.m., they were back in their booth, clearly tired, dejectedly tossing their toys back and forth to one another when Jacqueline went to go refill William's coffee. When she arrived in front of William, she found him hypnotized by what was going on over at the table with the children. At first, she made no move to interrupt his daze, simply hanging near him to observe what he was so transfixed by. She followed his eyeline to watch the smaller of the two children walk a toy soldier to the edge of the red rectangular table and simply push it off. The plastic man collided with the floor, and when it hit the surface, William flinched. It was a clear reaction, though, and when he noticed Jacqueline standing nearby, he attempted to comport himself as if it didn't happen.

"More coffee?" she offered.

"Sure," William said, and she noticed that the hand holding the coffee mug was shaking. With her back now to the table with the family, she heard the children sending their toy sailing off the surface to the ground again and noticed William flinch for a second time and close his eyes. She cocked her own head to the side.

"Are you okay?" she asked, the question flying from her mouth.

William didn't answer. He instead cleared his throat and said, "Do you mind distracting me for a little while?"

Dollar signs sprouted into Jacqueline's eyes. She wasn't sure exactly what he meant by that, but for the right price, right now, she was open. "What did you have in mind?" she asked, being cautious.

William gestured to the empty booth seat across from him, inviting her to sit. "Can you?" he asked.

Jacqueline looked briefly over both shoulders, deciding that it was both late enough and dead enough that she could skirt the rules just this once. William's body had a slight tremor, and she resisted the urge to reach out her own hand to steady his. She slid into the booth, sitting opposite him, and watched him drag his eyes away from the table with the rambunctious family.

"Friends of yours?" she asked, eyebrows raised, head inclined toward the table he insistently stared at.

"Hardly," he said with a gruffness. "I wish they'd get those kids under control."

She smiled. "They had three cups of hot cocoa each, so that's not likely anytime soon. They're tired, sure, but too wired."

William grunted in response. Jacqueline waited for him to say something else, confused as to why he'd ask her to sit down. They sat in uncomfortable silence for a full minute while William Carter Jr. stared at his hands flat on the table. "I just hate to hear crashing. I hate when I see things falling," he said finally, still not looking up.

"Are you military or something?" Jacqueline asked.

William raised his eyes to meet hers and shook his head. "No, just don't like it."

Jacqueline shrugged. "Hard to have quiet in a city like this," she said.

"Hard but not impossible," William offered with a wry smile. "I'm William Carter Jr." he said, still not moving his hands from the table.

"Jacqueline," she said, echoing his formal tone. An odd man, he was.

"So what are you? A student?" William said, sizing up Jacqueline's youth.

"I'm an actress," she said, jutting out her chin defensively.

"Oh yeah?" William asked, sitting up straighter. Jacqueline swallowed, knowing what question would come next. "Have I seen you in anything?" he said curiously.

"This diner," she said, folding her arms.

"That bad, huh?" William said, sitting back against the red vinyl booth and sliding his hands from on top of the table to clutch them at his sides. The kids sent their toys flying off the table for the tenth time.

"It's been slow," Jacqueline replied deferentially.

"Success sometimes is," William agreed.

"What do you do?" she asked.

"Well, I guess that depends on the day," he said. "I'm an entrepreneur in global real estate."

"What does that mean, exactly?" Jacqueline asked, her real estate knowledge limited to the terms of her boardinghouse lease.

"I provide people with housing, and with the materials to build housing in other countries," William replied. The family he was facing put on their coats to leave. The father held up two twenties, more than enough to cover the meal and Jacqueline's tip, and left the money on the table. Jacqueline swiveled her body to wave goodbye.

"Your work sounds impressive," she said, turning back to William.

"It will be," he assured her.

"What do you mean by 'It will be,' Bill?" she asked.

He cleared his throat. "It's actually just William," he said.

Jacqueline respected this. She was never Jackie, the discount version of her luxury name.

"Right, sorry. You hardly ever meet full namers these days," she replied.

"It's the one part of myself that I share with my father," he said.

Jacqueline nodded. "And where's he?"

"Boston. We're . . . not close," William finished.

Jacqueline nodded again. "I know how it is."

"It's not like—he didn't abandon us or anything. It's just complicated."

"Sure," Jacqueline said noncommittally.

"My father . . . he was a janitor, and then he was a groundskeeper and worked at my school," William said.

"Well, that doesn't sound so bad," Jacqueline said, waiting for the gotcha.

"No, it's not, in theory. It's just that, well, now my life is very different. I—well, you know how if you're going somewhere and you need to get there fast, it's easier to get there if you aren't carrying anything?" he asked, holding her gaze.

She frowned. He was getting kind of tongue-tied. "Okay," she said cautiously.

"I couldn't carry anything. I'm trying to do something that's kind of . . . crazy. I want . . . I want to make a billion dollars." As the words left William's mouth, he sat a bit straighter, jutting his chin out defiantly.

Jacqueline started laughing, waiting for him to join in. When he didn't, she realized that it wasn't a joke.

"Well, why do you need a billion?" she asked, still astonished at the number. The sheer scale of so much money seemed unfathomable. Who actively pursued a billion dollars? Why would anyone ever need that much money? She had never heard anyone say that number out loud before. It sounded absurd.

"I think something happens when you get a billion dollars. A million dollars won't save you from a lot, but a billion might," he said.

"What do you need saving from?"

"Don't know yet," he said, shrugging, "but it doesn't hurt to be prepared."

Jacqueline considered this. It was a staggering amount of money to think about: one billion dollars, but at the same time, she could also use some saving at the moment.

For the first time, William left her a handsome tip that night, as she predicted he might. She thought about their interaction and his earnest pursuit of something that seemed unnecessarily excessive. Somehow, though, her time with him made her feel energized. She was after something impossible too.

Jacqueline liked to remember what was real before she said what wasn't. The truth could be a terrific anchor for fantasy, what every great actress knew. Sitting in front of a camera, Jacqueline looked her daughter in the eye and with total confidence said, "Well, I met your father at a fundraiser, as you know."

<DATE>: April 17, 2015
<FROM>: najenkins@harvard.edu
<TO>: Ken.Carter@gmail.com

<SUBJECT>: Club Research

Dear Ms. Carter,

Thank you for your inquiry. We regret to inform you that we have no documentation of a "secret club" or "extracurricular" for Black students at Harvard between the years of 1963 and 1970.

We have many organizations that help to foster community for our Black students, including the Harvard Black Students Association, BlackC.A.S.T., and the Africa Caucus. All of these are officially affiliated with the university. If there was an additional organization dedicated to the Black experience, we have no knowledge of it.

Unfortunately, Professor Hill died in 2005.

Best of luck with your research,
Naomi Jenkins

African American Students Department Head

CHAPTER 18

William Carter Jr.

New York City, May 2015

Kofi had been on William Carter Jr.'s mind ever since it had been mentioned that someone was looking for leads on him. For years, William had been on high alert about Kofi, but as his wealth and status grew, an inverse relationship formed with his paranoia. It reduced. William had told Jacqueline that the Kofi information was well contained because that's what he wanted to be true.

"It's contained for now," he'd said to her just the night before, unsure if he could even trust that statement.

As he sat in a new briefing with this specialist, who had nothing to say but that personal IP addresses were not readily traceable and that increased search traffic on the name was not necessarily any cause for alarm, William instructed him to go to the ends of the earth to find out what was going on.

"Oh and sir?" the new specialist said, his cheeks reddening in front of an impatient William, whose assistant had already rapped twice on the door. "It turns out that your, er, daughter is interviewing your former classmates and friends about you for your birthday. That's why a lot of them have been contacted. It's harmless and sweet. I think the surprise is ruined now. Sorry about that," he said dutifully before gathering several folders and exiting William's office.

"I hate surprises," William muttered to himself before opening his office door to go outside for a smoke.

This information about Kennedy was welcome because the alternative theory that he was spinning was that some do-gooder reporter was poking around in order to dispute his legacy. There were definitely several things in his past that he didn't want anyone to find. Specifically, he hoped that the truth about Kofi wouldn't come to light, not that there was anything to find. He'd done his best to make sure of that.

Unlike what he experienced with his boarding school roommate, Russell, William didn't enjoy a comfortable friendship with Kofi Asare, and that was primarily because he seethed with jealously at the way Kofi had seamlessly integrated himself into the Harvard community. *Seamlessly* was a relative term, of course, since Kofi was still a dark-skinned Black boy on the historied Cambridge campus, but he had experiences and resources that William did not. Firstly, Kofi had lived in several different places all over the world. His father owned a hotel in Ghana and traveled abroad frequently, especially to European locales like France and Switzerland. And while living in an Accra hotel paled in comparison to, say, traveling to Luxembourg's châteaus, it was certainly more acceptable than the modest Roxbury quarters that William sometimes called home.

Secondly, by the nature of his father's work, Kofi was skilled in charm. He could readily converse on a range of topics with sparkling humor. He spoke three languages fluently and was sharply dressed for every occasion. He would jokingly refer to William as "brother" because a couple of their Harvard classmates assumed they were related. Well, William thought it was a joke, and it was in the context of Harvard. But for Kofi, his father had always said that Black people, especially the ones in the Caribbean or America, were always family to the ones from Africa. The joke part was that they looked absolutely nothing alike, not to mention had different accents and totally opposite dispositions. All this fueled William's anger toward his roommate in a way he couldn't articulate, even though the boys were generally civil to each other.

Kofi came to Harvard to study architecture, and ultimately his desire was to become a full-time designer of residential buildings. His goal was to double major in engineering so that he could marry the tactical and artistic parts of the process to oversee building in Ghana. William, in contrast, was increasingly steered toward economics and business by Professor Hill. To retaliate against Kofi's effortless ease at assimilating into Harvard, William kept the club a secret from Kofi. Technically speaking, this was antithetical to what Professor Hill was trying to achieve by bringing Black Harvard students together, but William Carter Jr. reasoned that the group was for *American* students. And besides, he'd been instructed to keep the club a secret. There was no need to take a risk bringing in someone like Kofi.

At the end of their freshman year, Kofi found an off-campus apartment that he convinced his father to lease for him. Since it was no cost to him, he asked if William wanted to continue rooming with him for free. William, for his part, was stunned by his roommate's generosity and realized that perhaps the animosity he harbored toward Kofi was a one-way thing. He was lucky indeed. It was a deal that he found almost impossible to pass up, considering how obsessed he was with saving money. Thanks to Kofi, William was able to sail through his remaining three years at Harvard.

At the same time, William had become Professor Hill's protégé, allowing himself to be dressed, influenced, and guided by this man whom he trusted like his own father. He distanced himself even more from his family, who, though less than thirty minutes away, rarely saw him.

Professor Hill, during one of his meetings, had once told the group of students he'd gathered, "You'll hear the motto of 'All for one and one for all,' or that 'When one wins, we all win.' That's simply not true. You lot in this room right now, you're the best there is, and you can't let yourself be dragged down by anyone else who couldn't make it here. It's your life, your destiny, and you don't have to carry anyone else's burdens." William, now a senior beginning his spring semester, had smiled when he'd heard this, words that affirmed the types of feelings he secretly harbored.

Meanwhile, Kofi had been struggling with what he was trying to accomplish for his structural engineering elective that year, confiding to his roommate in their apartment one night last year. William had listened closely, pushing aside his jealousy, wondering how he could put what he was about to learn to his advantage.

Kofi wanted to create a solution for the many manufacturing problems with building materials in Ghana. His ultimate goal was to make something simple enough that the parts needed for homes wouldn't need to come from multiple sources or factories. Currently they were made ad hoc when someone bought land and decided to build, which was common for middle-class people wanting to be homeowners. To avoid paying price-gouging developers, people needed cash for their own land, but then building the home became incredibly costly as well. The constant customization produced a bottleneck that slowed the entire home-building process down significantly. When materials were sourced outside of the country, as was often the necessity, there were extensive shipping problems and delays, and so if it were possible to make something that could be seamlessly produced within the existing infrastructure, it would help to accelerate the housing market. His architecture brain also told him that these things needed to be beautiful as well as functional. And he was attempting to counteract the age-old criticism that he'd heard his entire life from his own boarding school peers: Africa was backward and primitive.

He was stumbling with aesthetics, not able to come up with something that his professors found to be appealing enough. The problem was that anything that was affordable and structurally sound enough was hideous. The most beautiful materials with the most inspirational lines and curves had costs that far outweighed what would be perceived as "affordable" housing. He thought that he found a breakthrough when he'd produced LEGO-like block fixtures that would fit into one another, easily built upon. It offered marginal customization, but if the idea was to get as many people as possible into the safest and most inexpensive housing, this was the best he could do for the moment.

For his engineering elective final, he spent the remaining weeks in May constructing a miniature replica of what he wanted these buildings to look like. The apartment smelled like rubber cement and paint, as Kofi was pulling all-nighters repeatedly to make sure that the project was exactly how he'd imagined it. Conversely, William was breezing through his economics exams, even having a grade high enough in one class to exempt him from a final.

One night, William was in his bedroom balancing his personal finance budget when he heard a humongous crash come from the living room. When he ran over to the main space, he saw Kofi just staring at the carnage all over the floor. William had watched Kofi carefully build his model for his final. It had been a rendering of an apartment complex with six buildings built completely out of the original blocklike structures that he'd envisioned for the project. In the center was a diorama version of a park with native fruit trees. William was impressed with the scale and detail of it, that Kofi was thoughtful enough to show how nature would be integrated into the space. And now Kofi's vision was in pieces all over their living room floor.

"What the—" William tried to make eye contact with Kofi and instead found a blank, unreachable person on the other end. Without further warning, Kofi let out a sudden, severe scream, one that made the hairs on William's arms stand up, and then began to weep. Kofi's tears flowed freely as he got a glass of water from the tap and then walked to his room.

William Carter Jr. let an hour go by before gently knocking on Kofi's door and pushing it open. Once inside, he found Kofi seated silently on the bed, withdrawn, eyes puffy and blank. William hesitated slightly before pushing himself inside and sitting next to Kofi on the bed. They sat together, staring at the same bare white wall before Kofi finally spoke in a whisper.

"I worked on this project forever," he said. "I was so careful. I got to the final early. I was prepared, ready. I was nervous but I was ready. I don't even remember what I said. It was just seventeen minutes of talking that they threw away. I met with four professors and the architecture department head. They told me to wait outside and that when they called me back in, I would receive my grade. So I waited outside. Barely took them five minutes. They called me back in and gave me a D." He paused, hanging his head again. "A D isn't failing, but it might as well be. They said that the project was 'imaginative but impractical.' I couldn't even say anything else, I was so upset. I just thanked them and left."

"What are you going to do now?" William asked him.

"Nothing?" Kofi responded. "What can I do?"

"You could probably appeal. It—" William made eye contact with Kofi, caught the frost of his icy gaze, and stopped talking. He knew before the suggestion left his mouth that it would be a futile effort. The administration's decision would stand.

William felt a wave of conflicting emotions bubbling to the surface. On one hand, he had never thought of Kofi as a friend, but on the other, it was strange to see him in such a broken, demoralized state.

"Kofi," he said, "I think I know someone who can help."

When Kofi didn't respond, William sprang into action nonetheless. He gave Kofi a chaste pat on his knee and rose to his feet to exit his bedroom. When he shut the door, William looked around their apartment. He began picking up the pieces of the model. He picked up two blue pieces that were stuck together and held them close to his face for inspection. He didn't quite know what he was looking at, but it was kind of fascinating, like a toy. He tried to build back what he could by putting together the things that made the most sense, sort of like doing a 3D puzzle. When he was done, he left the partially repaired model on the living room poker table, but not before picking up the stuck-together blue modules he'd first noticed. He slipped them into his back pocket and headed to Professor Hill's for one of their private chats.

Acquisition Memorandum

Ross Financial

Please note that Ross Financial will be looking to put forth a proposition to acquire a new company headed by two Harvard graduates. The company partners are interested in expanding into new territories and will be vetting the sale with an on-site visit to Accra, Ghana.

With sizable market cap and an untapped market, we believe that this is a huge financial opportunity. William Carter Jr. and Kofi Asare will be the lead executives and will need Ross Financial resources and support. The offer ceiling has been decided at $5 million with Ross Financial assuming a loss for the first three years.

Please find attached the documentation that further details their qualifications and their business plan. Headquarters will move from Massachusetts to New York imminently. An analysis on viability will be completed after the visit.

CHAPTER 19

William Carter Jr.

Ghana, September 1968

The very first time William boarded a plane, he was going to London. Well, he was going to Ghana, but the trip required a stop in London first. He was traveling separately from Kofi, set to meet up and stay in Accra, the country's capital and largest city. Kofi had already been there for some time, and William swallowed his anxiety over the impending reunion. Kofi's meltdown over his D grade the previous year had nearly derailed his chances of finishing the architecture program, prompting William to turn to the only person on campus that he trusted, Professor Hill, to intervene.

Professor Hill, upon coming to their shared apartment, stopped to stare at the remainder of the smashed model on their poker table and stepped over the destroyed pieces on his way into Kofi's bedroom. He shut the door when he entered Kofi's room, and on the other side, William heard their muffled voices. Almost two hours later, Professor Hill and Kofi emerged from the room and shook hands in the living room, the older man clapping Kofi on the shoulder with the parting message of, "I'll check on you in a week."

With a nod to William, who sat on their fraying secondhand futon pretending to read, he left. William took in his roommate's appearance, which was, if he was being truthful, derelict. But what he did notice, once he was able to get past the unkempt Afro and facial hair, was a familiar light in Kofi's eyes, one that had been almost extinguished by the burden of failure. William waited for Kofi to speak first.

"Professor Hill thinks that it could work," he said.

William already knew this because he was the one who'd disclosed to Professor Hill that he thought he found something worth investing in. William nodded. "I think it could as well. You just needed to get in front of someone with vision," he said.

Kofi looked up at the ceiling and scratched the hairy underside of his neck. "Why didn't you think I should meet him before? You didn't tell him you had a roommate from Ghana? Am I not also a Black man at Harvard?" he asked.

William had hoped to avoid this subject. "Look," he began, trying his best to sound honest and forthright. "I messed up. I thought that I could just have something for me. I didn't think about you, not because I wanted to exclude you, but because I thought that it might feel weird for you to be with all these American guys and our American issues. But after what happened with your final, I realized that we're all going through the same shit, that we have to stick together." He emphatically dragged his pointer finger back and forth between their chests.

William's intentions were far from altruistic. He'd only just realized that Kofi's idea had enormous potential to be a functional business. While Kofi was sulking in his room, William was running numbers, and with his findings, he approached Professor Hill to get his feedback. First and foremost, they needed to convince Kofi that his idea was a viable business, regardless of what his professors decreed.

A year later, William was in the clouds on the way to Ghana to see if his instincts would prove correct. Additionally, William was attending business school so that he could stay in Cambridge working alongside Professor Hill and Kofi on this project and also so that he could learn more about how to make and manage money. It was one thing to have a great idea, but it was another thing to give that idea longevity and power.

When he touched down in London, he hated the dryness in his mouth. His teeth felt coated because he skipped his nightly brushing to be on the flight. It was a strange thing to wake up in a totally new place. His next flight was a few hours away, so he had time to waste in Heathrow. He spent a small fortune acquiring hygiene products at the airport shops and used the bathroom to freshen up. The rest of the time he spent at the gate, observing the other travelers in the airport. What he noticed most was that his next plane to Accra had the highest concentration of Black people of any other flight in the terminal. He smiled in amusement, looking at women wearing kente cloth in various shades of the rainbow, his eyes pleasantly taking in colors and textures that he was unaccustomed to seeing. He was self-conscious about how closely he had adhered to Western dress, wearing a tweed sport coat that he got two years prior from another one of Professor Hill's protégés. When he landed in Accra after nearly eight hours in the sky, he was knocked out by the air, thick with humidity.

He retrieved his bags, carefully navigating around taxi drivers who immediately identified him as an outsider based on the lost expression on his face and the stress sweat emitting from under his clothes. They hounded him with offers to chauffeur him into the city center. He confidently walked through the crowds until he spotted Kofi, standing among large families waiting to greet arriving cousins like the Prodigal Son.

"Brother!" Kofi exclaimed, bringing William Carter Jr. in for a hug and clapping his back roughly.

William, thinking about how his sweaty, unwashed body must smell, extricated himself in a dignified way and said, "Hi."

"Let me help you with your bags," Kofi said, reaching down to grab the handle of William's suitcase, a lender from a classmate. Kofi, the habitual traveler, was adept at navigating through the crowds with bags, much better than William, who was now carrying nothing and still one

127

step behind. When they reached the car that would take them to the hotel where they were staying, generously provided by Kofi's parents, who were currently away on business, William was surprised to find it to be a luxury vehicle while all the other cars in the lot seemed to be about seven to ten years old. Sitting in the black Mercedes with the Ghanaian flags violently flapping in the wind as they moved, William Carter Jr. felt special. It was clear that many eyes were on them, wondering who these two young and important men were, and he pocketed that memory, wanting to retain that feeling for as long as possible.

They arrived after forty minutes in a quieter, primarily residential neighborhood of the city where the hotel was. More like an estate, it was one of the most beautiful buildings William Carter Jr. had ever seen. Well, at least from the inside. From the outside, it had the stark and clinical appearance of an ordinary public school, but the inside, stunning. Stately and impeccably decorated, he was shocked to see that the entryway led to a courtyard with an ornate fountain and a walkway lined with palm trees. The residences, as Kofi referred to them, were in the back and slightly detached from the main building.

William was eager to settle in and freshen up. After Kofi showed him to his room, he collapsed on the double bed, which was a lot firmer than he expected, and closed his eyes briefly. No one had mentioned to him how exhausting travel would be.

He didn't realize he had fallen asleep until a knock on his door was followed by an older woman poking her head in to find him fully clothed and only half on the bed. He shot up and tried to look alert. "So sorry, Mr. Carter," she said in accented English. "I just wanted to let you know dinner will be served in thirty minutes."

William blinked rapidly to get his bearings and then remembered that he had flown here over the last day and was overdue for a meal. "Yes, of course, thank you, Miss . . ." His voice trailed off because he realized he had no idea who this woman was.

"Gifty," she said with a smile.

"Gifty," William repeated back.

"Yes, sir," she said.

William Carter Jr. hurried to freshen up and got lost on the way to the dining room. When he arrived flushed and out of breath, the meal was already underway. It was a relatively small group composed of Professor Hill, who'd arrived two days before, Kofi, and two other men that William did not recognize—white men—and he looked at them with a bewildered smile. Both men, closer to Professor Hill's age than his own, were also sweating a lot and looked worse for wear because of it. One had a comb-over haircut that was pathetically drooping due to the heat. The other's face was flushed a deep pink, bordering on red.

"Nice of you to join us," said Professor Hill, who was big on punctuality.

William Carter Jr. tried to slow his breathing while Kofi jumped in on his behalf. "It's a big place, and I didn't get to give him a tour, so he probably got a little lost," Kofi offered.

William nodded.

"Well, now that you're here, I'd like you to meet our partners on this from Ross Financial, Mr. David Ross and Mr. Charles Werner."

William shook hands with each of the men, noting that Werner was the one with the comb-over and Ross was the one with the hot flashes. William had not known that there would be other men present, but he was able to recover from his shock fairly quickly. The dinner was all business. The two men, William gathered, were interested in helping finance the homes that Kofi had envisioned for his project. They were here on a scouting mission. They wanted to see what the potential opportunities were in the market and to observe the current issues in the hopes that they might be able to help facilitate a solution. Over the next few days, they would be traveling with the group to existing building sites, eager to learn the ways Kofi planned to revolutionize the current real estate landscape.

Each of these interactions would unfold like an elaborate job interview, but at that first dinner, William observed the men, evaluating their responses and endeavoring to impress them, but mostly he was ready to learn. The white men, for what they lacked in adaptability, made up for in expertise. David Ross introduced their business by telling William and Kofi, "Ross Financial oversees $100 million in assets a year. Our primary holdings are in industries that have traditional resource markets: lumber, steel, oil, et cetera. But we've recently had a lot of success with real estate and are looking for a chance to expand into a new global market. That's where you young men come in."

As if rehearsed, Charles Werner took his turn to speak. "Originally, we were testing the Caribbean, but weather problems deterred the research team from really thinking anything there could have sustainable potential. So when Professor Hill reached out and said we had the opportunity to get in on the ground floor on something big in Africa, well, we just had to get on the plane. And as you can see, we really want to be here," he said with a laugh, dabbing a napkin at the few hairs plastered across his head.

"You've really impressed us, Kofi, with your ingenuity and ideas. There's huge potential here for expansion beyond residential to commercial or retail spaces. We can really modernize Accra," Ross said.

William Carter Jr. watched Kofi bristle and braced himself for how he might respond. "Well, it's already a modern place," he said.

"Oh sure, sure," Werner said, waving his hand dismissively. "I think what he meant to say is that the future of the city is potentially in your hands. This idea could be revolutionary. It could make a lot of Western people actually want to live here, show them the possibilities."

Kofi gave the men a tight-lipped smile, a vein bulging in his neck.

Kofi did the majority of the talking about his vision for what he wanted to accomplish in Accra and why. "My primary goal," Kofi said, "is preservation of the landscape while also making housing that's functional and beautiful. It's ambitious, I know, but throughout my time in school, I've studied how this exact kind of thing has been done across the world. It really takes someone with a brave vision and also uncompromising values to make it happen. I think it's easy to get distracted with profit margins and projections, but this is really about people for me. Homes are sacred. This is my homeland. I've been gone for a long time, but what was that all for if I can't make a difference here?" Kofi then made pointed eye contact with everyone at the table. William Carter Jr. hated when Kofi did this, merging business with his personal philosophies. While William tuned this out, he tried to discern how the Ross Financial men were responding to the pitch. They seemed engaged and interested, even as they also seemed physically very uncomfortable.

Professor Hill interjected. "And of course there's no reason we can't do all of that and make a little profit," he said with a laugh. The Ross Financial men joined in before expertly maneuvering the conversation to looking into government contracts that might help to subsidize some of the work.

Kofi shook his head at this. "Too much corruption. You have to grease the palms of a lot of men in order to get them to do what you want," he said.

David Ross chuckled. "Is that something unique to Ghana?"

Charles Werner joined in. "The entire world has some greasy palms."

Kofi didn't appear to like the joke but let out a strained, cordial laugh anyway.

When the food arrived, William and the men chased the spices burning their way down their esophagi with copious amounts of water. Gifty had made several trips to fill up their glasses, and by the second course, William had to excuse himself to relieve his bladder. When he returned to the table, the conversation was still centered around the unnamed potential real estate development. Tomorrow, they would all embark on a research trip to see what was already in place and where Accra's strengths and weaknesses were. It was the first meal that William Carter Jr. had ever had where eating was the secondary activity and not the central one. He would later come to understand that this was what was known as a business dinner.

When David Ross and Charles Werner announced their retirement for the evening, Professor Hill stood up as they did before they exited the table. A beat too late, Kofi and William did the same. When they were all alone, Kofi slouched back in his chair, his body limp with exhaustion.

Professor Hill clapped his hands together. "Well, that's off to a great start!"

Kofi let his neck rest against the back of his chair and hung his head, letting gravity pull it down though his gaze remained up. He didn't reply.

"Do you think," Kofi began, a cautious edge to his voice, "that these men are the best partners for what we're trying to do?"

William allowed himself a sideways glance at Professor Hill, who seemed like he was expecting this question. The older man rested his elbows on the table and tented his fingers. "What are we trying to do?" he asked.

Kofi sat himself upright. "Well, we're trying to make a difference in Ghana, for housing, for people who need safe places to live that aren't going to be so expensive that they can never afford them."

Professor Hill was quiet for a moment. "Isn't it funny that we need money to do that?" he asked.

"What is that saying, 'Not all money is good money'?" Kofi asked.

"What do you need it to be good for?" Professor Hill replied, a slight hint of irritation creeping into his voice.

William cleared his throat to jump in. "I think what Professor Hill is trying to say is that maybe we don't need to be hyperfocused on the source. If your intention is to do this, then the reality is that we need capital, and these men have capital and are willing to share it. You don't have to be friends with them, just partners."

"I just think there might be another way," Kofi said.

"What's that?" William said, playing his role of friend and confidant well.

"Perhaps it's self-funded at the onset, and then we try to bring in some money later," Kofi offered.

Professor Hill's features rearranged into a confused frown. "You think that you have the means to self-fund a building project in Africa . . . as a twenty-three-year-old?"

"Well, no, not me exactly and not right now, but William is in business school, and he's going to make a ton of money one day, and I think that maybe that's the answer," Kofi said, looking at William intently.

William's eyebrows raised. The idea that they would try to embark on a business venture with money they didn't currently have wasn't very good business. He made a mental note to keep Kofi far away from the financials.

"Kofi, let me be frank with you," Professor Hill said. "This isn't really something you want to wait on. People are going to hear about Ross Financial being here, and that is going to cause them to talk, and talking leads to investigations, and investigations lead to someone else stealing this opportunity right out from under you. Something I always try to impress upon my students is that no one is going to hand you anything; you have to take it. You have to seize every opportunity and every moment, and that is how you win. You can worry about the way that it *feels* later."

William caught Gifty's eyes as she emerged from who even knew where (the shadows, he supposed) to clear the remainder of the table while the three remained locked in silent debate.

Kofi and William found themselves in quiet reflection, and Professor Hill took that as his own cue to go to bed. "Gentlemen," he said with a nod as he slid his chair back, "to be continued tomorrow."

Both William and Kofi mumbled good night and sat with each other for a few more minutes while Kofi tried again to plead his case for eliminating the influence of Ross Financial from this project and William Carter Jr. just grew weary. He, too, opted to go to bed instead of talking in circles about the moral equivocation in exposing Ghanaian real estate to white American business partners. It was clear by the end of their conversation where Kofi's position was, but what frustrated William was that that position almost assured that they wouldn't have a company at all. An imperfect company was better than nothing. What in all the world was perfect anyway? William dragged himself to his room, exhausted, and it took every last ounce of his energy not to fall asleep again on top of his bed with his clothes on.

The next morning, the crew convened for breakfast at seven and set off via chartered van to look at various locations for building sites in, around, and outside of the city. The men were also interested in visiting potential factories that would be overseeing the production and manufacturing of Kofi's modules, which would be proprietary to this company. Most factories didn't seem equipped to handle the load for the size and scale of the potential project, which seemed like another problem that only money could solve. By the end of the day, they all returned back to the hotel, the two Ross partners sunburnt and spent and the Harvard crew in silent disharmony. Still, they agreed to meet up for another dinner.

That night it was more of the same, the men pitching themselves to Kofi, but with some incentives to sweeten the deal this time. It seemed like Professor Hill had coached them on what to say to entice him to sign on, which included founding an architecture program at a local school to inspire the next generation of Ghanaian architects and engineers. Kofi seemed to soften but not bend. William felt he would have to be the one to take the deal over the finish line.

Professor Hill had already promised to place William Carter Jr. at Ross Financial, where he could oversee the funding from the inside. Kofi would be the one on the ground in Ghana, returned home as was his desire. The proposal had appeal, but the idea that Ross Financial would own 51 percent of the still unnamed company was a nonstarter for Kofi. He only wanted to agree if there was a clear exit plan from Ross Financial, who also had to pledge to be hands-off with any and all creative decisions. These demands placed everything at a standstill. Eventually, after Gifty brought out dessert, they were talked out enough that everyone agreed to go straight to bed.

But sometime in the middle of the night, William heard his door-knob jiggle, followed by a knock. "Hello?" he whispered urgently, thinking he might be about to get kidnapped.

"It's me. Let me in," Kofi whispered back. William threw off the thin blanket that had been covering him and opened up his mosquito net to get out of bed and go to the door. On the other side, he found Kofi, fully dressed. William blinked rapidly, not trusting his senses.

"What time is it?" he groaned as he stepped aside to let Kofi enter his room.

"I don't know. It's late. Look, I wanna show you something. But we have to go now, and I don't want anyone else to know, so get dressed and hurry up," Kofi whispered.

William, too jet-lagged to protest, did as he was told and put on the same clothes that he wore to dinner earlier and his sneakers.

"Okay, now be quiet," Kofi emphasized in a whisper as they snuck through William's door, and he shut it behind them slowly, making sure not to slam it.

They tiptoed down the hallway in silence. Kofi was leading William through the kitchen on their way out the back door when William jumped to find Gifty sitting at a table with a magazine.

"Can't sleep?" Gifty asked pleasantly, not thinking twice about why these two were sneaking around the hotel at one in the morning.

"Just need some fresh air," Kofi said with a smile. "We're good!"

Gifty nodded and waved them off.

When they got outside of the hotel, William was surprised to see how quiet the city was at this hour. He and Kofi walked side by side for several blocks until his curiosity got the better of him.

"Where are we going?" William demanded, stopping to face Kofi and pulling on his arm.

"You'll see. It's not much farther," Kofi replied.

In another fifteen minutes, they arrived at what William could only describe as corporate ruins. The building they stood in front of rose at least one hundred feet in the air but had no windows, the night wind ripping through empty crevices. It was an eerie, concrete, haunted tower. There was a makeshift fence surrounding the area, erected haphazardly as if someone quit on the job halfway through. Kofi walked toward an area where the fence had collapsed and motioned for William to follow him.

"What is this place?" William Carter Jr. asked, looking around to check that they were truly alone.

"This," Kofi began as he marched through overgrown weeds toward the entrance of the building, "is a project started by an American real estate company that promised to build office spaces here in Ghana and then decided not to finish."

"Why does it look like this?" William asked.

"Insurance," Kofi said, as if that was the only explanation needed.

William trailed Kofi into the building and up into the stairwell as they climbed higher. "Insurance. What does that mean?" he asked.

"It means that they still own the land and can collect money on a project that's incomplete because they insured it, but as you can see, this project is not getting done. This has been here since I was a kid. I came here last night to see if I wanted to bring you here as well so you can see what happens when people say they want to work within Ghana, but all they really want is money."

William was quiet as they reached the eleventh floor. "Break," he huffed out, and Kofi mercifully made an exit through a sheet of plastic blowing in the wind to reveal a large empty floor space containing nothing but cement and a few stray tools.

"Everyone who was contracted to work on this project was stiffed," Kofi said. "Just discarded."

"That's not going to happen with our project. I can see where you're going," William countered.

"How do you know that? Do you know David and Charles? Do you think they care about if our work ends up like this?" Kofi said, his eyes flashing with accusation.

William raised his hands in surrender. He didn't realize just how personally Kofi was taking all this.

"Okay, so what are you saying?" he asked.

Kofi led William to the vacant rectangle where a window should have been and he sat, legs dangling over the edge.

"I'm saying we need to do this. You and me. Just us. I can't let this go and be controlled by people who don't care. You think David and Charles have ever visited Ghana before? You think they're coming back?" Kofi said.

William was quiet. Who cared? He'd never been to Ghana before. He didn't know if or when he was coming back. That shouldn't affect whether or not they could do business.

"We can't do this alone, though. I know you know that," William answered.

"We can try," Kofi said.

They could try, and they would likely fail, which William wasn't terribly excited to do. William and Kofi had a plan, or at least the semblance of one, that would allow each of them to get what he wanted. With Kofi's plan, neither of them would get anything. They would have nothing, be nothing. All their efforts would be for nothing.

William looked out into the night while he relished the coolness of the wind that blew through the opening where they sat, this nighttime meeting stirring up his anxiety. William stood and leaned against the decaying brick frame. "I think we should take their deal," he said.

Kofi groaned. "No," he said firmly, standing to indicate his resolve.

"No?" William asked incredulously.

"No," Kofi repeated. "It's my project. It's my idea, and this isn't how I want to do this."

William felt his blood go hot, anger coursing through him. "Your project?" he spat at Kofi. "You mean the thing you threw away and *I* saved?"

Kofi hung his head and shook it. "There's no company without my plans. I'm sorry, but this isn't the way that this should be done."

"Bullshit," William murmured. Having this argument in the middle of the night was pointless. He began to walk away.

William turned to shoot another venomous look at his roommate and noticed the brick he was standing on was wobbling violently. Kofi's right foot slipped from beneath him in the place that he stood. Kofi's eyes widened with fear, and he reached his left hand out to William, using his right to grab on to the wall. William reflexively stepped back, a decision that he would think about every day for the rest of his life. Kofi's right hand missed the wall and found nothing but air. For a split second, he was suspended, quite beautifully, regally, in the frame of the ruins before the bricks gave way and he hurled toward the ground. William watched in abject horror as his roommate plummeted several dozen feet down and landed with his limbs in a grotesque, unnatural contortion on a dusty wasteland. William stood motionless for several minutes, listening to nothing but the chilling silence of his own racing thoughts.

As the initial shock subsided, panic set in, and he began to hyperventilate, frantically looking around him. The sandy floor showed two sets of footprints, and he quickly removed his sweatshirt to use as a broom to sweep his away. He walked backward, erasing his own presence as he retraced his steps the exact same way that he and Kofi entered. When he got to the stairwell, he looked around to see if he'd touched anything that might contain his fingerprints. There were no doors, the building so unfinished and haphazard that it was just a shell.

He raced down the stairs to the ground level and rounded the building to check on Kofi's body. Kofi's eyes and mouth were still open, a reminder that death had grabbed him by surprise. William felt bile rising up in his throat but refrained from vomiting, aware that he shouldn't leave any evidence of his presence behind. He took one last glance at Kofi's broken body, and then he ran. He, who was almost always picked last for every sport or game or activity, sprinted down the streets of Accra, having no real idea as to the way back to the hotel but letting his intuition and pure adrenaline guide him.

When he returned to the hotel, sweating, panting, and crying, he headed straight for Professor Hill's room and knocked frantically on the door. His sweatshirt dangled limply in his hand, covered in dust and dirt.

Professor Hill's alarmed and confused face greeted him from the other side of the door as he swung it open. "What in the . . . ," he asked upon viewing William's ragged appearance.

In response, William choked out a sob and fell into the room, a trail of dirt and sweat following him. As the door closed, he looked behind him and saw Gifty's questioning face staring right back.

The Harvard Crimson

October 10, 1968

Kofi Asare lost his life in a tragic accident in his home country of Ghana on September 22, 1968. Throughout his time on campus, he was an extremely loved and cherished student. He was working on completing a dream project of bringing innovation in the housing market to his beloved Ghana when he died.

Kofi is survived by his mother, father, and two younger sisters. His memory will be honored by his family privately in Accra.

A memorial for Kofi will be held on the Harvard campus next week.

If any students are struggling with thoughts of self-harm, please contact the Health Center for help.

CHAPTER 20

Kennedy Carter

Boston, May 2015

Kennedy stifled her cough as the dust from Harvard's newspaper archives coated her nose and throat. She looked around to make sure that she wasn't disturbing any working students. She wanted to be as discreet as possible. She had secured special access to do a library search once she told admins that she was working on a gift for her father. Now, she sat cross-legged on a hard wooden chair, with several copies of printed and faded student newspapers. The internal search for Kofi Asare left her with fewer than a dozen hits. The one that she wasn't expecting to see was his obituary. Kennedy stared at the photocopy of the tiny newspaper clipping that detailed Kofi Asare's death and reread it, reflecting on the tragedy of his suicide. But even more importantly, the line that stood out to her most was the one that said, "He was working on completing a dream project of bringing innovation in the housing market to his beloved Ghana when he died"—a line that was especially strange since that was exactly what the Carter Corporation ended up doing.

It was then that she realized that she didn't even know the full scope of what her father's company was responsible for. Housing was definitely a piece of it, but by this point, there were now many complex components, a moneymaking diapason. She squinted down at the paper. Tashia's sending her that photograph of her father and this man, Kofi, had set her hunting, and now she was confused about what she found.

The video was still incomplete, and while she was able to tack this library visit on, the real reason she was there was to see her brother. She pushed aside her thoughts about Kofi. She checked her phone and pressed his name for the sixth time that day. Asher had been dodging her again, and when she showed up on the Harvard campus and pounded on his door after being let up to his high-rise by security, she found him hungover and half-dressed.

"Your knock sounds like the police" was all he said before stepping aside to let her into the apartment.

"Nice to see you too," Kennedy replied, trying to keep her spirits up. "Are you going to be ready to film today?"

Asher chuckled. "Do you have a hair of the dog?"

Kennedy displayed her empty palms.

Asher turned his back on her and went into the kitchen to make himself a Bloody Mary.

"Hey, I wanna ask you something," Kennedy prompted, a chill going down her spine as she remembered her nightmare about the plane crash.

"Yeah?" Asher asked as he took a giant sip from a tall glass with red liquid, his mood already improving.

"Have you ever heard the name Kofi Asare?"

"Uh, no. Why? He's someone you're trying to get with?"

"He's Dad's old college roommate . . . but . . . he died, maybe by accident, or maybe by suicide."

"Depressing," Asher said.

"Yeah. This is his campus obituary that I found." Kennedy offered the photocopy to her brother.

"Wow, it's so short," Asher said.

"I guess when you die young, that's what happens," Kennedy replied.

Asher shrugged. "What are you even doing with this?"

"It's weird, but when I started talking to all Dad's friends and everything for this video, I was trying to make it special, and so I wanted to include some stuff that no one knew about him. And then I found this, and I don't know. It just seems weird, is all. I was wondering if you ever heard the name."

"You think Dad wants things in a birthday video that no one knows about? Come on, Ken. Are you new here?"

"Yeah, no. I know," Kennedy said, her cheeks heating up with embarrassment. "It's stupid."

Asher drained his glass and set it down on the table. "Okay, so are we doing this or what?" he said.

Kennedy moved around him to set up her camera and two chairs facing one another. She sat down and waited for Asher to face her. Her finger hovered over the record button. "Wait," she said. "Can I ask you something off the record?"

Asher rolled his eyes dramatically. "What 'record'?" he said, using air quotes. "This isn't CNN!"

"Well, I know," Kennedy said. "I was just wondering something."

"Yeah?" he asked impatiently.

"Billionaires . . . ," she started to say.

She had to think of the right way to phrase this. She thought back to the first time she was asked to consider the morality of a billion dollars and it was all because of something Tashia had said. Kennedy had been in love with a classmate her senior year. This boy, who was white, was a fit lacrosse player with hair to match the sport, a floppy shag with bangs and sides that flipped up on the ends. His name was Ollie Abbott.

Ollie Abbott was a Dalton lifer. His father was a geriatric rock star who, in his third marriage, married Ollie's mom for a whole two years, long enough for her to bear two children. Ollie's older brother was a stoner who ended up at Stanford. Ollie's father was based in London, and so their fractured family, ever expanding because there was also a fourth and fifth wife, the latest with no kids, was often featured in tabloids. Ollie was traditionally handsome, his symmetrical features defiled when he took a baseball to the face in the seventh grade, shifting his nose slightly to the left.

He'd declined plastic surgery to fix it, eager to shed the pretty-boy card he'd been dealt by having a pretty mother. Ollie was pleasant and popular, striking that perfect balance between studious and athletic. He also had an atypical rebellious streak, which meant that he did things like playing the saxophone instead of something expected from the musical offspring of a rock star, like the guitar or drums. He was a jock, sure, but he wanted people to think of him as an artist, which was how he ended up in the film club with Kennedy.

His advances were innocent enough to begin with. He spent junior year sitting close to her at lunch or letting their arms brush in art class. These gestures were so subtle most of the time that Kennedy had to talk herself out of thinking it meant something more than it did. At first, she was so unsettled by his proximity because it happened so quickly, his placing himself in her orbit, but with consistency and familiarity, she developed a crush.

After several months, she worked up the courage to initiate contact. She dedicated many hours of thought per day to imagining their conversations and interactions beyond what she was actually experiencing. She found herself wanting to be carried away by the fantasy that this person, whom she had known for years, was here all along, yearning to be with her. And as for Ollie, he was a closet romantic, leaving her notes in her locker and finding opportunities for them to be together, bringing her candy after school and seeking her out at parties on the weekends.

When they became seniors and Ollie still didn't have a girlfriend, Kennedy figured that she could soak up as much of their good time as possible. It was well known that his plans would take him to Providence next year. Ollie had asked her out on little dates, creating magical private moments all over the city for them to build a world of inside jokes and core memories. They rode the Roosevelt Island tram just because. They took the subway to the Financial District and roamed the deserted Seaport. They laughed when Ollie got pooped on by a pigeon in Washington Square Park, and they ducked under scaffolding when the skies opened up, staying there for hours talking in the rain.

"I never thought that you liked me," Ollie had confessed. He flipped his wet hair out of his eyes.

"Really? Why not?" Kennedy closed her umbrella and faced him.

"I don't know," he said. "You're very . . . reserved." Kennedy considered him. She was indeed reserved in a way, guarded even.

"Yeah, I could see that," she said. "I guess that's the only way I know how to be. My family is . . . complicated." Ollie waited patiently for her to continue, and after a beat, she did. "There's a lot of attention on us, on me, sometimes, and it can be a lot. I guess I don't want to ever give people a reason to talk about us more."

"I get that," Ollie responded. "Do you feel close to many people?"

Kennedy shook her head. "Not really. I mean, it's weird, and I guess now that I'm thinking about it, maybe it's because I don't let anyone get that close." In Ollie, Kennedy soon realized she'd found a willing, sensitive vessel into which she could pour her repressed desires for companionship. Her friend Tashia, however, didn't approve of the union, telling Kennedy one day that Ollie was nothing "but a manipulative, entitled asshole. You can do better."

But Kennedy ignored her friend's warning because she was in love, even daring to dream that she could one day take Ollie home to her parents, though she knew there'd be some controversy. Her parents didn't have any hard-and-fast rules about dating for their children, but they had opinions. One of those opinions was definitely that it was a bad look to be publicly fraternizing with a white boy. Her father and mother had white friends and even business partners, but romantically, optically, Blackness was the standard. It was fine to aspire to whiteness in a superficial way, just not to let it in too close. The Carters were a

Black dynasty, a new one, and they desired to remain this way through as many generations as possible. This wasn't so much explicitly communicated to their children as it was suggested, and Kennedy, ever eager to pick up on cues from her parents, generally didn't want to rock the boat. But with Ollie, she'd take the chance.

Ollie had been with her in the library one day, softly holding her hand under an old oak table. The feeling of his thumb grazing her skin gave her goose bumps. Kennedy liked the contrast of their arms next to one another—hers warm and brown, and his pale and pink. Kennedy was trying to remain focused on her science homework but with him always felt distracted, almost dangerously so. She kept sneaking sideways glances at him after reading every few words when she realized that she was retaining nothing. The bell rang, signifying the start of the next class.

"Shit," Ollie said, looking at his planner, gathering his books. "I have that history paper due today. I totally forgot about it."

Kennedy and Ollie weren't in the same history class, but because they were in the same year, they were both studying American history. "Well, don't you have math next? Can you work on it in there?" Kennedy asked, trying to ease his panic.

Ollie cracked his neck and grabbed a little bit of his hair and tugged. "Maybe," he said. "I just didn't read the chapter, and I really have no idea what I can passably say about the New Deal."

Kennedy chewed the inside of her cheek. "Well, I finished my paper. Do you want to take a look at mine, for notes only?" she said, aware that her New Deal paper had been done for a week.

"Yes, yes, yes," Ollie said enthusiastically. "That would save my life."

Kennedy reached into her bag and extracted a laminated folder, in which she had her own paper typed up, ready to hand in. "Okay, I need it back after lunch," she said. He took it appreciatively and gave her a one-armed side hug before jogging off to his next class.

Later in the day, when she turned in her paper, she didn't know that he'd copied several of her words verbatim. The most egregious offense was a careful analogy that she'd made between driving on a highway and the federal government. She had written, "The New Deal created a new operational system for the American government to interfere with the economy when necessary. It functioned like driving down a highway by establishing conditions for the government to influence the financial lives of Americans by entering and exiting in ways that would be safe and cause minimal damage." A few days later, both Ollie and Kennedy were called in by their respective history teachers. As it turned out, the analogy was so specific that one of the history teachers had brought it up to the other, exposing their deception.

"I assume you both know why we've called you in here," Kennedy's history teacher said.

When Kennedy and Ollie said nothing, he continued. "You both have remarkably similar papers on the New Deal, and we'd like to give you the opportunity to explain."

Kennedy stifled a gasp and fixed her face into an impassable stare, just like she'd watched her mother do over so many years. Ollie wasn't so skilled at controlling his emotions and immediately said, "I mean, I have no idea why. Kennedy and I are study partners. I let her take a peek at my paper, but that's it."

Kennedy did a double take, whipping her head around to look at her boyfriend before looking back at both of their teachers. He prudently avoided eye contact with her and looked only at the teachers. "That's not—" Kennedy began, but Ollie interrupted her.

"I don't think it was intentional, but maybe there was some confusion," he said.

"Confusion?" Ollie's history teacher said, asking for clarification.

"Confusion about only using the paper for notes and not using any of the actual work. I think it's just such a stressful time for everyone; it's hard to keep a lot straight," he said. Ollie looked down, contrite.

Kennedy was stunned. She couldn't even get any words out, and as she listened to her teachers detail the "next steps," which would include "an investigation and disciplinary action if appropriate," she felt her lungs deflate and her chest tighten as her heart seemed to grow too big for her body. She imagined it popping like a balloon, and all the blood that it was pumping spilling, pooling all over her insides.

In the midst of her shock, she said nothing to the history teachers.

Her parents were informed by the school of this indiscretion by a conference call with both her mother and father and their legal team. The headmaster's voice replayed in her burning ears, even years later: "Plagiarism is a violation of the school's code of conduct. I have appealed to the board, based on your generous history with the school and her stellar record so far as a lifer, that she not be expelled but allowed to continue her education at home privately and receive her diploma separately."

That would always stick with Kennedy as the moment that her parents had revoked their love and replaced it with disappointment. They had realized that all their funding and donations and time and energy poured into the school meant nothing at all because she made one dumb choice.

Kennedy was never officially expelled. She wasn't even suspended from Dalton. Officially, she transitioned to a homeschooling model in order to pursue an unspecified independent study. She would graduate with her class but spent the day that she would have accepted her diploma tapping through photos of her beaming ex-classmates on social media. At her father's urging, she withdrew her applications to colleges, citing a medical emergency, and took a gap year to work on creative projects and reapply to schools. All this was done without her input. Her father, try as he might, could not stop the speculation and gossip among their community and the press. William Carter Jr. was livid to encounter something that his money could not fix. Her parents had never even asked her if the allegations were true.

The one person who reached out to her was Tashia, and Kennedy felt a brick of guilt settle on her conscience because she hadn't heeded her friend's warnings. But selflessly, Tashia sat with Kennedy as she cried. As Kennedy threw herself a pity party and wallowed as everything that she thought she cared about dissolved into nothing, Tashia called to check in every day. Before William Jr. made Kennedy withdraw her applications to college, she had been applying to Harvard. That was the only place she wanted to go. She'd wanted to stake a claim at the school that had formed her father, but he, afraid that Harvard might get wind of the scandal and paranoid about how it might reflect on him, expressly forbid Kennedy from pursuing enrollment there. Despite the scandal, Kennedy tried to tell herself her academic prospects were still bright. She could already speak two languages fluently and one conversationally, and her grades, so long as she completed her coursework and sat for her AP exams, would mean that she would receive honors.

"Dishonorable honors. What use is any of this when I am not even allowed to show my face at school? I don't think it matters on paper that I got a few awards," Kennedy said to Tashia as Tashia braided Kennedy's hair into neat straight back braids. Kennedy had been gone from school for a month, and the uncertainty she felt in the future was heavy.

"Your dad's blood money can't do anything else?" Tashia said in response.

"Blood money?" Kennedy questioned, doing a double take. Tashia had some radical views but had never so much as suggested that she thought William Carter Jr. was guilty of something nefarious.

Tashia shrugged. "Isn't any fortune worth more than a billion dollars blood money?"

And now, years later, this was something Kennedy was constantly wondering about, thinking about Kofi Asare and the roadblocks she encountered investigating her father's history. Now was her chance to ask Asher the same question.

"Is a billion dollars blood money?" she asked her brother, taking the tripod stand from its carrying case.

Asher looked at her confused. "What a random question," he said. "I mean, does it matter?"

Kennedy was quiet. She didn't know if it mattered. She just had a weird feeling that she was getting closer to finding out that a billion-dollar fortune just might be dirty in some way.

Then surprisingly out of nowhere, Asher said, "All construction businesses suffer accidents. That's what insurance is for."

This response wasn't what she was expecting at all. Her brother, so obtuse, so out of touch with administrative affairs, knew about construction regulations and insurance?

"Actually, never mind," Kennedy said in response. "Let's get started." She fitted the camera to her tripod and adjusted the light. Asher was looking at his phone with a bored expression, which she ignored.

Her finger hovered over the record button. "Are you good to go?" she asked him. Asher dramatically dragged his eyes from his cell phone screen before tossing it aside. Kennedy called out, "Action!" and watched him immediately straighten his spine and produce a grin that spread all the way to his canines, ready to share how proud he was to be a Carter.

September 24, 1993

Invoice

#2382

Billed to:

Carter Corporation

26 Wall Street

44th Floor

New York NY, 10001

From: Gifty Obeng

Item:

$20,000

Consulting:

Payment Information

Ecobank of Ghana

Swift Code HAGHA28171

Account Number: 118827161

CHAPTER 21

Asher Bennett Carter

Boston, May 2015

Asher knew what Kennedy was getting at but he wasn't obligated to give her any answer, because she, like most people, underestimated him. His was the art of weaponized incompetence. If he gave people nothing, nothing would be expected, and he had been quite successful so far. In any case, he wasn't about to admit to her that he knew that theirs was indeed blood money.

Asher was at least aware that their father's contribution to parenting would include imparting wisdom onto his children. Well, the William Carter Jr. brand of wisdom. He thought of his kids as permanent interns enrolled in his personal program of business acumen, a philosophy that deeply shaped their upbringing.

Asher was the first to reach eighteen, and therefore he was the first to deal with his father's expectations of what a Carter child should be. To William's surprise, Asher took great interest in how the company worked. The issue with that, though, was that Asher was negligent on a good day and foolish on a bad one, the circumstances created when a kid was given a map and told to follow directions without ever thinking for himself. That was Asher's problem: he could not think. He had no imaginative capabilities, and unfortunately, that was half the battle when it came to mastering what William had done.

The summer following his last year at Princeton, instead of doing his one-month penance at the Carter Corporation, as was the norm for both him and his sister, he voluntarily spent the whole summer there. He had planned to take the next year off, a decision acceptable to his father only if he was "learning something." Asher did plan on learning a few things, including what had changed about New York City night-life in the four years that he'd been away, but something surprising happened that summer. He took an actual interest in the company. He wanted to prove his dedication, demonstrate his willingness to learn. He tried in earnest to understand the complexities of the business, but it made his head hurt. He often found himself lost, but he'd also never felt closer to his father in his life since he had the ability to ask his father tons of direct questions. Something he hadn't done since childhood.

One night, they were working late in the office, the hum coming from the industrial air-conditioning providing a monotone soundtrack to their toil. "Can I ask something?" Asher said.

"Sure, son," his father said without looking up.

"Has anyone ever died because of our work?" he asked. Asher was too aware of the gossip surrounding the Carter Corporation, that there might be a history of controversial methods when it came to conducting business abroad. He had never asked before, but now seemed as good a time as any. He wanted to understand the full picture of what he was getting into.

His father, who was reviewing a contract, put down the paper that he was holding. "Has anyone ever died because of our work?" he said, repeating the question back to Asher. William Carter Jr. paused for a moment and rolled his neck. His eyes wandered around the room before they found Asher's.

"Not directly, but there have been accidents over the years. It's a real estate venture, and we do construction, so accidents happen," he finally said.

"Right, so anyone who's died, died in an accident?" Asher said.

"Yes, anyone who died, died in an accident," his father confirmed.

Asher nodded as his father stepped from behind his desk.

"Come, I want to show you something," William said, walking out of his office and heading down the hall. Asher followed closely behind his father as he passed the rows of empty cubicles and offices. They went into the records room, a library of sorts with blueprints of buildings and module designs and the changes made to them throughout the years. His father opened a low drawer of a wide file cabinet and bent over the opening. He emerged holding a folded piece of vellum that he slid out from a folder that said "1993." He then opened another drawer and did the same for a folder that said "2003." He walked Asher over to the island in the center, where he spread both pieces of paper out and lit the table from beneath.

The plans appeared nearly identical. It was a building in Accra, Ghana, called the Paradiso, a complex of high-end apartments near the city center. An early project of the Carter Corporation.

"So I brought these out so that I can show you something that we decided to do very early on. See these modules?" William Carter Jr. asked his son, pointing to the document from 1993.

Asher laser focused on them, and William Carter Jr. said, "And see these modules?" He pointed to blueprints from 2003. Asher nodded again.

"They're almost the same but different. The modules from 2003 have slightly rounder edges, wouldn't really fit the designs from 1993."

"Okay," Asher said, not understanding what any of this had to do with his original question.

"Do you know why that is?" William asked. For much of his life, everything with Asher's father seemed like a riddle. It was like playing Russian roulette and *Jeopardy!* simultaneously, always uncomfortable, rife with tension.

"Because . . ." Asher's voice trailed off as he waited for a good idea to solidify. "It had to be brought up to code?"

"Something like that," his father said, more patiently than he deserved. "We make the modules and build the buildings, but what a lot of people don't know is that we also sell the insurance policies. See, son, when I was building this business, I realized that if we stopped at modules and apartment complexes, we'd have a single point-of-sale problem. These people wouldn't be repeat customers. They'd buy their one unit and not buy again. Most homes will be owned for at least ten years. But if these homes have parts that only are under warranty for a certain number of years, let's say ten, then those parts need to be upgraded and paid for. It wouldn't make sense to upgrade to the same exact part, so we make little tweaks.

"If you look here," he continued, "you can see that in 1993, the edges of the modules are straight but in 2003 they're round. So the modules from 1993 and 2003 can't fit each other, and if you don't purchase insurance, which you purchase from us at a monthly premium, you risk having to pay for the entire upgrade because these parts will either break down or not fit when all the other parts get upgraded. We also work with a variety of factories and have a similar system for software. And that's how we developed sustained income."

Asher looked closer, seeing the subtle changes magnified by the glare of the lighted table.

"Okay, so we charge people every step of the way," he said. "We do the design, source the materials, manufacture the modules, and build, and then we also sell insurance for the individual units and everything inside them? That we also make."

"Exactly," William said. "We own over two hundred subsidiary companies. Now sometimes, these people aren't able to pay us, so *sometimes* accidents do happen. And a few times, faulty elevators or even a collapse, a fire, things like that. They have happened over the years but it's not often. All contractors know that that's a possibility, and we have amazing corporate insurance to insulate us for such instances. Of course, son, all of this is private information, items that should never be shared with the masses. Do you understand?"

"Yes . . . yes, of course. I got it, Dad," Asher said, surprised that this was all new information to him. Had he really been working here for the last four summers with no idea how the company even made money?

Yes, he had. And that's when Asher Carter briefly realized just how empty his brain was at times. He wanted to ask a follow-up question because something told him there had to be more to the story, but it wasn't like he was going to ask how every one of the two hundred subsidiaries functioned.

His father went to put back the files, and they walked side by side to return to his office. When they arrived, the nightly cleaning staff was in there. "Stanley!" his father greeted the janitor warmly. This was a famous trait of William Carter Jr.'s, one of the signature things that people would talk about at his funeral: his affinity for cleaning staff at offices. William famously paid the cleaning crews at the Carter Corporation as much as he paid senior managers. He liked to say it was in honor of his father, who'd been given a lucky break while working as a janitor. Stanley had been with the Carter Corporation for as long as Asher had been alive.

William prattled on good-naturedly with Stanley while Asher got lost in his own thoughts about the business structure of the Carter Corporation and what to do about the fact that he didn't understand how he'd ever be able to oversee something so complicated, and nor would he want to.

Still, it was nice to be with his father in this way, connected to something bigger than himself, and that's what he had planned to say in his interview for this video about his father's life. The muffled noises of Boston traffic floated up to his ears. "Just one second," Kennedy said, pausing to let an ambulance's siren subside.

Asher cracked the knuckles on his right hand and took a deep breath. As he sat across from Kennedy, reciting what he'd learned about the family business best he could, he was mindful of putting a positive spin on things while keeping more controversial matters close to his chest.

Asher tugged down the sleeves of his sweater and adjusted his Cartier watch. Today he was wearing a yellow-gold Tank with a brown alligator strap. It was a gift that he received on his thirteenth birthday. He sat slightly forward, belaboring his good posture. "The best part about my dad," he said, looking past Kennedy and directly into the camera, "is that he treats all of his employees incredibly well. He knows that everyone has value to the organization, and he wants to make sure that people feel that. I think what a lot of people don't know about him is that his humble beginnings made him more sensitive to the needs of everyday people. He really tries to improve lives and make them better."

"How does he do that?" Kennedy asked.

Asher broke character. "What do you mean, how? Who cares? That's a great sound bite. Use that."

"But it doesn't really say anything," Kennedy countered.

"Yes. It does," Asher shot back. He held out his left hand to her as he put down fingers for every point he made. "It says he's a good guy, that he treats people well, and that he made it from humble beginnings. All of this was in the brief, and Dad's public relations guy has been basically stalking me to make sure I stick to a script when we talk to anyone for any reason, so that's what I'm doing. And you probably should too, Ken. That's what we do in this family."

CHAPTER 22

William Carter Jr.

New York City, December 1989

William Carter Jr. became a billionaire, yes, but he had suffered to get there. How much suffering anyone else was aware of was entirely up to him. He couldn't even really remember when he started rewriting his story. His version had completely painted over the truth as soon as he had arrived in New York after graduating from Harvard Business School. But sometimes, despite his best efforts, he was still haunted by the night Kofi died in Accra.

Behind the closed doors of his room in the hotel, Professor Hill listened to William's frantic explanation of the events and formulated a plan. Kofi, an emotional artist on the brink of realizing one of his greatest dreams, became overwhelmed by the pressure. He'd been prone to emotional outbursts, maybe even had a chemical imbalance. Tragically, he jumped to his death in Ghana at a construction site that would mirror the residential development he wanted to make.

To help make their story more believable, Professor Hill and William forged a suicide note, tracing Kofi's signature at the bottom. And then they went to bed.

The next day, when Kofi was absent from breakfast, Professor Hill made an excuse and suggested to the rest of the party that they proceed with the schedule so as not to lose any more time. The men had drained their coffee cups, and when Kofi still hadn't arrived downstairs, Professor Hill said, "Well, perhaps he's not feeling well. William, you knocked on his door this morning, yes?"

William nodded vigorously. "Yes, I knocked, and he must still be sleeping."

Mr. Ross suggested waiting. "We can give him a few more minutes, perhaps," he said generously. He then looked around for Gifty to refill their water glasses, his rubicund face already making it look like he'd run several miles that morning. William, who'd become jumpy from the rush of adrenaline and lack of sleep, displayed uncharacteristic alacrity, trying to distract himself with jaunty chatter.

"There's some real promise coming out of South Africa with manufacturing," he said to fill the silence, alluding to the research he'd been doing on successful construction markets in other African nations.

"You know, there is," Ross agreed. "We'd have to use a different approach, of course, since a lot of what we're doing will need brandnew infrastructure, but that's a great point. What do you think about the Ivory Coast?"

Another ten minutes passed before they decided they were finally ready to get going without Kofi. The foursome toured a factory on the outskirts of the city and met with a government official about tax subsidies that might be available to an American business looking to set production up in Ghana.

When they returned to the hotel, it was swarmed with police. Kofi hadn't been found yet, but they'd opened his room and found it empty, so the assumption was that he was indeed missing. William, Professor Hill, Mr. Ross, and Mr. Werner all cooperated with the investigation, telling the police the series of events that had happened the night before. Well, for William and Professor Hill, not everything.

The increased activity around the hotel caused the gentlemen to want to dine independently for dinner, so everyone remained sequestered in their rooms until the next morning. William experienced another sleepless night, though this time he didn't leave his room. He paced back and forth over the ocher floor, the limestone heating up from his energy. By midmorning the next day, the police had returned to say that a witness had found a body that fit Kofi's description. The word "witness" had seized William with dread, but the police said that the person who'd happened upon the body said he had no idea when, why, or how Kofi died. The police searched Kofi's room, where they found a hastily scrawled note, detailing his personal struggles, all but confirming that he had jumped to his death.

Once the authorities declared that Kofi was dead, hotel staff members held each other as they cried in the hallways, except for Gifty, who remained stone-faced and skeptical. William avoided eye contact, knowing that she saw him and Kofi leave together the night of his death. He spoke with the police again and fed them the story that he'd rehearsed with Professor Hill: They'd gone up to bed separately, and Kofi must have snuck out at some point during the night. William, a chronic insomniac, wandered into Professor Hill's room during the night after a bad dream. After talking with him for one hour, he returned to his own room, where he remained for the rest of the night. He hadn't seen Kofi since dinner.

Assuming then that Kofi's death was a suicide, the police asked for a complete picture of his mental health. William filled them in on the pressures they were under at Harvard, that his final project had been a failure, and that this trip was a last-ditch attempt to see if it could be a feasible business. Kofi was stressed and scared and maybe depressed, but William couldn't say so for sure.

The police interviewed everyone else in the hotel, and William held his breath as they took Gifty into the private room where they were conducting their meetings. When they'd concluded their search, satisfied that the case was an open-and-shut suicide, they said they would be informing Kofi's family and that the Asares would likely arrive the next day, exactly when the American party planned on departing.

Professor Hill asked William how he'd like to proceed in terms of the business, and William was more than ready to give the deal the green light. Kofi's death was a tragedy for his personal life but an opportunity for his professional one. He saw an easier path forward without Kofi and his incessant moral agenda.

All the men changed their tickets to be on the same flight out, citing that they would give the family time and space to grieve privately. On the plane, they upgraded William's ticket so that he flew first-class so they could hammer out further details. They decided that William, now the sole owner of the project, would receive 51 percent of the company and Ross Financial would own the remaining 49 percent, generously giving him a controlling share. Had Kofi been alive, William and he would have to split that percentage, but that was no longer a concern. Because Kofi was so adamant about not trusting Ross Financial, William fought for the majority so that he could honor his wishes, somewhat. That was for Kofi. Plus, William was well aware that Ross Financial needed him, optically at least, for legitimacy in pushing their way into Accra. They had really needed Kofi, but William, now his proxy, was the second-best thing. This gave him leverage, more than he should have had, and he could acknowledge that.

On the plane, sitting in a plush cushioned seat, William listened to Ross and Werner present their ideal timeline.

"So within three years, we want to break ground on the first building. It should take an additional seven to eight months to complete from there. We're hoping to get at least fifty residents to sign up by the end of year one. What do you think?" Ross said to William. It was an ambitious plan, but he was an ambitious guy.

"I think we should also consider the marketing for this property. We need to make sure that someone local—someone whom people trust—lives in the building and advocates for us. Kofi would have been that person, may he rest in peace, but I think we can get someone else who will serve the same purpose." William did not want that person to be himself. He could appreciate that his skin color would only get him so far here. Besides, he was not planning on ever returning to Ghana.

"Great idea," Ross said before lifting his glass of champagne to his lips. Across the aisle, Professor Hill used his hand to hide his smile. William could feel that he was on the right path.

"William," Werner interjected, "we want to be clear that Ross Financial is also going to be providing the initial capital. We don't expect you to front any money immediately, but we're happy to pay you an appropriate salary. We also have subdivisions at the firm for investment and money management if you're interested. Since we need to begin production on an aggressive timeline, it's best to keep everything contained and under one umbrella for now. Production factories should be opened and producing materials for the future builds within a year."

Since this was essentially an acquisition, William would work under the Ross Financial umbrella and simultaneously run the corporation independently. It sounded perfect. It was almost better this way, with Kofi not able to object to every little thing. When the plane landed back in New York, William was already fantasizing about his success as he and Professor Hill traveled on to Boston. He stopped at a newsstand and picked up a pack of cigarettes to soothe his nerves.

Because he was still in business school, William couldn't move to New York right away. He sat in classrooms being lectured on organizational behavior and globalization. He was focused but eager to make his escape. Though he remained on Harvard's campus, he kept to himself, not socializing with anyone except for Professor Hill. And since he could now afford to live alone, he didn't have a roommate in the new apartment that he moved to. William found a reasonably priced studio that was a twenty-minute walk to campus, and though that was somewhat out of the way, he thought it an appropriate exchange for not being in prison.

William completed his last year of business school in Cambridge while working full-time on the development of this new entity in

Ghana, which made his life a little more intense than the average student. He also began to distance himself further from his family, visiting less frequently and keeping his correspondence with his parents brief and vague. During that time, William became something akin to a monk, his private penance for Kofi. He couldn't and wouldn't enjoy himself. He would suffer, knowing what he'd done to achieve success.

Even as he boxed up all of Kofi's things and sent them to his family overseas, he never cried. Kofi's death was an accident, and as Professor Hill had assured him, there was nothing else he could have done. But Professor Hill wasn't with them that night. William knew there was more that he could have done. He could have listened to Kofi to start with instead of meeting his objections with outright dismissal. He could have controlled his anger so that Kofi didn't have to get defensive, and he could have reached out his hand as he was falling. He could have moved quickly and grabbed his shirt and pulled him back toward more stable footing. He could have at least tried.

William adopted a parsimonious existence, refusing to spend money on anything and putting all his funds and energy into the formation of the company. By the time he graduated, two factories were producing the module parts for homes, and they had purchased several acres of land on which to start building in the next two years.

Upon his arrival to New York, William started at Ross Financial with a generous salary, especially for someone who'd never had any real money. He moved himself into a new studio apartment close to the offices. When they finally broke ground on the first development site, sending a sizable stream of income into his bank account, he bought himself a small van Gogh drawing at auction, which became the only thing that hung on his wall for years. He didn't even like the ugly thing but figured it was impressive to say that he owned quality art, a piece of history, remembering Professor Hill's lessons.

Five years after he'd graduated, and the first year that they turned profitable, William received a million-dollar bonus. The feeling when it came was hollow, like he'd expected, and at the same time like he'd just eaten an enormous meal but was still hungry. He thought that it should have felt like winning the lottery, and he reached for a memory where his father had won some small sum and allowed him and Walter to get whatever they wanted. He could get whatever he wanted, and yet he didn't want one specific item. He just wanted more.

He invested the money like Ross and Werner had advised, pouring it back into Wall Street like he'd seen so many others do. Predictably, it multiplied. At a yearly return of almost 9 percent, he now had enough cash to significantly invest in stateside real estate, which he did by buying a building in Chelsea. He thus became a landlord, and while his money was in the market and soon in as many properties as he could get his hands on, he watched his dollars grow. It wasn't easy for him to get a loan; not many banks were willing to lend thousands to a Black man who didn't come from wealth, but the association with Ross Financial and the relationships that he built there began to help him as he knew it would.

Not at first, but slowly, $1.1 million became 1.2, and became 1.4, and became 1.6. He was obsessed with its expansion. He would routinely go into a branch to check the number in any one of his many bank accounts, and each digit thrilled him. The opposite of a gadabout, he did not look for many outlets for socializing or spending. With the new financial abundance, he founded a separate company, one to help train sales agents in Ghana so that there was a dedicated team to sell his properties. After that one exceeded one hundred employees, he sold that company to another brokerage and took that cash and invested it back into the market. All day he would ruminate over new ideas on how best to expand the business. He would constantly look for opportunities. The Ross team was overjoyed with his work and acquisitions and, in fact, began discussing the sale of their 49 percent of the Carter Corporation to Goldman Sachs, which was rumored to want to expand into non-Western markets. It was happening so fast, but William felt like a machine. He was able to calm his mind with focus on this very specific thing, and he found salvation.

He spent sleepless nights poring over the biographies of wealthy men with last names like Astor, Vanderbilt, and Rockefeller. It was through them that he tried to forge his new personality as an executive who commanded respect. He didn't take lovers, or indulge in a drug habit, or even drink much alcohol aside from the occasional cabernet during business dinners. He garnered a reputation as an especially serious person who appeared to be much older, which was exactly what William desired.

On a rainy Tuesday morning, as he sat in his private office reading over scouting materials for a new building site, his secretary told him that he had an urgent phone call. As he grabbed the receiver, bracing for some bad news out of Africa, he was relieved to hear Professor Hill on the other line from Cambridge.

"You need to get to campus. It's urgent," he said gruffly.

"Right now?" William asked him, looking out the window at the terrible weather.

"Right now," Professor Hill said before hanging up.

William held the phone away from his face and stared into the black holes that transmitted and received sound. If he didn't know any better, he would have thought he'd just gotten a ransom call. He grabbed his briefcase, coat, and umbrella and told his secretary to clear his calendar; he was leaving to attend to an emergency and would let her know when he'd be back in the office. He boarded a train at Penn Station and sat patiently for the few hours that it would take to get back to Harvard.

When he arrived, William took a taxi directly to Professor Hill's home, where the door was opened by a young Black girl. He did a double take, not expecting to see a female student in Professor Hill's midst, but a lot could change in two decades. He followed the nameless girl down a narrow hallway to Professor Hill's office, though he knew the route well. Everything about this place was so familiar, and he felt more at home here than he did anywhere else in the world.

When the door opened to Professor Hill's office, William was seized with dread. His heart dropped straight to his stomach when he saw his sullen-looking mentor seated across from the one person he expected to never see ever again: Gifty.

"Have a seat," Professor Hill said.

Gifty hadn't changed much from the last time he had seen her as he was loading his luggage into the car before departing Ghana. They'd made awkward eye contact through the days following Kofi's death, the knowledge that each of them had of that night ricocheting back and forth with a vigorous, forceful telepathy. William had artfully avoided conversation with her and thought that once he departed Ghana, he and Gifty would cease to know one another. So seeing her soft, round face, which had barely aged save for a few lines in the corners of her eyes, gave him a terrible shock.

William swallowed hard as he sat down in the chair next to Gifty opposite Professor Hill's desk. No one spoke. Gifty's expression seemed to be quite accusatory, though William wasn't sure how much of that was his own imagination. He bit some skin off his bottom lip as Professor Hill spoke.

"Gifty has come here to show us something that she has found amongst Kofi's . . ."—his voice trailed as he searched for a tactful word—". . . things," he finished after a beat.

William observed the slightest tremble in Gifty's hands as she opened the brown leather-bound book in her lap.

With horror, William recognized Kofi's elegant handwriting on several of the pages.

"I found this," she said in a small voice, very unlike the full and expressive image that William had of her in his memory.

"It's a journal of some kind," Professor Hill explained. "And it seems to indicate that Kofi had some serious objections to the project as well as Ross Financial's being a potential partner. It's dated." Professor Hill folded his hands and rested his mouth on them, piercing William with his gaze. His unspoken message: This is danger.

William's blood ran cold.

"The Carter Corporation is in all the papers in Accra," Gifty said.

Professor Hill nodded. "Quite right. The corporation is making a major difference in housing options for many residents in the area. It's a . . . wonderful accomplishment."

"I don't think that Kofi wanted it that way. Right here, he says so." Gifty paused to point at the pages in the diary. "And I think there was something funny about the way that he died. I saw him leave with you," she continued, extending a shaking finger in William's direction, eyes blazing. "And he didn't come back."

"Kofi's death was tragic, and I know it can be hard to accept when a loved one takes his own life," Professor Hill said. "It's a shock."

"It was a real shock," William echoed. William had never forgotten how Gifty looked at him that night, doubtful but restrained. Now she had a different look on her face. Like she wanted something. She had a knowing twinkle in her dark eyes, a tiny silver sliver that seemed to wink on its own, making eye contact difficult. Gifty still looked capable and strong. And worst of all, unflappable.

"So you're here all the way from Ghana . . . to Boston . . ." William quickly found his voice and added some edge, puffing himself up for a confrontation. He didn't know where this was going but he wanted her to know that he wasn't going to admit to anything. As far as she knew, Kofi had jumped. And yes, she saw them leave together and him return alone, but it had been many years since that happened, and all the authorities had seemed to move on, so why couldn't she? He put a stony facade to his face before saying, "Why?"

William noticed Professor Hill's eyes had widened in his direction.

"What he means to say is thank you for bringing this to our attention, and we'll take it into consideration for the future buildings," the older man said. "But right now, the ball is rolling on the projects that began before Kofi's death, and there's nothing we can do to stop that."

"I flew here to tell you that I know that you're lying about something. And that I can prove it," Gifty said, squaring up against William, finding her own edge.

"Ah, okay," Professor Hill said, stepping in again. "I think there might be a misunderstanding here. And that's perfectly fine. It's been some years. Memories can be complicated, details forgotten. Gifty, is there anything that we can do for you that would help, perhaps, to ease some of your . . . discomfort?"

Gifty gripped the brown leather book closer to her chest. "What do you mean?" she asked.

"I mean, perhaps, maybe, if you're amenable, we can find an agreement, an arrangement, if you will—that might help you feel more comfortable knowing that we're fulfilling Kofi's wishes."

Gifty's head tilted left, and she looked like a confused puppy hearing a new noise for the first time. William prepped himself for an explosive rejection of the bribe that Professor Hill was so blatantly trying to offer, but instead Gifty said, "I want five million dollars."

William barked out a hoarse laugh. "Five million? American dollars? Are you joking?"

Gifty gave him a blank stare of her own and said, "Not at all."

William felt his blood pressure increase. His feelings of anger and incredulity collided, and he felt lightheaded. Even with the rejection of every epicurean pleasure he occasionally craved, he still wasn't where he wanted to be in his career. And he most certainly didn't have $5 million, at least not yet.

"Gifty, will you excuse us?" Professor Hill said. "William and I would like to quickly discuss this request privately."

"No. I think this is really a take it or leave it matter. It also doesn't seem like *he* is taking me seriously," Gifty said, jabbing her thumb in William's direction.

William immediately straightened in his chair, trying his best not to let the colorful wave of expletives he was thinking escape from his mouth, trying his best to avoid the type of escalation that would lead to his ruin. "I assure you," he began, "I understand the seriousness of this situation, and I do believe that we can come to a resolution."

Since Gifty refused to allow the men to have a private conversation, Professor Hill and William had to employ a series of telepathic gestures to speak without speaking. Professor Hill inclined his head down and to the left, looking over his glasses at William. In turn, William let his shoulders sag a little and shook his head, feeling ridiculous. Then Professor Hill let his shoulders rise ever so slightly, which William recognized as a miniature shrug of surrender.

They agreed to "hire" Gifty on a consultant basis, giving her regular quarterly payments that would in the end exceed the five million she asked for so that they would incur all tax costs. She departed the next day a wealthy woman, the legal paperwork executed by Professor Hill. With the ink dry on her NDA, she handed over the diary that she brought with her, which also contained new drawings for modules and ideas that William found incredibly useful. He was upset with himself for not checking Kofi's room for something like this before he departed from Ghana all those years ago, but now there was nothing standing in the way between him and everything.

After they had sorted everything out with Gifty, Professor Hill requested that William stay over for the night. Though William had heard many of Professor Hill's lectures over the years, none was as urgent as the one he delivered that night.

"You almost lost everything," Professor Hill had started out, slamming his open palm down on the desk. "You can never be that reckless and confrontational. Have I taught you nothing?"

William opened his mouth to defend himself.

"Shut up," Professor Hill snapped at him, although he hadn't said anything yet. "Listen to me. You need to take this very seriously, extremely seriously. You need to become the best person in the world. I don't care what you do when no one's around, but everywhere else, people need to know that you're a good man—no, not even good. You need to be the best man."

William wasn't sure what he was going on about. "I—"

"Okay, here's what you need to do. You need to get married as soon as possible. Marriage is trust. It's stability. Family. I know you have feelings about your brother and parents because you come from nothing, but get over it. Make a new family. And make them perfect. You need to show everyone, and I mean *everyone*, that you're a humble, hardworking, deserving professional with incredible vision."

"Professor Hill, respectfully, I don't think Gifty is a threat, and I also don't think anyone is going to believe her even if she says anything. I mean, look!" William said as he held up the brown leather book. "This is all she had, and we have it now. I think it's all good."

"Do not be glib, William. That is beneath you. I'm telling you this for your own good. You might think this is over, but this is the very beginning. And thank God you have five million to give over time, but if you want to make more money, if you want to expand the corporation and continue to do so without external interference, you need to hear me now. People will start to question you and they will dig. Who knows what they'll find when they do? The best thing you can do is aim to control what people will believe."

"Okay, so I get a wife and family, and I'm magically protected?"

"No. You get a wife and a family and a charitable foundation, and you start scholarships, and you donate money to youth shelters, and you have yourself photographed feeding the homeless, and you have a stellar, squeaky clean, cause-no-trouble reputation because if you do not, they will destroy you however they can."

William was somewhat alarmed by this uptick of paranoia, but he kept listening, enraptured once again by his mentor's words.

"Anyone can get rich, William, but it takes a very smart man to stay rich. There are certain rules of fortune. You know this; I've taught you. When I first met you, I said to myself, 'That kid is smart and driven and beyond shrewd. He's going to create an amazing legacy.' And I don't want to be wrong."

The next morning, while the train rumbled back to Manhattan, William had racked his brain for how he could start to build his family, approaching the task as an affair of the head and not the heart. There were girls, sure, but none that he could think of as appropriate legacy carriers. The right candidate needed certain qualities. Young, for starters: a given. Beautiful, because image was the point. Agreeable, because he didn't want a home where he had to fight. Black, also a given, because he would never get respect otherwise from his community.

Upon arriving back in New York City as a man who'd suddenly been accused of murder, he stopped by the diner that he had been frequenting for years. William was buzzing, and when he reached for the door of the venue, his hands were slick with sweat. He had walked the whole way from Penn Station, the wind rushing by in his ears, dodging slower-walking folks with his own aggressive pace. He was going to get himself a wife.

He beelined for one of the only women he knew, the diner's pretty, young waitress, Jacqueline, who'd made several unsuccessful attempts to flirt with him in the past. After sitting down, he asked her to meet him outside on her break. "I can take my break now," she said, calling out behind her to someone named Carmen and instructing her to watch her tables.

"Everything okay?" she asked once she and William were outside and alone on the sidewalk.

"How would you like to be my wife?" William asked. He had thought about this on the train ride back from Boston. Jacqueline was stunningly gorgeous; everyone looked at her. Her beauty was wasted serving customers, but what if she didn't have to? William couldn't quite understand how she hadn't landed any acting or modeling jobs considering her looks, but that didn't deter what he felt. He sensed, despite her circumstances, that she and he were very alike.

This girl, and she still seemed like a girl even at twenty-nine, was going to be the one. Well, at least she was *someone* whom he could make into the one.

"Well—I—I barely know you," she replied.

"Look, we can hammer out specifics later. I don't want to make you uncomfortable, but I'm a rich man. I'm going to be richer. I need a partner who understands how to perform for a certain audience and won't cause trouble. My gut is usually right, and it's telling me that that's you, especially since you're a trained actress. This . . . well to be completely forthright, this is a business arrangement more than anything else. You can take some time to think about it, and my lawyers can draw up a prenup outlining any arrangements you'd like to specify."

Jacqueline Bennett clicked her teeth together. She was thinking. He could feel the wheels in her head creaking, trying to understand how this was the way that someone was asking her to marry him. She squinted her eyes at him. "Why?" she said finally.

"W-why?" William asked, repeating her question back and stumbling over the word.

Jacqueline didn't speak as she waited for him to answer.

"Because I need a wife," he said after a beat.

"Why?" Jacqueline asked again. William's heart fell as he wondered if this was a preview of what their married life would be like.

"Because a man with a family is a better image than a man without one," he said finally.

"Wow, a whole family too?" Jacqueline responded.

William gave her a lopsided smile and shrugged. "It kind of comes with the title, but please know, intimacy isn't my primary goal," he said.

Jacqueline nodded. She backed up until she was leaning against the building and looked at the sky. William mirrored her and watched the foot traffic and car traffic crawl by.

After a few seconds she said, "Okay."

"Okay?" William repeated.

"Okay as in yes," she said.

A verbal deal was as good as any. William didn't know whether to shake her hand or hug her. Instead, he said, "Do you have to go back inside?"

"No," Jacqueline replied, removing the white apron from around her waist and letting it fall to the sidewalk. "I quit."

William Carter Jr. and Jacqueline Bennett Announce Their Engagement

William Carter Jr. of Boston, Massachusetts, and Jacqueline Bennett of Elkin, Kentucky, are set to be wed. Carter Jr. is currently an executive with Ross Financial and oversees international building projects. Bennett is a former beauty queen and actress. The two met at an education fundraiser and spent several months dating before Carter Jr. popped the question.

William Carter Jr. is a graduate of The Galston School, Harvard College, and Harvard Business School. Jacqueline Bennett, fifteen years his junior, is looking forward to being a homemaker.

Their wedding will be a private ceremony held at East Side Episcopal.

CHAPTER 23

Jacqueline Bennett Carter

New York City, October 1991

Jacqueline was never overly concerned with the details of her courtship with William being muddled by external parties. There were plenty of weirder arrangements out there. She did, however, hold a secret close to her chest that threatened to dismantle everything that she'd built.

Six weeks before William's proposal (if it could even be called that), Jacqueline thought that she was getting her big break. She was almost officially broke but not quite, and after all her time in the Big Apple, she was counting on booking this new gig. She had a shot at a recurring role for a housekeeper on a daytime soap. She'd have to read for the part, but the official casting document specifically asked for a Negro actress. She never liked to go for those, truth be told, but at this point, she was desperate.

So her heart broke when the audition went poorly. The casting director said that Jacqueline was far too poised to be a maid, who in the script, was supposed to have hailed from the South. It was a role near perfect for her, but they simply didn't find her read believable enough. She was dismissed.

That night, she set out to get drunk. She was ready to give up on her dreams, sick to death of waitressing, of escorting, of working in general. And she was sick of being poor. Jacqueline was sitting alone at a bar downtown, far away from the places that she and Donna usually frequented. Her hair was blown straight and feathered out, a big brown halo around her head. She only got one gin martini deep before she ran into a client of hers whose company she actually enjoyed. Now Jacqueline could not recall his name, but his strong dark-olive Italian features were always making an appearance in her memory. This guy was a typical Jersey commuter, middle management and conservative. He was a gentleman, or so he liked to think, and he paid well for her time. They'd never had intercourse. Their arrangement was a strictly fellatio-fund exchange, since he considered penetration to be crossing the line to infidelity, but on this night, because they didn't plan to meet and because Jacqueline was hurtling toward despair, he wanted to comfort her. She must have seemed sad because he did ask her immediately what was wrong.

"Oh, I've just decided to waste my life in becoming an actress," she said to him.

He gave her a sad smile. "I'm sure you're not wasting it," he said.

"Well, I'm not doing it either," she said, tapping her self-painted Revlon red nails on the black lacquered bar. He swirled the ice in his lowball glass. She watched as his hand gripped it, his knuckles surprisingly worn for a man who didn't spend much time outdoors. She turned to face him and draped her arm over the back of her high bar seat. This wasn't how she usually behaved with him. She was too herself right now, had no energy to reach for a character. When he looked at her, he seemed to be expressing such care that it warmed her much more than the martini did.

"I used to win you know," she said, "all the time. I used to win pageants. I won so many back home that I was a local legend. That's how I got here, to New York. I won a lot of money as a kid, and I saved

175

up, and I made it all the way from Kentucky to the big city. I used to win all the time. Now all I do is lose."

"I'm sure you'll win again. That's just how it works. You can't win 'em all, right?" he said, attempting lightheartedness.

"I guess," she said noncommittally.

"What will make you feel better?" he said, looking at her through his jet-black lashes.

"Do you have a billion dollars?" she said, sighing.

"Not today," he said and laughed. "But I do have good advice, so tell me your problems for a change." And she did. As she detailed her string of rejections, she felt a loosening, like the stench of her failures was no longer as potent. She made some jokes, and he laughed at them. As it does, the comfort led to sex, for which he paid her a satisfactory $300. In the moment she hadn't been all that sure that she wasn't just acting sad to play at his sympathies. She had so often spent time confusing when she was acting and when she was not. She didn't expect to get paid, not really, but she was grateful for the money.

She wasn't in the habit of tracking her cycle, but she definitely missed it when it didn't show up. She kept giving herself one more day to get a period, but one never came. She didn't feel a baby. She didn't feel a heartbeat or a guest tenant in her uterus, a ridiculous thought, she realized, but she felt something she was pretty unfamiliar with, and that was fear. She didn't want to confirm her suspicions and thought that she might be able to pray her period into existence. When that never materialized, she had to know for sure. She cursed herself for her uncharacteristically blasé attitude toward protection with him. She stared into space on her bed in Hitchings House, reluctant to go get a pregnancy test she was sure would be positive. But finally she did, and she peed on it in the common bathroom and walked to her room with the test hidden under her sweatshirt. She rested it on the corner of her old secondhand desk and waited. A little plus appeared in the results box, and her breath caught.

If she hadn't already spent the $300, she might have not stayed pregnant, but since she had, she was short on options. She continued to work, showing up to the diner every single day, working doubles, hoping to exhaust herself into a miscarriage. She bought a pack of cigarettes and smoked as many as she could stand before she got sick. She knew these were half-hearted measures for terminating a pregnancy, but she had no one to talk to about this and no real knowledge about how to handle it.

To her own dismay, she remained with child. Four weeks into gestation, she accepted William Carter Jr.'s proposal, which felt more like brokering a sale. She accepted him because he was the one who planted the seed of a billion dollars. That would certainly solve a lot of problems for her, but a man who wanted a family so much so that he proposed to a stranger was almost too good to be true. She looked at him as her salvation. She didn't know him at all, but she knew he was practical and predictable, and that would be enough.

The week after they stood outside the diner and agreed to marry, they were married. It was a courtroom thing, downtown in a basement with long brown benches lining the walls. She wore a white pencil skirt with a matching blazer, a business suit for William's proclaimed business arrangement. William had given her cash to get something, and she picked the outfit before she started hyperventilating in Macy's in Herald Square because she was so overwhelmed with choices. William picked her up wearing a dark-gray suit, somber and serious.

She was sure they didn't look like they were in love. After the deed was done, William awkwardly held her shoulders and hesitated before giving her a chaste, closed-mouth kiss that was captured on camera for posterity. They posed for photos outside East Side Episcopal to make the event seem more romantic, riding uptown in a chauffeured town car. She'd signed many more documents in that week than she had ever even known existed. There was the prenuptial agreement, of course, which detailed that she was entitled to nothing but that she was required to bear heirs. The unborn heirs would be the sole recipients to the Carter fortune, and they would decide what part of it their mother could have, if any. This was an interesting stipulation, and the only reason that she agreed to it was because she was already carrying what she hoped to pass off as Carter kin. This was already a gamble, and she wanted to ensure that there were no hiccups with the larger plan she needed to make work.

Then there was the nondisclosure agreement, which prohibited her from speaking with any members of the press unless preauthorized by William. Then there was the marriage license and name change documents, which officially made her Mrs. William Carter Jr. He'd allowed her to keep her maiden last name in the middle because he thought that it was phonetically appealing. The whole arrangement was so much more clinical than she expected, and in a lot of ways, that made the process easier. Everything was refreshingly up front on his end. On hers, she had to ensure the consummation of the marriage happened fairly quickly so as to maintain the continuity of the timeline. As the baby in her belly split cells and multiplied from a poppy seed to a lentil to a kiwi, she needed to make sure that William believed that in forty weeks or less, the child was his.

After the wedding, sitting across from one another in spacious leather seats, Jacqueline gave William a soft smile. She noticed that his jaw was set, uncomfortably so, the tension held there like a taut rubber band. She looked down at her left hand, where a slim gold band held a tasteful solitaire two-carat diamond and now a thicker gold band. She admired the classic gold band on William's left hand, a costume for a new play. "So we're on the way to the rest of our lives," she said because she thought she should. Her words seemed to startle William, who was looking out the window.

With great effort, he stretched to lean forward and pat her leg and said, "I guess so." William dropped his voice to a loud whisper. "Are you comfortable with having a—uh—wedding night?" he said.

Jacqueline smiled at his shyness. "I'm comfortable with that," she said, trying to sound confident and reassuring, knowing that they'd have to have sex soon in order for the timeline of the birth of her baby to appear acceptable.

"I got a suite for us at the Plaza," he said. "Have you been?"

"I have," Jacqueline answered, remembering several nights there with Donna and girls from acting class, hoping no one there would recognize her.

The newlyweds remained holed up in their room for the entire weekend, and it wasn't bad. William splurged on champagne and room service, and the high-thread-count sheets felt marvelous on Jacqueline's body. The time with William was fine; the sex they had, short and perfunctory. Adequate. Jacqueline expected nothing more. She didn't love him, no, but she loved what he was doing for her, and maybe she could love him one day. Years later, she would laugh at her girlish naivete.

After their weekend at the Plaza, Jacqueline moved in with her new husband. William relinquished his studio bachelor pad and within days got them a new home. This apartment, in a high-rise building in Midtown, chosen for its value to William's work commute, was on the fourteenth floor out of twenty-six. It had a living room, dining room, three bedrooms, and small quarters for staff, which they would have had if William was not hoarding his wealth. Though he had some money now, William was militant about how to spend it. He was determined to build up a fortune, not blow one. "We don't just want to be rich; we want to stay rich," he would say, more to himself because Jacqueline barely spent anything.

William was invested in keeping his home a private space, and Jacqueline soon learned he had a strict schedule that couldn't be disrupted by any means, making it impossible to host guests. That's exactly what he said before shutting off the light on his nightstand when she'd mentioned that her friend was coming to town. His obsession with privacy, a quirk bestowed upon him by his mentor, was something he took, like everything else, to an extreme. Jacqueline wasn't sure how much of it was in the interest of self-preservation and how much was just plain fear. Still, over time she learned to manage him the best she could. She was overly accommodating to his whims and idiosyncrasies, like she was with any client.

At William's direction, the Carters didn't have staff until much later. William allowed for the expense of a weekly housekeeper, who changed the bedding and did the laundry. They had a dishwasher, and Jacqueline had started learning to cook, but most nights they ate out. He was mostly content to leave the domestic responsibilities to her as long as she followed through on his wishes for privacy, presentation, and organization of the home, which she did perfectly. They lived on a deserted island up in the sky, and thankfully, Baby Asher's presence invited more opportunity for communal interaction as a family. But William was reticent about that too. As Asher grew into toddlerhood, William said that the boy needed to "make the right friends" so that he would be comfortable when he "attended the right schools" eventually. Going to random parks and playgrounds not frequented by the right people? Wasn't going to happen.

While William worked, Jacqueline remained at home with Asher all day, maintaining the house and learning how to navigate a neighborhood with an infant. William had also given her the task of researching the New York City Black Elite so as to complete his mission of becoming one of them.

The Black Elite, composed of an old guard as historic as America herself, were scattered all over the country, the power players on a team that William was hungry to join. The New York scene was interspersed with investment bankers, lawyers, doctors, and other highly paid professionals. This was long before those careers became pedestrian and powerless, but at the time it was impressive for African Americans to achieve such professions against all odds, especially in the United States. They attended schools like Morehouse and Spelman but also Harvard and Yale. In this department, she was at a deficit. William, on the other hand, had been tangentially included in their ranks by virtue of attending Harvard, but since he had no pedigree, he was woefully excluded from most of their private socializing.

That's where Jacqueline could help. What she lacked in impressive family history and education, she made up for in European features and pleasantly medium-tone skin. She hated this, an old echo from pageants coming back to haunt her. When she first started competing, she was told by every other older woman to stay out of the sun, to wear a hat, to wear long sleeves and gloves. She in fact passed out in the July heat at a church picnic when she was twelve, trying not to get too dark so that she could win a pageant the next month. She woke up dazed, surrounded by people fanning her red face. She pulled at the gloves and dress, desperate to break free. "Oh no, baby," she heard an older woman say. "Don't you have to be up on that stage soon? Can't let you get too black."

Jacqueline didn't know then that she was destined for motherhood, but she'd sworn that she would never do that to her own children, finding such ideas beyond repugnant. Still, when dealing with the elite world, she was aware of the currency of her complexion, that she'd garnered favor with her looks, and that was just one more box checked. She resented it, but she'd learned a long time ago to work with what she had. She reluctantly recognized that Asher, who was blowing spit bubbles in his playpen, a shade lighter than her, was in an even better position for social mobility.

At first, Jacqueline was afraid that Asher's appearance, so fair and so lean, would make William question his parentage, a wager she made the day she decided to become William's wife while already pregnant. But William seemed to be willfully blind to the ways that he and his son had few genetic similarities, immediately declaring his love for the infant at his birth. The only thing that he had ever said about it was a single comment made the day after Asher had been born. William turned over the infant's tiny hand, which was balled up into a fist encased in a gray cashmere mitten to mitigate scratching, and pushed up the edge of the onesie to expose a tiny wrist. While running his finger gently across his pale skin, he said, "His veins almost look blue, don't they?"

After Asher was born, Helen Hudson, now known as Helen Neal, called unexpectedly to let Jacqueline know that she was coming to New York City. Jacqueline and Helen had managed sporadic contact over the years, letters here and there and the occasional phone call to catch up, but their close friendship had ended when Jacqueline secretly boarded a bus to Manhattan without telling anyone.

Helen was now a mother of two, and as she promised, began having children almost immediately upon graduating high school. She had one girl and one boy and was an active member at Zion Baptist Church in Louisville where Martin Luther King Jr.'s brother, A. D. King, was famously a minister, as she never failed to mention. Helen and her husband had moved to and settled in Louisville, making a comfortable life for themselves and their charming offspring. Exactly what she said she was going to do. The consistency in Helen's ambitions and how her life looked was impressive. For Jacqueline, who'd done almost the complete opposite of what she set out to do, her life was a combination of envy and embarrassment.

"Girl, I didn't know that you'd become so bougie," Helen said to Jacqueline as they sat in Freds at Barneys for lunch, shopping bags at their feet, Jacqueline bouncing one-year-old Asher in her lap.

In the moment, Jacqueline had laughed off the comment, declaring, "Honey, I'm still the same girl from Elkin, don't you worry." Still, Jacqueline had heard herself when she spoke, how her southern accent was nowhere to be found. She also was aware that the places that she had taken Helen to on that trip were telling a different story. She was not the same girl from Elkin, and when she recounted what happened as she sat across from William at the dinner table later that night, his reaction startled her.

"She said 'bougie'?" William questioned. "She actually said that?"

Jacqueline had moved on from Helen's comment, wanting to give William more context. She started to tell him about how a sales associate at Barneys had suggested that Jacqueline and Helen could not afford to shop there. But William was stuck on bougie, even though the racist sales associate was far more offensive.

To meet her oldest friend, Jacqueline had selected a black A-line Alaïa skirt with a matching cropped cardigan. She wanted something that felt both understated and impressive, and this was perfect. Or it was perfect until Asher left an explosion of soupy shit all over the whole thing at the exact moment she was carrying him to his stroller in order to leave. Years later, she would hardly believe she once parented so closely as to be covered in her own child's feces. But in that moment, between the baby's cries, his need to be held, and her rapidly fraying nerves, the zeal to dress to impress completely evaporated.

As a backup, she'd set Asher down in his crib, quickly showered, and grabbed one of William's Harvard sweatshirts, something that he barely ever wore anymore since he spent most of his time in a suit, pairing it with a pair of Levi's jeans and sneakers. She grabbed a baseball hat as well to conceal the fact that she'd run out of time to do her hair, disappointed that, yet again, another New York plan had fallen apart. Fifteen minutes later, when Jacqueline had met Helen in front of Barneys and the two had walked into the store, an older white sales associate had immediately looked Jacqueline's disheveled outfit up and down and said, "Is there anything I can help you find? Perhaps six would be a good place to start."

The sixth floor was where the most casual and contemporary clothes were found. To which Jacqueline had replied, "Thank you, but I'm fine on three. My regular associate, Carolyn, usually does pulls for me."

Back home, and with Helen, Jacqueline had called the white woman racist, pure and simple. But later, at dinner, William wasn't convinced.

"That shop girl doesn't know you or who you are," he declared. "She's judging you based on what she saw, and you know better than to walk into Barneys looking any kind of way."

William was gearing up for a lecture and barely noticed how his wife shrank back at his words. "But your childhood best friend coming to visit you in New York and insulting you like that is really what you should be upset about," William continued.

"I don't think she meant what she said in a mean way," Jacqueline said softly.

"Didn't she?" William asked.

"Well, no—she was just saying that she thinks I've become different living in New York, and I have. I've changed."

"She didn't say that though. If she wanted to say you're different, she would've said that. What she said was 'I didn't know that you'd become so bougie.' That's an insult."

"Don't be so sensitive. It's not an insult. It was just an observation," Jacqueline said.

William took notice that she was getting defensive, but neither would take themselves out of the moment enough to calm down. Jacqueline didn't enjoy arguing with William either, especially because he was so skilled at speaking that she often found herself outmatched. William also never wanted to take it easy on her, thinking that every opportunity was one for learning.

"Jacqueline, what do you think the word 'bougie' means?" William asked. He placed his fork and knife down on his plate and calmly waited for her response.

"It's just slang, William. It means fancy, rich, kind of showy. She didn't mean anything by it."

"That's not what bougie means," William said before reaching for his wineglass. He was entering into some kind of performance now, bolstered by the fact that he found her definition of bougie to be unsatisfactory.

"Bougie is a derivative of the word *bourgeoisie*. The bourgeoisie represent the middle class, a middle class trying to emulate what they *think* it means to be a part of the aristocracy. But these people don't know. They don't have seats at the table. The bourgeoisie live outside of the confines of court. They're relying on gossip and observation to ascertain what they imagine an aristocratic life looks like. They get a distilled version of what it means to be an elevated member of society, and then they dress themselves up and parade as such so that they're able to feel important."

"William, there's no way she meant it like that, okay?" Jacqueline said.

"There's no other way she could have meant it, Jacqueline. Bougie is being used as a weapon. It signifies that you don't belong just as much as that Barneys woman who said you don't belong. Saying that you became bougie means that she thinks this is a learned behavior and that you don't deserve class mobility because it isn't consistent with her opinion of you. Don't you see that?"

"I didn't know that dinner needed to include a history lesson," she replied.

"We're *living* history, Jacqueline. Us. When I become a billionaire . . . how many Black billionaires do you think there are?" he asked.

He didn't wait for her to respond. "There are none currently. There are two men born in the United States other than me who might get close and amass a fortune of one billion dollars or more. Just two. And do you know how many billionaires there are in the world? The whole world? Eighty. Out of billions of people, only eighty have a billion dollars. That is history, and I will not be convinced that we're pathetically mimicking the aristocracy when we are the aristocracy."

"Okay, William. I get it," Jacqueline said finally, conceding to her husband and hoping that would satiate his need to argue.

"I don't think you should be spending any more time with Helen," William said, picking up his fork and knife and resuming his dinner. It wasn't just important for Asher to have the right friends, but Jacqueline had to as well. He'd given her a luxurious life, and most days this was something she found comforting, even freeing in some cases. Someone who made all critical decisions and gave her a life of extreme comfort was what she thought every woman prayed for, but she'd never quite counted on it coming with so many restrictions. Donna had told her a long time ago, "You have to just let them lead"—*them* being the men—and in most cases, Jacqueline was happy to do that. But sometimes William was simply too much.

Some weeks after this discussion, William broached the topic with Jacqueline about her returning to school. He felt that it would be a crucial part of the kindergarten application process that both of Asher's parents were college graduates. He suggested that she apply to and enroll in Columbia because it looked better for the children to have two Ivy League–educated parents. William said that he would "take care" of the admissions process, that a Black student interested in continuing her education would be a noble endeavor, and he knew "many people who would want to support this."

Just like he said, Jacqueline was accepted to Columbia's Division of Special Programs, a school she entered under the private tutelage of someone who spent their career as an actor in London's West End. Jacqueline would be earning not a degree, but a certificate in theatrical arts, although no official materials would ever say as much. She and William diligently worked on Asher's kindergarten applications, which read "William Carter Jr., Harvard College, Harvard Business School and Jacqueline Bennett Carter, Columbia University." This was as much as anyone needed to know. William had assumed that his résumé would help to legitimize Jacqueline's, and like he had on many things in the last few years, he had bet right.

Now in her thirties, she was pleased that she no longer had to waitress and experience the train delays and commuting drama that living in Harlem resulted in, but that also meant that her acting dreams had dried up. She *was* still acting, she supposed, but taking on the role of mother. But now that she had officially transitioned out of her twenties? Her career on screen or stage was definitely over before it began. She did mourn what could have been, but after a depressing number of years sharing a run-down dormitory with all those other girls clamoring for a new life in some way, Jacqueline told herself that she had ultimately lucked out—that if she played her cards right as wife to this complex man who yearned for status, she would have access to a grand stage that would encompass the world.

CHAPTER 24

William Carter Jr.

New York City, June 2015

William was reviewing a draft of the speech that he was to give at his seventieth birthday. The main event was now only three weeks away, and everything was falling into place. In his study in his New York City apartment, he was surrounded by memories of what he had built. He glanced at the framed photograph of him with Barack Obama, a snapshot taken in Hawaii. There was also him and Warren Buffett laughing on the tarmac after touching down in Sun Valley. Him and David and Charles from Ross Financial encased in a weighty Baccarat crystal frame.

And then for some reason, another picture popped into his head, the Polaroid that had been taken of him and Kofi on the first day of their trip in Ghana. He hadn't seen that picture in years, the physical copy lost to time, but he saw it in his mind. William wasn't hallucinating, per se, but every day since the first time he'd heard Kofi's name in years, he had the feeling that he was constantly being chased. He reached more frequently for his cigarettes, his hand trembling as he extracted one from the pack and smoked it out on the patio of his personal office. He noticed that his heart would race, that he would begin to perspire and get short of breath. He tried to disguise this as best he could as to be able to camouflage any weakness. He had assured Jacqueline that everything was contained, but he didn't know truthfully if that was the case.

With only three weeks to go to the Vineyard party, one of his men on the ground reported that Gifty had been making some peculiar movements outside of her normal routine. She was as slow as could be expected at her age, taking long walks outside the gates of her considerably large home. It was strange in and of itself. She had been unofficially retired for decades, but according to paperwork filed with the IRS, she was officially a Carter Corporate consultant. Even though they had a contract, the fact that she wanted to blackmail him at all made William want to keep a close eye on her whereabouts and, more importantly, on any potential additional evidence that she might've had that suggested that he killed Kofi.

According to his sources, Gifty's daughter had taken a meeting last year with a local teacher, which was strange, and William didn't know why exactly, but it was giving him a feeling of unease. There was a part of him that wanted to inform Jacqueline about this, but he knew that she was very busy planning his birthday party, and after so many years, he had finally learned to stop micromanaging her.

It had never occurred to William that he would need to work at being a husband. Marriage in his head was a binary, like a light switch. It was either on or off, married or not. What happened in the middle was a great mystery, but when Professor Hill had suggested that getting married would aid in the establishment of his reputation, he couldn't argue with the logic. With Jacqueline, he saw an opportunity and stepped into it, the intuitive sense that he'd begun to hone over the years working efficiently for him even outside of the office. It was an arrangement to begin with, but along the way, his feelings had evolved. He grew very fond of her and remained so to this day, sometimes fascinated by her sparkling wit and emotional intelligence, how she could work a room far more effortlessly than William ever could, and how she spoke to him with respect, maybe even care, even when he knew he was behaving like an idiot. They had a great partnership, and he'd never regretted his decision to make her his wife.

During the early days of their marriage, with Jacqueline being so low maintenance, William was able to focus on growing his business. He attended a Harvard Club lunch two years after their wedding where two gentlemen, both white and older than he, had been describing tactics for dodging their spouses. The Jewish music executive said, "I have to make up studio sessions just to get out of going to another Central Park Conservatory fundraiser. They have enough of my funds, and they need me too? No way."

Across the table, a white-haired WASP agreed, "Why do you think I am golfing Saturdays *and* Sundays? Hell, I'll go golf in Australia. Twenty-four hours to fly there and nine hours on the green uninterrupted? Bliss."

William cut into his steak and listened good-naturedly but did not really have anything of measure to add. He left that lunch and phoned a hoary Professor Hill to recount to him what was said.

Professor Hill had laughed, "William, your wife is a saint, and not because she doesn't care about golf or the trees in Central Park. She's good because she works hard and she has agreed to align with your goal. Look how far you've been able to go with her help." And that was the truth. He had needed Jacqueline's help in the beginning, and he still did.

When he signed with Ross Financial, he was aware that Kofi's ideas would help to give him a stable financial foundation, but that wasn't enough to take him to the next level. Building projects took years to get off the ground, especially abroad, and it was a singular point-of-sale. It was guaranteed revenue, but there was an inherent limit to how much he could make based upon how much could be built, and so he had a problem that needed a solution. From listening to the issues on the ground in Ghana and poring over detailed reports of the market, he assessed that there was a lack of functional technology that stood in between him being able to maximize the potential of the factories that produced the modules for his properties.

To solve this problem, he recruited more factories to produce different modules so he could expand into more industries. There was no reason that these modules had to be specific to architecture. In fact, it was actually better if they were not. By automating production for other things he needed to help his business, he not only decreased the time it took to build new properties but also created a new industry that only served him in the end. He easily adapted to production for things like automobile parts, medical machinery, and even consumer goods.

His vision involved implanting complex systems of software into manufacturing facilities. This required clients to set up a subscription service, garnering a guaranteed monthly income for the initial cost of membership. Thereafter, anytime there were updates (and of course there were always updates), each additional service incurred another fee. Contracts minimally required a five-year commitment, and in that time, he generated tens of millions, if not hundreds of millions, in additional profits.

Getting clients to sign on to this was a barrier he was confident that he could handle by, as Kofi had not liked to admit all those years ago, greasing the palms of several strategic government partners who could all but make it illegal for a production facility to not have this technology. And at Professor Hill's direction, he significantly increased his charitable contributions in Ghana. He opened a school. He opened a facility for women specifically to be able to work and earn money. He named a hospital wing after Kofi and gave money to mental health. He also helped to fund the police force and befriended some judges too, because it was important to have them as allies.

William realized he was composing a kind of symphony. He never considered himself very artistic, but this was art, and it would have been impossible without his steadfast co-captain, Jacqueline. It was intricate and complex and beautiful, and best of all, all these things working in tandem reduced his taxable income. In the meantime, he continued paying Gifty as a consultant even after the $5 million payment was completed, because keeping her quiet and happy was key to his success.

He wasn't totally sure about the requirements of husband and father outside of providing, but he was certain that providing was at the top of his priority list. He was still in constant contact with Professor Hill, who received a 10 percent finder's fee on all William's endeavors. Hill provided all the introductions to necessary experts, who also aided in guiding William in positioning himself optimally for the lifestyle that he was seeking and the legacy that he was determined to create.

William would have never guessed that decades later, after accomplishing all that he'd set to accomplish as a young man, the concept of legacy would trouble him deeply. Outside of thinking about Kofi, the other preoccupation giving him anxiety as his birthday approached was the colossal disappointment he was experiencing over his children. He hovered the cursor over the lines in the speech that read "Of course, my greatest achievement is being a father." He knew this was what he was supposed to say, but his children had caused him a great deal of stress so far. He couldn't find himself in them on most days, physically or otherwise.

He'd begun to notice their exaggerated shortcomings when they were young, how Asher seemed to epitomize imbecilic behavior at times, and how Kennedy seemed lost in her daydreams. Now that he was older, it was abundantly clear that they were ill equipped for a life without him at the helm. The first thing that activated his distaste for his own children was how careless they were. Never in a million years did he believe that his children would have no regard for caring for their things (or his, for that matter) and how mad this would make him. It started when they were toddlers, their sticky, dirty handprints covering vintage wallpaper that constantly had to be replaced. When they were in middle school, he would notice how they scuffed up their shoes, creased them, stepped on the backs to get out of them, never tied them, and let them wear down to a holey imitation of their original form. This also never bothered them.

With technology they were worse. They broke, tossed around, or lost everything from cell phones to digital cameras to keyboards and gaming consoles. An entire drawer in Asher's desk was dedicated to being a graveyard for discarded devices. They abandoned their belongings all around the houses with no regard for how such a mess reflected on their character. They crashed cars (well, Asher did) and smashed devices and lost jewelry and accessories. William realized, entirely too late to do anything about it, that this was because his children were extremely certain that they could just get something new whenever they felt like it. Somewhere along the way, he realized, in cementing his vision of being among the elite, his children became just like the kids he went to Galston and Harvard with—spoiled rotten, obnoxious in how they related to exquisite things. They didn't appreciate the art lining the walls that he'd won in auctions, beating out major museums and private institutions. They didn't care about Watcha Cove's mesmerizing scenic views. They didn't interact with the world that he built for them with any kind of veneration. And it was such a profound disappointment.

William was not sure how to rectify this, and by the time that he noticed how problematic it was, it was too late to correct. Forcing gratitude on them as teenagers would just result in eye rolls and snide commentary. They already had to do community service through school and Jack and Jill, and this was something that they did without complaint since it had been established as routine, but how could he make them see how lucky they were to be in their position?

He toyed with an extreme idea: dropping them off somewhere without any money or knowledge about where they were and letting them use their instincts in order to get home. An insane proposition, frankly. He brought this up to Jacqueline one night as they were both flossing over their separate sinks. "Like *Survivor*?" she asked him, slightly confused by the suggestion.

"Well, no," he said, wanting to persuade her. "More like . . . a way to cultivate resourcefulness."

"They're kids, William. Torture is not a mechanism for character development," she said, looking at herself in the mirror.

To some degree, he could acknowledge that this was correct, but on the other hand, it worried him that his children had limited life skills. They seemed to lack drive, ambition, and general grit. They could only do what they did in a very specific context, which was sanitized and predetermined. William found it distressing that they had been to all the places that he deemed them worthy to be in: summer camps for networking, ski trips in the Alps, summers spent on safari, but with each eye roll and bored glance they displayed, he grew more resentful. "We're here, we've made it!" he wanted to scream at them, but no matter how extreme the lesson, they would not learn. He'd once forced Asher to accompany him to a Carter Foundation Scholarship ceremony for kids his own age, hoping to see a spark of gratitude, but nothing came. Asher shook hands for five minutes and texted his friends for the rest of the time. They had grown up in such extreme comfort that they had no concept of struggle.

William had always imagined that his children would be smart, and with Asher, the most disappointing realization hit him. Asher was solidly average, and that was being generous. What Asher lacked in intelligence, though, he made up for in loyalty. The boy was as dedicated as they come. He would do whatever, whenever, no questions asked. In another life, he would have made an incredible soldier. William found this useful for the time being while he was vivacious and healthy, but the day would come eventually when he was gone and the Carter Corporation might also crumble if he wasn't careful. The first step toward making sure both children were ready for the world at large was enrollment in an elite four-year university. This was not a formula that William Carter Jr. had invented, just one that he had obviously seen work.

The night that Asher was accepted to Princeton, William had stopped working. He threw an impromptu party for the four Carters at home. He turned the stereo up to full volume, knowing that he would be reported to the co-op board. He let Asher and Kennedy drink alcohol. He was certain they were doing it already anyway. He laughed with his kids, and when they had all gotten tipsy, asked everyone if they wanted to go for a drive. He had to summon two separate SUVs, but they paired up and piled in and drove to the marina on the East Side. Asher stuck his head through the sunroof of the other car, and William watched him let out a guttural scream, arms outstretched and head back, just absolutely roaring with delight. When they arrived at the dock, a chartered boat was waiting to take them around the island, anywhere they wanted to go.

"Oh my God, Dad, how'd you do this?" Kennedy asked as she was removing her shoes and being helped on board. William answered by tapping the side of his nose and winking like a thin Black Kris Kringle. It had been years, decades since he had allowed himself such freedom. As the city receded behind them and all four Carters clinked their glasses together with giggles, William had to blink back his tears. He knew he was fulfilling the destiny he had set out to accomplish the moment that he accepted that he would leave home and enroll at Galston. The moment that he let Kofi plunge into the dark. The moment that he decided to make his own luck and choose himself and his future family.

PART 3

JOB POSTING:

CARTER CORPORATION CONSTRUCTION

Position: Construction specialist

Location: In region with strong preference for Accra, Ghana.

Language: The JOB SITE'S working language is English. TWI, FRENCH, OR ARABIC TRANSLATORS WELCOME.

Timeline: Applications will be reviewed on a rolling basis and the postings will remain open until filled.

CHAPTER 25

Ernest Morris

Accra, February 2014

Ernest Morris was itching with anticipation to start his life when he graduated from Princeton. It was difficult for him to determine if the experience was "worth it" given the tens of thousands in debt he took on after he returned the Carter Foundation Scholarship following his junior year. (This was coupled with the thousands that he already owed before college from when his mother put several bills in his name when he was in elementary school.) But he had his degree. He had heard that public service work could help wipe out student loan burden, and so he set out to find an opportunity that might mitigate some of his financial stress. A teaching-abroad program that was advertised within the Black Student Union on campus landed him in Accra, which was how he found himself living abroad for the last two years.

He wasn't any closer to the kind of future that he thought he was promised when he'd decided to make his way to New Jersey from Atlanta, but at least he didn't have to deal with cold weather anymore. He had no teaching certifications, but this would be achieved in tandem with his actually doing the job. The only thing he minded about Accra was the roads; the daring drivers on speeding dirt bikes made him dizzy. Aside from that, his life was good. At the school, his role was to teach math and English to nine-year-olds, and as much as this wasn't in his grand plan, it was something that he enjoyed.

He needed an escape from the last four years of his life, and he didn't know how much he craved an experience away from America, somewhere in a majority Black place. Living abroad hadn't seemed like an option for someone of his circumstances at first, but now as he enjoyed cold after-work beers with his colleagues from the Netherlands, the United Kingdom, and Guam, he felt inspired. He was pleased at the community that he was able to form and how much he felt fulfilled by the work that he was doing. He was thinking that he would like to extend his stay another year, but in a matter of months, his program was coming to an end, and he would have to figure out how he was going to deal with what was waiting for him at home.

In the meantime, he was trying to manage the needs of his students, discovering that his role as an educator wasn't limited to the classroom. One of his favorite students was a bright girl named Esi. She was well above average height for her age, so much so that her knees knocked against the standard desk often. She was responsive and agreeable in class, and though he knew he was not supposed to have favorites, her energy in the classroom was helpful and dependable.

Ernest grew concerned when Esi stopped coming to school one day. After twenty-one days of missed classes, he traveled to Esi's home to find out the reason for her extended absence. Esi answered the door and was visibly surprised to see Ernest. He quickly second-guessed his presence there, wondering if he'd crossed a line.

"Mr. Earn?" she asked, slightly skeptical.

"Hi, Esi," Ernest replied, now self-conscious about his motivation for being there. He hoped he didn't look as creepy as he'd started to feel.

"I just wanted to come by and check on you because you've been absent from school. Is everything all right?"

"Oh," Esi said as she looked down at the floor before stepping aside so that he could enter the house. Ernest hesitated in the doorway for a second before looking over his shoulder but decided that since he'd come all this way already, he might as well see what's going on. "I know I've been absent, but I can't come to school anymore," she said to him when he was finally inside.

Ernest stood uncomfortably in the hallway that led into a small living room. The home was an aluminum-sided, two-bedroom dwelling in a community called Bibu Estates. There were high walls enveloping each property, clearly delineating individualized small parcels of land. There was a gate to get inside, but no one had been guarding it, so he just walked in. Inside, the furniture seemed to be a mix of purchased and inherited items, the decor not really coalescing.

"Why's that, Esi?" he asked, hoping to coax her into sharing.

"My brother, I have to take care of him now," Esi said, looking down at the floor and pointing to an area in a bedroom partitioned off with a curtain.

"But you didn't have to take care of him before?"

Esi shook her head slowly. "He's older than me, but he was working on a construction site and—" She motioned again toward the curtain.

Ernest heard a faint whimpering sound coming from behind it. Esi beckoned him forward and put a finger to her lips. Ernest tiptoed behind her. She vented the fabric slightly to the side to reveal a boy who was unmistakably related to Esi, lying on a bed, twitching and groaning in his sleep. Ernest frowned and took in the surroundings. The boy couldn't be more than sixteen years old, and Ernest would not have thought anything was amiss until he noticed a bloody stump suspended by a makeshift sling where his right hand should have been. His intake of breath was sharp. Esi began to back away from her brother, and Ernest followed.

"Esi, what happened?" Ernest asked.

"My brother, he had a good job working for the CC. A few weeks ago, someone dropped something on his forearm, and it was injured so badly, it had to be amputated. He can't really do anything for himself now, and he has nightmares every time he sleeps. He's sleeping now, which is good, but I have to be here to take care of him because there's no one else to help," she said.

"What's the CC?" Ernest asked.

"The Carter Corporation, I think it's called. They do all the building around here," Esi replied.

Ernest felt his blood run cold at the mention of the Carter Corporation. He hadn't heard the name Carter since he'd left Princeton, since he himself had been bedridden and battered with no compassion. Since he had rejected the remaining last year of his scholarship and plunged himself into debt to pay for school. He couldn't believe these people had reached him all the way in Africa.

He'd known, of course, that the Carter Corporation had its roots in Ghana. This was a famous fact, a good bit of trivia that played well for identity politics. For his entire life, he had been aware of these American Black billionaires who'd made their fortune elsewhere. It was also just as known that whatever they did to make their money was always at the expense of other people. He just didn't expect for them to be children, or for him to be so close to one of their victims. He felt sick as he looked into Esi's eyes and saw her distress.

Briefly, he was lost in his memory of his own experience with Asher Carter. He wouldn't say he was obsessed, but for a time, a short one, he was certainly fixated on getting Asher to be involved with his on-campus initiatives, hoping his popularity and money could potentially do some good for other Black students at Princeton. But Asher had thwarted every attempt at connection, even after they'd met on good terms at Ernest's scholarship ceremony. Ernest eventually understood that Asher had no interest in connecting, and in fact avoided Ernest as much as he could. Ernest found himself watching Asher closely in their shared class, waiting for him to reveal anything interesting about himself, but

Asher was an astoundingly typical jock. He was handsome, tall, light skinned, and incredibly dull. Worse than that, he was dumb as a brick.

This guy, Ernest felt himself thinking, *is the son of a billionaire?* Ernest had spent the first few weeks of the semester surveying his new environment and classmates. He'd chosen Princeton because he wanted the best, and yet he found himself stunned that this population was what constituted the best. Most of the people he met seemed to be chosen by physical archetype from some sort of catalog and dropped in New Jersey with matching monogrammed everything.

Their sophomore year, instead of joining ranks with the Black student organizations that Ernest had beseeched Asher to be a part of, Asher had bickered for the eating club Ivy, which wasn't surprising, but irritating to Ernest all the same. Ernest declined to bicker for any eating clubs, knowing already that he was of a status so lowly and undesirable, he would retain more dignity in abstaining. Still, he had to admit that he wanted to be in the Ivy mix every now and again. Their parties were legendary but not advertised. For nonmembers to be granted admission, they required a pass. Passes were indiscriminately handed out to hot girls and very discriminately handed out to everyone else. Having the right look was sometimes half the battle, like getting access to an exclusive nightclub.

One person who very much didn't have the right look was Ernest Morris. On a particularly frigid night his junior year, he'd made the bold choice that he was going to accompany a friend to an Ivy party. "Come on, Ernest," his friend Madison Sanderson had all but begged. "I know you don't love it, but there's nothing else going on tonight. There'll be a DJ and drinks, and I'll be there," she said, shaking his shoulders affectionately. Ernest rolled his eyes dramatically, and the corners of his mouth downturned when he thought about rolling up to the Ivy house, but she was right: there *was* nothing else going on that night. He was six shots deep and just getting started, letting off some steam. He walked arm in arm with Madison across the campus to Ivy, where she'd been invited to the party and he would be attending as her plus-one.

Madison fell outside of the demographics of whom he might choose to typically befriend. She was a moneyed and slender white girl, but as a socialist bisexual from Vermont, she had won him over in their shared political science class by absolutely eviscerating a gun-loving good ole boy over his stance on American interference in developing nations. She wasn't perfect, but neither was he, and he figured that college was for making new relationships, so why not?

Ernest felt the tension the moment they walked up to Ivy's building. The two had zigzagged their way to the door, still linked at the elbows, laughing to keep the biting January cold at bay. The two underclassmen manning the door eyed Ernest when Madison gave her name and followed it up with "plus-one" before flashing her brilliant white smile, a feat of modern orthodontia and money. "Hmm," the chubbier kid closer to the left said, scanning the paper printout list. "You're here but . . ." He paused ceremoniously. "It doesn't say · plus-one."

His comrade looked over at the paper to confirm and then at Ernest. "Yeah, sorry, only her," he said with a shrug and a slight air of malice.

"Oh no, I definitely have a plus-one," Madison said. "Hold on, let me text." She swayed in place as she pulled her phone from her pocket and slid her glove off with those perfect teeth. She held the glove there in place, and Ernest watched the two guys watching her mouth. He stood on his tiptoes and craned his neck to see if he could confirm that the paper said that Madison did not have a plus-one.

The bigger of the two saw what Ernest was doing and snatched the paper close to his chest. "I think you should leave," he said, eyes narrowed.

Ernest took an unsteady step forward, closer to the door, and stood his ground. "Fine," he growled and reached for Madison to tell her that it was time to go. Ernest had a fuzzy memory of what occurred next due to the alcohol and the fact that he got a concussion.

According to eyewitness reports, Ernest made a move to take Madison's hand so that they could walk away, but she hesitated, thinking that she might be able to talk Ernest into the party if he just gave her a second. She was texting and said, "Hold on," glove still in her mouth so that her words muffled together, thus sounding more like a groan of protest to some.

Becoming increasingly irritated and cold, Ernest pulled a bit more forcefully on Madison's hand, which was when all hell broke loose.

Before Ernest knew what was happening, he was on the ground. From beneath these two beasts, he kicked his legs up and threw his arms in the direction that felt best. With his glasses knocked off, he could see nothing. The two Ivy members, both white, were seen beating the shit out of Ernest Morris, the dusting of snow almost permanently underfoot from January to March momentarily speckled with Ernest's blood. His two assailants were screaming profanities, and he couldn't be sure if he heard the N-word, but a report of the incident would say that it was dropped.

No one stepped forward to come to his rescue as he heard Madison's voice screaming in panic. He felt the heat of the lights from the campus police car before his limp body was lifted onto an orange spine board stretcher and carted away. The last thing that Ernest remembered seeing before he lost consciousness was a figure that he thought was Asher retreating along with the other party attendees as they shuffled inside. For years, he couldn't figure out why this image stuck with him even after everything else went dark, but it did.

The stories that emerged from that night might as well have been from a college fantasy fable. And in a matter of days, all conversations on campus had become centered around Ernest Morris.

"Oh my God, he totally tried to kidnap that girl. She wasn't safe, and it's so good they stepped in."

"Princeton is so fuckin' racist. Of course he got jumped."

"I heard he hates all eating clubs too. He's got, like, a vendetta."

"He wasn't even invited. Why was he here?"

"He wasn't doing anything, and they jumped him."

"They didn't jump him! It was self-defense."

Ernest felt bile rising in his throat remembering waking up in the hospital with bruises and fractured bones and an even more destroyed sense of pride. The boys who jumped him had never been charged for what they did, even after Madison explained that she was in no danger. Their families were responsible for major endowments to the school. It was all an unfortunate misunderstanding that they prayed Ernest would put behind him.

He turned back to Esi.

"I'm going to write a note to your parents, and if they could get in touch with me, that would be great. I would love to talk to them about what happened and see if I can help," he said.

When he left, he was seething with anger, his emotions from college that he thought that he had abandoned rushing to the surface. He knew what it felt like to be hurt physically and feel powerless for recourse, and it was seeming like these people, the Richie Riches of the world, were responsible for the maiming of more than one innocent body, and he was sick of them getting away with it.

The next week, Esi's mother came down to the school to speak with him. He was surprised to hear her voice when he was cleaning the classroom at the end of the day and nearly dropped the books he was holding when she walked into the room. Esi's mother was only a few years older than him but looked like she could have been his mother. He stood leaning against a wood table that doubled as his teaching desk while she took an uncomfortable seat across from him in one of the children's desks.

"Mr. Ernest," she began, "my daughter gave me your note and asked me to come see you. I want you to know that we want her to go to school, but my son cannot be alone right now. I work. My husband is not here." She paused to take in a breath. Ernest blinked rapidly. He didn't feel equipped to handle the weight of these problems. He wasn't even a real teacher.

"If I may," he said, briefly interjecting, "Esi said that her brother was injured in an accident. There might be a way to get his employer to help subsidize his care."

Esi's mother shook her head. "Ah, no. That's not possible."

"Why not?" Ernest asked.

"The contract is pretty strict on the company's responsibilities, and workplace injury just is not covered. Things happen a lot. These buildings are going up so fast that there's not any time for safety checks. That's why so many young people work them."

Ernest nodded. "And this is the Carter Corporation, correct? Based out of America?"

"Yes. They've been here for many years. They do a lot in Ghana, all over. They built this school."

Ernest couldn't disguise his shock. He felt disconnected from his body and immediately immobilized. He was under the impression that this school was the result of donations from various entities and individuals. They did commercials regularly, having the kids pose with their new water filters or books. There was nothing anywhere to indicate that this school was founded or funded by the Carter Corporation. He would have never worked here if that was the case. Where else could they possibly control?

He pressed his fingernails into his fists as hard as he could in a fight to keep himself present.

"Mr. Ernest?" Esi's mother's firm voice brought him back to the room, but his thoughts were still reeling.

"I'm sorry," he apologized. "I didn't know that."

Esi's mother nodded. "They do a lot here, but I don't think they'll be able to help. As I said, this kind of situation, it's very common."

Ernest considered what she said. While he didn't know how deep the Carter Corporation ties went, his suggestion was more so to have the company take more responsibility, but now he was sure that something more drastic needed to happen. Not only was this corporation unethical, immoral, and secretive but also damaging to a population of people that they actively pretended to be helping. It was diabolical.

He thought about his own time stuck in a hospital bed with no recourse and was filled with rage. He couldn't let this happen to more people. He had to tell someone about this, anyone.

When Esi's mother departed and he was left alone with his thoughts, he immediately went home and accessed a message board, where he posted asking for personal accounts and stories from other people nearby who'd been injured by Carter Corporation construction sites. By the time he went to bed that night, he had no responses, but when he woke up in the morning, a dozen accounts had replied with their own stories that covered everything from permanent disabilities to death. Of course, all the accounts were anonymous, so Ernest didn't know who they were. When he fired off private messages, the trails went cold. No one was willing to come forward on the record, which was going to be a major problem for him if he was ever going to be able to tell someone else about the depravity of the Carters.

From then on, Ernest spent his nights and weekends working within the community to gather intelligence. It gave him a chance to better work on his Twi, which was admittedly weak. When conversing with older people who had been around to understand life before the invasion of the Carter Corporation, this was especially important. Most conversations were a hybrid of the languages, Ernest trying to clumsily translate while someone detailed their observations. Eventually people began to divulge to him because they thought that they were unloading to a friend.

One man asked Ernest to meet him at a café four villages away from where he lived and spoke to him while wearing a baseball cap and sunglasses, eager to protect his identity and safety. He was a middle-class father who spent much of his education abroad before returning to

Accra. "The Corporation does a lot of things that are all technically legal but exploitative," he told Ernest. "They make people pay rent sometimes years in advance, two to five years sometimes. They also make you pay an additional fee to renew your lease, and they get away with that because buying a home is so expensive. When the Carter Corporation bought the lands that they own, they could get entire plots for around two hundred and fifty dollars, and now that same plot might be worth thirty thousand dollars."

"So the whole setup is that they bought land for cheap and now it's very expensive?" Ernest asked.

The man lowered and shook his head. "I wish it were that simple. Homeownership is very difficult here but also very important. Most people are renters, so whoever controls the rental market controls everything. These private developers have made life impossible, and they always come out on top. They have the backing of the government, of law enforcement, and the press. They pretty much do whatever they like because how's anyone going to stop them? Carter Corporation was just the first, but they aren't the only ones. And because housing is already so hard to find, people just pay so they don't have to move and start all over again."

"What about private houses?" Ernest asked him, wondering about the tiny bungalow that Esi and her family lived in.

"Developers do those too, but if you make enough money, you can purchase a plot of land and self-build. The problem is a lot of the building materials also come from the Carter Corporation, and so they set the prices on those too, and they're very high. They bought factories years ago that do all of the production for building materials, so that market also belongs to them."

By the end of this conversation, Ernest had had four cups of very strong coffee, and his hand was shaking over his notepad. He wasn't sure if that was the caffeine or his disgust. Ernest was sick at how far and wide the reach of the Carter Corporation went. When his teaching contract was up at the end of the term, he had spoken with seventeen families whose lives were permanently damaged by working for or because of the Carter Corporation.

He opted not to renew his teaching contract and took a chance to return to America, to New York this time, so that he could get one step closer to amassing evidence to expose the Carter Corporation for its crimes.

Copy Carter: Billionaire Kid Booted from Dalton Over Copycat Scandal

New York City, March 12, 2013

Kennedy Carter has allegedly been booted from Dalton over a plagiarism accusation. The school would not release an official statement, but a source says that Carter will complete the remainder of her senior year at home and has rescinded college applications. Unconfirmed allegations say that Carter and another student turned in identical papers. The identity of the other student has not been revealed. The Carter Corporation has stated that Kennedy Carter will be taking a gap year as was always intended. Dalton could not be reached for comment.

CHAPTER 26

Tashia Carter

New York City, March 2015

Tashia Carter considered herself to be an exceptionally helpful person. She answered phone calls on the first or second ring, always, because she thought it reduced stress for the person making the call. She rushed to help pick things up if someone dropped them. She let people go ahead of her if they seemed to be in a hurry. This was a very un–New York way of life, but she intentionally cultivated this part of herself because she thought it was a good thing to do.

The downside of all this, though, was that people always knew they could ask her for help. She was currently enrolled as a double major at Columbia, working on building a historical photo archive of Black students across the Ivy League. Still sensitive about the experience she had at Dalton, she wanted to expand her art and concentrate on the forgotten students who'd done remarkable things. When Kennedy had texted her, letting her know that she was working on something to debut at her dad's birthday, Tashia just knew that being asked for help wouldn't be far behind. Initially she thought that she wouldn't be able to contribute, but as part of her research, she traveled across the Northeast to all the Ivy League universities to gather their archival imagery of

Black students and rephotograph them as a way of contextualizing their experiences with her own. In doing so, at Harvard she had stumbled upon a photo of Kennedy Carter's father as a student.

The picture was from the early seventies and taken in Ghana with a man named Kofi, who Kennedy had since discovered had died by suicide shortly after graduating. Her heart sank, weighed down by the pressure that she knew that Kofi had to be feeling, a pressure that she was all too familiar with. At present, she was trying to complete an ambitious photography project that would hopefully catapult her to the next level. She dared to dream about potential careers as a professional photographer that would allow her to pay off her debt, be a caring daughter, sister, and friend while also working as Kennedy's unofficial assistant, a volunteer position she hadn't really asked for. It was hard for her to say no to Kennedy, whom Tashia considered to be as helpless and pitiful as a newborn animal.

Tashia smiled to herself as she thought back to when she and Kennedy were technically enemies. Tashia arrived at Dalton already pretty secure in her attitudes, preferences, and tastes, so she almost immediately felt extremely skeptical of the way that the other Black students had been inducted into the culture of the school and the Upper East Side as a whole. She had come from a grade school where murals of radical Black leaders like Malcolm X and Huey P. Newton covered the walls. The school was over 80 percent Black and Latino, meaning that oftentimes, overheard conversations were conducted in Spanglish. Tashia hadn't needed a tutor or a nanny to teach her another language. She had sharpened her vocabulary the old-fashioned way by making friends and listening.

By comparison, Dalton was multilingual in a different way. The culture was so insistently formal that sometimes, even as a native English speaker, she was finding herself struggling through literature classes. For the first time in her young life, Tashia felt herself not enjoying school. A quick learner and a serious student, Tashia prided herself on being a model academic. Her intelligence was rewarded with praise and attention from her teachers and respect from her classmates. She liked that everyone always knew she did the homework, that when the teacher asked a question, she would almost always be able to respond with the right answer. But when she arrived at Dalton, she found herself panicking, feeling very behind the curve even though she did all the summer reading. Her grades after the first four weeks of the term were distressingly average. When she logged on to her student portal, which was a sophisticated program accessible on all the Dalton-issued laptops, she was looking at letters of the alphabet that she never associated with grades, and yet right there were a cluster of Cs and Bs, making her question her whole life.

Aside from the fact that she needed a glossary for a whole new set of terms that she was learning (words like Bridgehampton, Upper School, Lululemon), she even found socializing to be a strain. A rabid basketball fan, Tashia found that she most naturally gravitated toward the boys, the jocks, simple creatures only interested in sharing their knowledge of sports statistics. Unbeknownst to her, though, this would make her an enemy to girls who were eager for their attention. The girls treated Tashia with a frosty indifference, making it clear in their own coded way that she was unwelcome. This was just as well for Tashia, who didn't feel like she needed to play nice with these little princesses anyway, with Kennedy Carter being the most annoying princess of all.

Tashia made her disdain for the celebration or elevation of all things white-coded pretty clear from the start, and it became important to her to distance herself from Kennedy, the other Carter specifically, whom she saw as a walking betrayal of their Black roots. One day in October, a month into the start of the school year, both Carter girls in their introductory biology class had been paired with one other girl and one boy to diagram the body of a marsupial to later present to the class.

In the moment, Kennedy said, "Do you think we should, like, draw something really big or work on something on the computer?"

And what Tashia repeated was, "Do like you like think like we like should like draw like something like really big like or like work on like some like sort like of like digital like rendering that like costs like a million like dollars?" It was like a bad *SNL* skit, Tashia clearly trying to insinuate that Kennedy talked like a white girl.

Tashia immediately watched Kennedy flinch and felt a sting of shame. Kennedy forced out a laugh, which Tashia thought was an admirable attempt to appear good-natured. The other two students in their group were certainly waiting on Kennedy to dictate how they would react. Upon seeing that she wasn't going to be openly contemptuous, they chuckled weakly.

"Well, I actually like the idea of, um, a big drawing," said the boy, somewhat self-conscious.

"Same," the girl agreed, and Kennedy nodded enthusiastically.

Tashia's heart soon thawed when it came to Kennedy, realizing that her fellow Carter was just as scared and lonely as she sometimes felt. Kennedy turned out to be a deeply sensitive girl with an astounding knowledge of old-school films and TV shows for someone her age. She often treated Tashia to peace offerings throughout the semester, ranging from lending her driver to take her all the way home to the Bronx or buying her camping gear for the class trip when Tashia said she didn't have any.

As Tashia's grades gradually improved and she accepted Dalton for what it was, she tried to be a helpful person in Kennedy's life by explaining to her the nuances of some of the racial divides at school that the girls experienced over the years, including countless microaggressions from some of the white girls. And Tashia was sure that wannabe Backstreet Boy Ollie, Kennedy's boyfriend during their senior year, was just trying to have a Black girl on the low, wanting to hide her in order to escape other people's judgment. Tashia thought this was clearly evident by how he was adamant about "keeping things casual."

"You really gonna let that white boy keep you as a dirty little secret?" she had said to her friend while stuffing pretzel sticks in her mouth as they sat in the student center.

"Shhhhh!" Kennedy's eyes widened, and she leaned in toward Tashia, looking around to see if they'd been overheard. "It's not like that," she whispered.

"I think it is," Tashia whispered back, wishing for once that her friend would stop caring so much about what people thought of her.

Kennedy rolled her eyes. "Not everything is about that," Kennedy whispered back to Tashia with an edge to her words.

"I know that's what you think," Tashia said, leaving the meaning of her words hanging there for Kennedy to do something with.

Over time, Tashia had come to understand that Kennedy lived a very different life than she did, and this was something she knew, but she had never really seen the application of it so clearly. These were Tashia's people for only a limited amount of time, but Kennedy would have to deal with them forever. Tashia would be free from this place, these people, their snobbery and petty authorities, but Kennedy would not.

That's why Tashia didn't gloat when Ollie plagiarized Kennedy's paper and got her in trouble. After doing everything in her power not to retaliate when she saw him at school (another Black girl getting expelled just wouldn't be acceptable), Tashia called Kennedy every day after her parents pulled her out of Dalton. She went over to her apartment and waited in the sprawling and silent mirrored lobby to be let upstairs. When she stepped out of the elevator and turned to the only door on the floor, she began unlacing her sneakers. A housekeeper opened the door and greeted Tashia, taking her shoes in one hand and her backpack in the other. It had become so routine to Tashia by that point that she didn't even question the ritual. The first time it was strange, but she was surprised at what she could get used to. After being kicked out of Dalton, Kennedy stayed upstairs in her room, bundled in bed like a fictional sick person, like she thought she was an injured soldier with amnesia.

Tashia rolled her eyes. "Kennedy, get *up*," she said, pulling at her limp wrist when Kennedy didn't move.

She allowed herself to be forced into an upright seated position, but she didn't get up from the bed. "I can't," she squeaked out.

Tashia fingered Kennedy's embroidered bedding. Tiny hand-sewn rosettes bloomed under her hands. She sighed.

"You have to," she said looking into Kennedy's withdrawn eyes, "because if this is the worst thing that's ever happened to you in your life, your life's actually . . . fine, so come on."

Kennedy was better soon after that, and by the end of the week, she was bathing regularly and had agreed to go outside so long as they went to Tashia's Bronx neighborhood where no one knew her. They took Kennedy's car up, and her security followed a few paces behind as they looped through St. Mary's Park. Tashia saw Kennedy come back to herself. Tashia just listened as Kennedy cried on her shoulder and vented about being betrayed, wanting to do everything she could to help out her emotionally fragile friend.

Just like now. As she was in a coffee shop in Washington Heights, flipping through images that she collected, she noticed the barista staring at her. She had bought a single black coffee three and a half hours ago, but the place was empty, so she didn't really understand his hyper-focused attention. She stared back at him defiantly. If he wanted her to buy something else, she was going to make him say it. She tore her eyes away and went back to recording the dates of the photographs on her laptop screen with renewed concentration, which was how she didn't notice the barista inching closer to her table before he was right beside her. She jumped when she felt him very near.

"Sorry," he said. "I didn't mean to scare you."

Tashia caught her breath. "No, it's all right."

"Can I ask what you're working on?" he said, taking a pointed look at her screen.

She reflexively shut the laptop and then apologized, feeling awkward and fumbling. "Oh, it's a photography project, sort of a Black history retrospective. It's about the isolation of Black students at Ivy League universities."

"Wow, no way. That's crazy," he said. "I went to Princeton."

Tashia immediately perked up. They spent the next twenty minutes talking excitedly about her project, his feelings about having gone from a majority Black city to Princeton and then all the way to Ghana. She shared with him her thesis and why she wanted to preserve these images. She told him about the rumor she uncovered about a secret society for Black men at Harvard throughout the sixties and seventies. After another customer came in and began loudly clearing his throat for service, Ernest realized that he had to get up and go back to work. He asked Tashia for her number. She hesitated just for a moment but then agreed. He was skinny and dorky but cute in his own way.

"What's your name?" she asked as he was going back to the register.

"Ernest, Ernest Morris," he said with a big smile before turning to the customer.

CHAPTER 27

Kennedy Carter

Watcha Cove, June 2015

Kennedy was back in her Watcha Cove bedroom, pacing back and forth while the interview that she'd done with her mother in New York uploaded to her external hard drive. She'd made the quick trip from seeing Asher in Cambridge over to Watcha Cove. It wasn't staffed right now, but she only needed a few days. She would leave the coverings on the furniture, even. She stopped walking to stare out the window at the waning moon. She sighed out loud, frustrated with her lack of progress on completing her mission. Her mother, she knew, would not be the person to ask about Kofi. Her parents had met well after college at a fundraiser, as her mother had just asserted on camera.

Kennedy walked over and checked the progress: 43 percent. She pulled out her notebook to review the dates that she had written down and anything that was confirmed by anyone already interviewed for her project. So far Kennedy knew this: her father had a college roommate who died by suicide. He had never spoken about it or mentioned it ever, and that could be because the death traumatized him. The other strange part was that his corporation had been paying millions of dollars over the last few decades to a woman whose last known occupation was "housekeeper." She had never heard of or met Gifty Obeng before either. When she paid a service to verify Gifty's identity, she found that Gifty had been working as a housekeeper and property manager at the hotel owned by Kofi's family. Earlier in the spring, when she had finally tracked Gifty down and spoken with her, her daughter intervened and mentioned an NDA. Her last advice was to "find Kofi." She had found Kofi, but that was no help since he was dead. Curiously, years after Kofi's death, Gifty began her tenure at the Carter Corporation. Kennedy called Tashia, who wasn't arriving at the Vineyard until next week for the party but was happy to mull over facts on the phone.

"So you're saying you think this is all related?" Tashia asked.

"I know it sounds like a detective movie, but you have to admit that's pretty weird," Kennedy said.

"Well . . . did you talk to anyone else about it?" Tashia asked, trying to appeal to Kennedy's logic.

"I mean, I tried my brother; he was no help. I don't think I can ask my mom. She only talks about herself, and I can't ask my dad without blowing the whole surprise open, so I'm on my own, I guess," she said, sliding from her bed to her floor.

She looked around her room at Watcha Cove. It was a museum of "good taste," which meant that she often had to struggle to get comfortable, like she was doing now.

"Ken, I don't want this to sound insensitive, but have you considered that maybe none of this matters for the tribute video?" Tashia asked gently.

Kennedy had considered this. The project that she wanted to make was almost complete, but making art that was ultimately dishonest felt wrong. She had wanted to tell an epic, emotional, and hulking story of her father's life, which could not be done without talking about the Carter Corporation. He had long ago merged his professional life with his personal life, and they were now a unified entity, forever inosculated. Now, even with every single person checked off the preapproved list of interview subjects, she was feeling like the piece fell short. It was a surface video, promotional and shallow, and she hated watching it. She knew that there was more to this than what she had, but she just didn't know how to put everything together.

"Let's change the subject," Kennedy offered, tired of thinking about the same thing she had been thinking about for weeks now. "How are you?"

"Thought you'd never ask," Tashia said. "I'm seeing a new guy. I mean, it's only been like two months or whatever, but so far so good. I mean, you know how it is. I wasn't sure if it was just a situationship, but it feels like maybe it's something good. I've been holding my breath hoping that it didn't implode, but now it's like we are together like all of the time. I met him in a coffee shop, totally randomly, but he went to Princeton, so he had such an interesting perspective on my photo project. And he's sweet and funny, and I think it's going well. He's actually here now." Kennedy could hear the levity in her friend's voice, and she lit up too.

"Oh my God!" Kennedy exclaimed. "I can't believe I have been rambling on about nothing when you have a real-life update to share. That's amazing, Tashia. I'm really happy for you. I can't wait to meet him." Kennedy smiled. It was good that her friend was finding some happiness. She deserved it. She didn't want to bring the mood down by insisting that they continue to hash out the sketchy details of her father's past. "Tell me everything," Kennedy said.

As Tashia revealed more details about her new boyfriend, Kennedy laughed to herself when Tashia said that she, at first, thought this guy "might be a weirdo."

"Of course you did," Kennedy replied, knowing that because Tashia was a naturally skeptical person and had an innate distrust of men overall, this would be the case. Back in high school, when Kennedy had fallen for Ollie, Tashia repeatedly told her that he wasn't worth all the trouble that he was making. In the end, she was right, of course, but Kennedy had to learn that the hard way, the very hard way. Kennedy remembered thinking, *Tashia was right; he deserted me*, as she sat crying on a conference call with both her parents and their legal counsel. The room had fallen deathly silent. Even Kennedy's audible cries had ceased. Kennedy remembered that she could hear her own heartbeat thumping in her ears. She saw herself, totally out of her own body, sitting at a long glass table. Kennedy was limp, her tears silently falling, the only sound escaping was her uneven breaths. Jacqueline and William looked at their daughter in disbelief.

Kennedy never spoke to Ollie again. She was sure that he was enjoying his life at Brown, also not thinking about her. She felt triply betrayed, and it was significant because she understood then that she was utterly alone.

Forty minutes later, when Tashia and Kennedy had wrapped up their phone call, Kennedy wandered downstairs at the Vineyard house and found herself in her father's office. It was late afternoon, and the light was flooding through the paned windows and bathing the room in an atmosphere that she could only describe as abundant. She figured that now was as good a time as any to do the snooping that she came to Watcha Cove to do. When she was younger, all the offices in all the homes were considered to be off-limits, but she'd been sneaking into her father's offices for years now.

In the center of the room sat a large antique executive desk with drawers on each side. Some of them were locked and some weren't, but she knew where the keys were stored. Her parents seemed to believe that neither she nor Asher would ever violate their rules, like circus animals who'd been trained to only do one thing and kept doing it long after their retirement. For her, at this point, she had to get some answers, so she turned to the built-ins, located the trick book where her father kept his desk keys, and removed a heavy Cartier key ring. She briefly held up the weighty object and wondered how much it cost. It wasn't even gold. It was plated. She tried each key in each of the drawers, and when she had all of them opened, she began to comb through their contents.

The first thing Kennedy found in a folder were plans for an underground nuclear bunker. She put those aside. Next, she found various invoices for the Watcha Cove property. She found security clearance forms for friends who'd stayed at the house when they were not there, lists of important numbers and local services. She also found some Carter Corporation documents that she couldn't make sense of. Some of them looked like quarterly earnings and projections, but some of them were also org charts and invoices, all outdated. She gripped the bridge of her nose, not knowing what she was looking for exactly. As she returned the files to their respective drawers, she hit something with a folder. Upon closer inspection, she discovered that it was another key, this one taped to the inside of the drawer.

She held up the key and examined it. Now that she had a new key, she had to find what it kept. Her eyes scanned the office. This felt like a sinister scavenger hunt, trying to guess where her father would hide something that he clearly did not want another person to see. She walked the perimeter of the office, checking carefully for any potential hiding spots. As expected, everything was neat, orderly, and organized. Kennedy opened the only closet in the office and noticed a plain gray box on a shelf. She stood on her tiptoes to pull down the box and saw that it was fastened with a tiny gold lock. When she tried the key in the lock, it fit flush, and when she turned it to the right and heard a satisfying click, her heart began racing.

Inside the box, she found a handwritten note with several passwords. She assumed these number combinations corresponded to accounts that she was not interested in accessing, although she was surprised to see such a flimsy method used for their safekeeping. Watcha Cove was guarded twenty-four seven, as were all the Carter properties, but any person could have done what she did this afternoon and found this. She moved those papers aside and found herself holding a medium-size brown leather journal. Inside it was embossed on the bottom with faded lettering. She traced the letters K O F I. Kennedy dropped the book out of shock. She went to pick it up again and read it cover to cover over the next twenty minutes. Kofi's thoughts and musings came pouring out all over the pages, even as she felt guilty reading the private thoughts of someone who was dead.

When she got to the last entry, it read: *I do not feel right about working with these men. I know that we need money for funding, but money cannot be the only thing that dictates this decision. We have to think about legacy and what we are leaving behind. Future generations will inherit the consequences of this decision. I am going to speak about this with William tonight.*

Kennedy frowned at that, her skin bunching together between her brows. The *Crimson* article detailing Kofi's suicide flashed in her mind. Perhaps his reservations about founding what became the Carter Corporation caused him to jump to his death. This entry didn't seem like the ramblings of someone on the brink of taking their own life, but what did Kennedy know? An uneasy feeling swept over her as she moved the journal aside. The last things in the box were some plans that she didn't know what to make of either. She took a photo of the pages that she wanted and carefully stacked everything back in the box the way that she'd found it.

Then she texted Tashia to call her back right away.

DNA TEST REPORT

Private and Confidential

Sample One: WCJ
Sample Two: ABC

Combined Paternity Index: 0   Probability of Paternity: 0%

The alleged father is excluded as the biological father of the tested child.

CHAPTER 28

Asher Bennett Carter

New York City, May 2015

Asher gazed at the turbulent East River as his chauffeured SUV cruised down the FDR on his way to the Carter Corporation headquarters. It was the end of May, and with the close of his term approaching fast and his grades still worse than a popped squash ball, his time was up, and he knew it. He wouldn't be able to outrun the clock on his inadequacies at Harvard Business School being exposed. He came home to New York City to get ahead of it, and to perhaps create a diversion of sorts to buy himself more time with his father in particular.

He thought he might ask his father for funding to finally get his startup, Squash Lodge, off the ground. He would provide the ABCs of squash basics. Coincidentally, that was also his name, which is something he would promote in his deck. He only needed $3 million or so and his plan was to pitch it to his father as a real-life business application and then somehow prove to Harvard that he could use founding a company as an independent study of sorts. He had managed to finesse something similar last year when his grades first returned as less than desirable. Plus, if he already had a business, the MBA would follow. It was real-life learning, and Harvard loved stuff like that, going rogue or whatever. It was bold, fresh, unexpected.

He was going to say all this to his father, and he thought about how best to approach the topic while he sat at his father's office, waiting to go in. Well, he sat in the waiting area *outside* of his father's office. He, like always, needed an appointment to go see him. William Carter Jr. didn't do surprise visits and drive-bys, not even for his kids. Asher had already been offered four or more beverages, which he had declined, and was impatiently shaking his left foot waiting to be called for his turn. The Carter Corporation employees weren't discreet in their gawking, taking extra-slow walks by the clear glass to get a glimpse at the returning heir apparent.

Asher hadn't wanted to make the rounds. The last time that he was in the office was last summer during his mandatory servitude to the family business. For at least four weeks of every summer since they were twelve, each Carter child was required to show up to learn the ropes at the company headquarters. Neither sibling was qualified to do anything serious connected to the family business, but their father thought of it as immersion therapy, that simply being on the premises would inspire them to be better. At first, this was the kind of thing that Asher grumbled about until college, when Tatum first suggested that he would take over the company one day. She sat with him in his off-campus apartment dreamily imagining the future. They would live in New York, obviously. She would work in art, perhaps as a dealer, perhaps in curation. Asher nodded along, partially giving this conversation his attention. Tatum had to ask him twice what he wanted to do.

"Oh, I don't really know yet," Asher said noncommittally.

"You don't?" she asked. "You're not just going to go work for your dad?"

He hated that that was what was expected. He wanted to be his own CEO, to have the chance to be the self-made man that his father would respect. Asher jumped when his name was called by his father's third assistant, and he was, at last, ushered into the office. William didn't look at Asher when he walked into the room, leaving Asher to make the choice of where he would sit: the couch in front of the large burl coffee table or the two chairs directly across from where his father was. Asher tried to nonchalantly wander toward the furniture that he wanted to sit in, waiting for any sign of objection from his father. William didn't show any immediate interest in where Asher sat, so he finally just chose the couch, sitting with an exaggerated delay. William looked over at his son and spoke first.

"I assume you have come here to ask me to help you not fail out of business school," William said.

Asher choked on his own response. His father's already being aware of his failure wasn't desirable, thwarting any opportunity he had to maneuver strategically. William raised his eyebrows as his gaze bore into his son. Asher tried to control his heartbeat.

"Dad, I—I was going to tell you that I needed some help," he sputtered.

William raised his hand. "Save it. You need more than *some* help. But I want you to first convince me why I should give it."

Asher inhaled audibly. He had to play this right. He should have anticipated that there'd be no windup, that he'd be shot right into action from the moment he entered this arena. In the end, he just hung his head in shame and said, "I'm sorry, Dad."

William stared back blankly. "Asher, this isn't something that I'll fix for you. You're an adult now with all the tools at your disposal to turn this around. Your sister also went through some difficulties at school, but she had to suffer the consequences and now understands how to better adapt."

His sister. Asher perked up at the mention of Kennedy, remembering that her little project could be his get-out-of-jail-free card. "I know, Dad, and I have a plan on how to graduate, and I will. I'm not going to let you down. Not like Kennedy."

"So why are you in my office?"

"Well, actually, it's about Kennedy," Asher began, feigning hesitation. "She's working on something. She said it's a birthday tribute for you, a video about your accomplishments and whatnot, but she's been asking a lot of strange questions. It's like she's gathering intelligence on you and the company, and it just seems weird. I thought you should know."

"What kind of intelligence?" William asked, his attention now totally focused on his son.

"Company origins, your relationships with old classmates, how you think about yourself and money, what the company does. Stuff like that. I don't think she knows anything you don't want her to know, but she's been doing this for a while, so I thought I should tell you." Asher tried to look contrite, as if he felt a bit uncomfortable snitching on his sister.

"I see," William said carefully. "Well, I already know, but perhaps you can be of assistance. Asher, you do know a great deal more than your sister about this corporation, and I trust that you'll ensure that that information doesn't fall into the wrong hands for any reason."

Asher locked eyes with his father and nodded. He had been keeping the secrets, dodging Kennedy's questions, and intentionally minimizing any inconsistencies that emerged from her research. He felt, again, that he'd earned his father's trust, that he was given marching orders and he wouldn't fail. He left the office with no immediate solution but with a renewed energy to use Kennedy's video as leverage for their father's affection. At least that was his plan until he stumbled into the penthouse that night, drunk and high. Wandering past the library on his way up to his room, he caught the tail end of a conversation between his parents.

Growing up, Kennedy was the eavesdropper, Asher too big and noisy to be subtle. But since he did want to know if his dad was going to intervene on his behalf with Harvard, he snuck quietly closer to the door and held his breath to listen. The beer he was holding was sweating in his hand. He got to the door too late to hear what his mother said first, but his father's words shocked him. He clutched his drink tighter to ground himself.

"I had him tested at least ten years ago," William said. "Jacqueline, the boy is dumb. It's an insult to me that you thought that I wouldn't notice that. And he's very physically fit. He's tall. He's all . . . brawn. I tested him, and I found out. It doesn't change anything for me. He's my son and that's that, but I knew. I never asked you about it because, well, what does it matter now?"

Outside the door, the boy in question did a double take. He was very physically fit, but surely his father couldn't be talking about him . . . about his not being a Carter. Right?

"I guess it doesn't," his mother replied. "But this stuff about Kofi potentially coming out is not great. Are you sure Kennedy doesn't know anything? This new activity surely can't really all be from her . . ." Their voices muffled after that and dropped to a decibel that he could no longer hear.

Kofi? Who's Kofi? Asher wondered to himself. Somewhere deep in his mind, he had a vision of his sister telling him that name, but he just couldn't remember why. He was receiving far too much new information. His head began to swim and his entire worldview upended. Was he *not* his father's son? Why would his father know something like this and never say anything? What did that mean for his future? What did that mean for his inheritance? Surely that was based on the fact that he was a legitimate Carter.

Asher realized he'd never had so many thoughts in such rapid succession. He was getting a headache. He slid down the wall in the hallway to catch his breath. He looked right at a painted portrait of all four Carters, something done around his time in middle school. He stared at his own immortalized young face, slightly lighter than the others, hair texture a bit different, but that was normal for Black families, surely. Wasn't it?

He felt suffocated by the toxicity of these secrets. He'd come here believing that his biggest issue in life was that he might not make it to a graduation ceremony, and now he had to question who he was, his own family history, his mother and father's lies. Asher walked in a daze to his room and decided to do what he always did when he was confused, which was often. He did nothing.

Asher reclined horizontally on his bed and stared up at the vaulted ceiling. His was the bedroom with the skylight, and through the upward-facing window, he could see neighboring buildings and a bit of the sky. He thought about what his life would be like if he wasn't a Carter, thought about what would change for him. Surely, it was bad. He would be stripped of everything, not only his name but his security detail, his driver, his apartment, his credit cards, his access to cash, his club memberships, his cars, his watches, his art, his stock holdings, his boat that he never used. He wondered if he might be allowed to keep the vintage diamond-accented squash-racket lapel pin he received for his high school graduation, but just in case, he would take it back to Boston with him.

He was tipsy, but he followed his thoughts down the spiral of this waking nightmare and found himself suddenly sober. He would have to get a job, a real one. Asher ran from the bed to his bathroom, where he waved his hand forcefully in front of the toilet seat to trigger the auto-open and vomited. He rested his head against the gleaming white TOTO ceramic and closed his eyes. There was no way he was going to ever tell anyone what he'd just heard.

CHAPTER 29

Ernest Morris

New York City, May 2015

Ernest Morris couldn't believe his luck. He had been afraid that his pursuit of justice against the Carter family at large would have to be sidelined permanently, but then in walked Tashia Carter (no relation), and suddenly his quest was given new life. He hadn't known who Tashia was and just thought that she was a pretty girl. He wasn't even looking for a girlfriend, but when the opportunity to talk to her presented itself, he was glad that he took it. Tashia just happened to be best friends with Kennedy Carter, the youngest (and apparently outcast) Carter child. If glee was an emotion that he could feel, he would have been gleeful. From what he understood, Tashia and Kennedy were in regular communication, and Tashia was even helping Kennedy work on some celebratory video about her father's life. This last part was especially nauseating to him since he'd discovered that her father orchestrated a regulatory monopoly over real estate in Accra, but now he saw the opportunity to potentially get more information that no one else would ever know in order to finally put a stop to William Carter Jr.'s prolonged reign of terror.

He couldn't act too curious while Tashia and Kennedy spoke on the phone if he was nearby. He knew it would be suspicious to be hovering around while his girlfriend was having a conversation with someone else, so instead he would strategically place himself nearby Tashia and busy himself with a menial task while she just happened to be on the phone. This meant that he had at least a one-sided account of what they talked about. He recorded what he learned in a notebook and then transferred these notes to his computer once he got home and was alone.

So far, he had discovered two very crucial things: 1. A man named Kofi was William Carter Jr.'s business partner, but he died by suicide shortly before the launch of the Carter Corporation. 2. His death might not have been a suicide. Ernest looked at this information and began the laborious task of establishing a proper timeline. Every time he ran into a slight roadblock, his fury was reignited by the resentment that he still felt toward Asher Carter.

Though it had been years since their last interaction, the shame and humiliation that he felt at Asher's hand still felt present. Ernest felt that Asher had made him deliberately insignificant, that he could not find a single brain cell to dedicate to remembering his name, even though in some odd, roundabout way, they should have been bonded together by the Carter Foundation Scholarship. It haunted him on a daily basis, a persistent gnawing ache that he sought to silence once and for all by taking away all the things that made Asher feel superior: his money, power, and credibility. He once had a belief that there was a humanity within the Carters that he might be able to stoke into something useful and productive, but that fantasy was quickly flattened by the reality of Asher's depravity.

After his brutal beating his junior year of college, Ernest Morris was released from the hospital after three days. In the time that he was in there, he did a lot of thinking and concluded that it would be appropriate to call for the expulsion of the two Ivy members who assaulted him. Two friends of his at the BSU heard his argument but tried to coax him to be realistic.

"They're not going to get expelled," Travis said when Ernest had told him how he wanted to resolve this dispute with the university.

"I don't know, I think he might have a legitimate case," Travis's girlfriend, Nandi, said. "I mean, it's a really serious accusation, and they fucked him up for no reason."

"They *think* they had a reason," Travis responded.

"Okay, but not a great one, and not one that warranted that kind of beating. I mean, they sent him to the hospital," she replied.

"Look at where we are. Do you think that Princeton is going to expel two white Ivy kids because of one fight?"

Ernest, laid up on bed rest, listened to all this silently. He took everyone's opinion into consideration, but ultimately he wanted to do what was right, and what was right was not rolling over. Other students of color, but not Asher Carter, flocked to support Ernest Morris, whom they agreed had been racially profiled and unfairly targeted by bigoted white Ivy members.

"Oh, you don't know?" Nandi had asked Ernest when he expressed disappointment over not having Asher's support. Ernest stared blankly in response, and Nandi sighed dramatically. "The Carters are like the worst kind of colonizers because they look like the oppressed but they're not. They literally don't care about anyone or anything except making more money, and they will do anything to do that." Ernest felt his stomach lurch. It was really only because of the Carters that he could afford to be at Princeton at all.

They picketed outside Ivy for days after the incident. Multiple times a day, Asher would cross the picket line and hear insults like "coon" and "traitor" being hurled at him, but he stared back with this helpless look that seemed to communicate: *What do you want me to do? I have to eat.* Asher's reaction inspired nothing in Ernest but tactile disgust.

On day three of the picketing, Ernest couldn't stand to be ignored by this person whom he'd expected so much more from. William Carter

Jr. had invested in him, had selected him out of thousands of candidates, but to his son, he was invisible. Ernest hobbled over to Asher to confront him personally. Ernest was not looking for another fight, but he wasn't alone so he wasn't afraid.

"Hey!" Ernest called out.

At first, Asher seemed content to ignore him, but Ernest yelled again and then dragged his injured leg behind him in a bid to catch up to Asher,

"Hey, man," Asher greeted him, an obvious attempt at diplomacy. "I'm kinda heading in for dinner." He lifted his chin toward the house where he saw his white girlfriend was already past the picketers.

"Yeah, I noticed that. You've been walking past us for days like we're not even here. That's pretty fucked-up, man," Ernest said, the heat of his anger rising off his body. For some reason, he wanted Asher to care. He really wanted that. He wanted his sympathy and attention. He wanted mostly the ancillary support that would come along with Asher's sympathy and attention, which would compound on itself and perhaps actually change something about the systemic rot that was the dining club system. He needed an inside man to care about this so that those on the outside might have a chance, but Asher wasn't that man. Far from it.

Asher's face collapsed into confusion. "Yeah, well, a guy's gotta eat," he said, finally trying to sidestep his adversary.

"We could use your support over here," Ernest said, planting himself firmly in Asher's path.

"Excuse me?" Asher asked, wanting to confirm that he heard what he thought he heard.

"Do you condone the systemic discrimination and racial profiling of the Ivy Club?" Ernest asked him.

"The what?" Asher asked in disbelief. His eyes roamed wildly, looking for a way out. The picketers had quieted and were tuned in to Asher and Ernest's conversation, which had taken center stage.

"Are you aware that this eating club has a documented history of abuse toward students of color and that they escape accountability constantly because of the agenda of this university and other interested parties to protect its members?" Ernest said.

"Agenda? Do you hear yourself, bro? Eating clubs aren't even affiliated with the university." Asher scoffed, rolling his eyes.

"I mean, I guess you wouldn't know a thing about that, though, would you? Since your dad made his millions—sorry billions—doing God knows what all over the world for profit. Yeah, cooning runs right in your family."

A few members of the crowd called out their agreement in solidarity. Asher was becoming visibly uncomfortable.

"Okay, I don't know what you heard, but that's crazy, and my dad is a celebrated philanthropist," Asher said, his rehearsed response rolling fluidly off his tongue. "People are always really critical of someone who makes it when he comes from nothing, but he's done everything he can to help other people, Black people especially. He supports the community at every opportunity."

"You really believe that, don't you? But you don't care about us. You haven't been taught to. You've got blood on your hands for walking into Ivy and breaking bread with the assholes who put an innocent Black man in the hospital," Ernest said, his voice rising.

Ernest could see Asher's face flush. He felt his own temperature rising as well. Ernest knew he would lose a physical fight with Asher, but he was ready, even though he was still recuperating. This smug asshole had spent years ignoring him, letting people belittle him, and all the while pretending to be a pillar of "Black excellence." He was a fraud.

Ernest inched closer to Asher, just to close the gap between them, to test his resolve. Asher didn't flinch, instead shortening the space between them.

Suddenly a slim white hand was between them, and Ernest inhaled a fragrant floral scent. Shampoo, he assumed. When he looked down, he saw that the hand belonged to Tatum. "Time to go, babe," she said, leading Asher away.

"Yeah, better go inside your white tower with your white girlfriend. Sorry, did we say too much? Don't want to blow your cover, Incognegro!" Ernest called out to Asher's back.

With that, Asher turned around and charged at Ernest. Tatum was yelling his name, but Asher was not stopping. His fists were balled, and Ernest squared himself, bracing for impact. When he was back in front of Ernest, breathing hard, Asher reached into his pocket and groped for something. Ernest's face collapsed into confusion as Asher slipped his wallet from his pants and opened the brown leather bifold. Asher quickly counted off ten hundred-dollar bills and flattened them with an open palm straight onto Ernest's chest.

"A donation," Asher said, "for your hospital bills. I imagine they were pretty high." Without another word, he turned and walked into Ivy.

Ernest was mortified. The bills fell to the ground, and he bent down to pick them up and pocketed them because it was true: he needed the money, and that was the worst part. Shortly after, he took out a personal loan to pay for the remainder of his education and told the Carter Foundation that their funding was no longer needed. He did not want a dime from these people, but every day since then, he wanted to take everything from Asher Carter.

He sat with this memory while he opened the folders containing what he'd found on his laptop. He made a careful list detailing the human rights violations, labor violations, governmental interference, and theft that he had compiled about the Carter Corporation. William Carter Jr. had successfully been performing a magic trick for decades. His sleight of hand was so sophisticated that it had taken Ernest months to organize all the illegal and immoral ways that he was conducting business and turning a profit, at that. A Daedalian enterprise. William Carter Jr. controlled the police, "elected officials," and had even made it impossible for competition to emerge in Accra, all but ensuring that he was the only business in town. He had done all this while establishing a network of charter schools, museums, and cultural touchstones that had most people convinced that he meant no harm.

He might have fooled a lot of people, but he had not fooled Ernest. Ernest knew that this kind of selfishness was hereditary, and he had seen it spread through Asher. He had wondered if Kennedy was the same, and he asked Tashia gently about her friend and her family while they were smoking weed on his couch one night. He counted on times when her guard was down to be able to question her about the Carters.

"Aren't all billionaires quite evil?" was how he put it.

Tashia seemed to consider him. She exhaled a little stream of gray smoke. "Yes, technically, I guess. Kennedy isn't really a billionaire though, at least not yet. It's complicated. She's . . . never really lived a normal life. She's like an alien. It used to really upset me, but now I think I understand her better. She's doing the best she can, like everyone else. I also think being in that family is hard-core. Like, her parents are crazy, and so once you understand that, it's kind of hard to be mad at her."

Ernest didn't understand this. He was raised by a single mother in poverty and had struggled most of his life. He resented the idea that he should even try to understand it, that somehow the wealth of the Carters protected them from any kind of critique. He couldn't say this, though, so he took the joint she had passed him and said instead, "That's nice of you." He found it tragic that he couldn't share with Tashia what he was thinking about doing, her sympathy for Kennedy like a shield. She was too close to see the flaws. He wasn't, though.

Ernest had only been dating Tashia for a few weeks when he felt he finally had enough evidence to demonstrate that the Carter Corporation was an advanced and highly developed criminal enterprise. She had inadvertently shared so much about helping her best friend repair her tragic relationship with her family with a video project that he himself felt like a producer. He considered the implication of what it would do to his relationship with Tashia to use the information that she had told him in confidence, but it was a personal sacrifice that he had to make to restore order to the world, or at least he could try. He started calling journalists. He first started with financial reporters, the *Wall Street Journal*, *Forbes*, the *Financial Times*, and they all declined to meet with him. He didn't want to send his documentation over email because he didn't want to risk his work being intercepted. He also went national to CNN, MSNBC, ABC, and NBC. He sent dozens of emails over a five-week period and got no responses. His desperation and impatience were increasing at the same rate, and so he reached out to a friend from Princeton, a journalism intern at the *Huffington Post* and the one person who he thought would be on his side.

Madison Sanderson was still radiant and met him after he closed up the coffee shop one night, and they walked toward Ernest's apartment. She was now a brunette with bangs, a mature makeover for her new life in the city as a serious reporter. Ernest gave Madison the briefest of summaries about what he was trying to do, and before he could finish, Madison interrupted. "So you're talking about the Carter Corporation here?" she said, her voice dropping to a hurried whisper.

Ernest nodded and opened his mouth to continue talking, and Madison stopped him again. "That's never going anywhere. William Carter Jr.'s old school. He's got eyes and ears everywhere. There's never, ever been any bad media coverage about him. The guy is untouchable."

"Well, yeah, but only because people don't have the right information, and I don't think that anyone has been looking in the right places. It's really dark, what I've found," he said.

Madison's face displayed pity. "Okay, so . . . everyone knows that already. No one cares."

Ernest couldn't believe that no one cared. Someone had to care. He'd seen people get taken down before: sex offenders, tax evaders, violent criminals. "I mean, you can't get away with this stuff, can you?" he asked Madison in a small voice.

"I think you kind of can when you're a billionaire. Look, Earn, I know you have an axe to grind with the Carters, but my advice is to just let this go. It's not worth it. Like you said, no one's biting, and you're not even getting paid for this. You're broke! Why don't you figure out a way to make money and stop chasing this dead end?"

"You really think it's a dead end?" Ernest asked dejectedly.

"I don't think anyone is ever going to run the story that William Carter Jr., premiere family man and entrepreneur, is a monster running his company like a thug, no," Madison said with finality.

Ernest felt his stomach twist and quickly made an excuse as to why he had to go home. Madison gave him a sad hug and told him to "take care," and he felt the pangs of shame for letting her see how ingenuous he was in this area. The rest of the walk left him fuming. It was disgusting to him that he had hard evidence that the Carter Corporation was harming people in Ghana right now and could prove it, but no one cared. When he was a senior in high school, the Carter Scholarship Foundation had published part of an essay of his on their website alongside his photo. They had used him, his life and story, as a cover for their horrible business practices, and now he was powerless.

When he got home that night to the drab studio that he rented on the upper Upper West Side, he opened another anonymous account on the same message board, started a thread titled "Carter Corporation Crimes: Exposed," and typed up the introduction to what he knew. Again, he went to bed that night angry, but when he woke up in the morning, he had over forty responses from other people who seemed to agree with him, who knew that William Carter Jr. represented everything wrong with the myth of the self-made man. He was a greedy capitalist, and maybe this would be the way to take him down: by using the voices of the people.

Ernest called out sick at the coffee shop so that he could buy a web domain and publish his own findings directly, which he did without setting the site live. It scared him to do so, but he let the fear drive him. He thought that it might be good if his identity was discovered; then Asher would know that he hadn't bested him after all, that he wasn't able to do whatever he wanted all the time without repercussions. It was finally time for him to pay Asher back.

May 6, 2015
<TO>: h00drobbinh00d@gmail.com
<FROM>: customercare@websiteregistry.com

<SUBJECT>: Your Domain

Congratulations, EEEM

You have successfully registered the website CarterCrimes.com. To verify your email to begin using your new domain, please click here.

Your yearly subscription fee is $800.00. You are currently enrolled in autopay. To change this or to enter new billing information, please access your client dashboard.

Our customer care team is available to assist with any questions, so please do not hesitate to reach out.

CHAPTER 30

Tashia Carter

New York City, July 2015

The heat in New York was stifling as the weekend for William Carter Jr.'s birthday party approached. Tashia's thighs rubbed together uncomfortably as she hunted through photo libraries, some without air-conditioning, in the fresh July hell. She couldn't wait to get out of here. Tashia had mixed feelings about whether or not to ask Kennedy if she could bring Ernest as her plus-one. Technically, Tashia was a plus-one, and plus-ones don't bring plus-ones, but she was sure it was going to be an amazing weekend, and it wasn't like the Carter family couldn't handle extra head count.

She and Ernest had been spending a ton of time together over the last few months. There were frequent stays at each other's apartments, and she was starting to feel very comfortable with him. He was curious and engaged. He asked a lot of questions, which was a refreshing and different experience from other men that she had encountered. He had taken a genuine interest in her project, carefully examining old photographs and speaking about his own time at Princeton with an openness that she found refreshing. From what she gathered, he'd had it tough there. He hadn't gone to a high school like hers, so he was somewhat unprepared for the levels of insulation around socializing that would be difficult to penetrate as an outsider. He'd felt slapped with the label of intruder, and she could relate to that. She found that he was still hardened by this experience, even after spending so much time in Ghana trying to reclaim a sense of identity.

She, too, discussed with him the awkwardness she felt at Dalton, how Kennedy was her first rich friend, and the way that she marveled at her life at first. "So, the first time that I went to Kennedy's house, she let me use her personal driver to get home. And I don't mean her family's driver; I mean her personal one. All of the Carters have their own personal drivers and cars," she said to Ernest early into their courtship at his apartment after he'd made her dinner.

"That is so—" he said.

"I know," Tashia interrupted with a shrug. "But it is what it is."

"So what did you think about that?" Ernest asked neutrally.

"Well, I was a kid. I thought it was weird and cool at the same time. But it wasn't until later that I found out why exactly they all had cars," Tashia said with another shrug.

"Security, or is it just because they have money to burn?" Ernest questioned with a smirk.

Tashia laughed. "Surprisingly, no. So listen to this: Everyone in the family had personal drivers and security details because of an incident that happened when Kennedy was really little. Her dad had just bought his first Rolls-Royce, and he was driving the family around when he got a flat tire. I mean, you know how dads are: they always want to show they can do something or whatever. So he goes to change the tire himself in the street, and there he is—sleeves rolled up and everything—when here come two of New York's finest. They immediately ask for identification and whatnot, and when he tells them that the Rolls-Royce is his car, Kennedy and her brother and her mom have to watch as the cops shine a flashlight in his eyes and ask for proof."

"Well, that happens to us all, I guess," Ernest said, betraying no emotion either way.

"Her dad got so mad, apparently. I think Kennedy is probably going to drop this story in her video," Tashia said, getting more animated. She noticed that Ernest wasn't reacting to this recounting in the same good-natured way that he usually listened to her stories. He seemed less than amused, so she upped the theatricality. She accessed a deep voice to mimic William Carter Jr.

"You know how he talks. He would have a British accent if he could. He goes, 'My taxes are paying for them to be this stupid!' He was furious that the cops dared to question that his hard-earned money could afford him a Rolls-Royce. So then after that, he decided that driving himself was communicating that he was common, that he was low-class. Driving himself made him too accessible and vulnerable. So now, every Carter has a driver."

Ernest didn't seem remotely amused. "Yeah, well," he finally said, "that's a lot of gas."

"Oh, come on." Tashia reached out and shook the top of his hand across the table. "That was supposed to be a silly story. I was just trying to tell you that I felt like an alien too."

Ernest maneuvered his hand on top and squeezed hers back. "No, I get it. I think it's just hard for me to imagine that much money."

"It's hard for me too," Tashia said. "And weird, which is really why the only thing you can do is laugh."

"Maybe not the *only* thing. How do Kennedy and her brother deal with it?" Ernest asked.

Tashia considered his question. "Differently. Kennedy doesn't really know when she's being an alien because she tries really hard, but every so often she gets exposed—like she didn't really know how to act in an airport for a long time because they always flew private. One time, in high school, I took her to a public pool in the Bronx, and she asked me who everyone else was because she thought they all had to be there for a party. She hadn't ever been to a community pool before. And Asher is a little less . . . aware. He's aware of himself, I guess, but he doesn't really think too hard about other people."

At this, Tashia could feel the mood shift, and she let Ernest change the subject and steer the conversation for the rest of the meal. It was hard to explain Kennedy to other people, and even though she recognized how ridiculous her life was, she also felt a responsibility to protect her. She was glad that she had gone with the car story and not a description of their apartment, or their Vineyard house, or the Aspen one, or the boats, or the art, including a Koons dog and something from the Ming dynasty that Kennedy and Asher also smashed by accident.

She was aware that many things about the Carters would be off-putting to people, and she'd heard them all. Some opinions were even legitimate critiques; like Ernest had said, it was a lot of gas. The excess was not necessarily something that she agreed with, but she also couldn't lie: her friendship with Kennedy had a way of demonstrating to her that life could be a lot easier. She did often have to fight the urge to push back or object if Kennedy parroted absurd things from her father, like a ventriloquist's dummy from another time. For example, William Carter Jr.'s feelings about racism wouldn't be something that she could share with Ernest.

Kennedy had expressed to Tashia that her father's opinion on racism was that it was an inevitable reality but not something that required too much devotion or energy. William wanted his children to be people first, not just Black people, because that was reductive and unfair. Kennedy had paraphrased her father's words to Tashia: *There is no use in trying to convince people who are determined to find fault with you over something you cannot control, and this goes both ways. You can't live for other people. Sometimes you have to choose the* me *over the* we. *There will be Black people who will want you to be a certain way. There will be white people who will want you to be a certain way. None of that matters. The only thing that matters and is useful is how you are able to process information that you have learned and how you are able to move forward in life.* She had not understood it when Kennedy presented it originally, and it was not something she wanted Ernest to know.

Tashia felt relief that she stopped sharing about the Carters that night at family chauffeurs without wading into systemic inequality. Kennedy said that her father resented how much his race was paraded in public, as if he also had another responsibility to martyr himself for his community, and she didn't want to have to do that either. This made Tashia cringe. For her, being Black was not like a T-shirt that she could put on or take off. It was an all-the-time thing, and she knew that it was for the Carters as well. But still, she found it very strange that they behaved as if Blackness was a temporary condition.

If ever Tashia broached this subject, Kennedy would imitate her father and say, "White people want to make us feel inferior because we are Black, and Black people want us to be a certain way to represent them, but it's all a fallacy. And as long as I know that, it can't hurt me."

At first, this was a big source of tension between them, with Tashia thinking that Kennedy thought herself exceptional. But over many conversations, over many years, Tashia saw how much pain it caused Kennedy to be so constantly judged, and she understood that it was easier for her to disengage with external perspectives and magnify a voice that she felt was stronger. To Kennedy, her father was larger than life. He wasn't an abstraction. He was real, but it was as if he were a living monument, and Tashia saw it in real time. This was not something that she could ever hope that Ernest would accept. For the most part, they didn't have to talk about the Carters. She didn't love to keep things from Ernest, but occasionally her friendship with Kennedy required keeping some secrets. The main thing that she couldn't tell Ernest was that being around the Carters was electrifying. Her friendship with Kennedy allowed her to inhabit a covert, exclusive world. There was the regular world, where she lived her everyday life filled with lines, waiting, stress, drama, and uncertainty. Then there was Kennedy's world, where everything was perfectly coordinated and private. They didn't wait. They didn't search or stress. They didn't even have to ask for anything, and yet things came, and it all felt like magic. This was embarrassing to admit, because obviously when she was with Kennedy, she was on borrowed time, but it was part of the reason why she would never give up her friendship with her, no matter what.

The air-conditioning hummed as Tashia debated with herself whether or not to text Kennedy about bringing Ernest to the party. Tashia was scrolling on her phone, waiting to find the right words, but it was dying. Ernest had already passed out, as he usually did well before her, and so she crept out of bed in search of her charger. On the way, she decided she should text Kennedy and ask if she could bring him to the Vineyard. He would have fun, and it would be nice for them to be together, but she thought that it might be strange to ask if they could both stay at Watcha Cove. She grabbed Ernest's laptop to quickly research motels on the Vineyard to price out if they could afford a weekend trip. She lifted the cover on Ernest's silver MacBook, which he always left on, and frowned when she looked at the open window. It seemed to be a website dedicated to exposing the Carter Corporation. A website owned by Ernest.

She began to shake as she read, her left hand covering her mouth as her right used the track pad to scroll. It appeared as if Ernest was behind a website responsible for publishing an investigation into her best friend's family. She gasped when she got to Kofi's name. At the top left corner of the webpage, there was a timestamp indicating when it had been published. These findings were published in May. At the bottom of a page was a web counter for traffic, and it recorded a pathetic thirty-four page views, which helped her breathe an exhale of relief. Even though few people had seen it, it did not make the duplicity of what Ernest was attempting to carry out any less unnerving. She glanced at the bed to check that he was still asleep and with a shaky hand set the page to private to make sure that no one else could see what she'd discovered before she could tell Kennedy what was going on.

Her eyes caught a direct quote from William Carter Jr. that he had, to Tashia's knowledge, only said to a very specific closed audience years before: "The key to a successful business is figuring out how to make a problem into a profit." It was something he had said to Kennedy's fifth-grade class, immortalized on video, taken by a camcorder but otherwise undocumented. The short clip, which Kennedy had sent to Tashia as a potential for the tribute video, featured dozens of glassy-eyed children listening to this man detail how he made millions and then billions. On that same day, he also said, "Everything is debt, and you need money to convince people they can lend you money." The latter was likely going to end up on the cutting room floor, but the former was something Kennedy was considering adding to her video.

Reading this, Tashia realized that Ernest had been mining her relationship with Kennedy for information about the Carters, but she just didn't know why. Why anyone would spend their time on something this extensive, this involved, this deceitful was beyond her scope of comprehension.

After the quote was an editorial note from Ernest, highlighting how William Carter Jr. was evading criticism about how Black billionaires and millionaires replicated a toxic form of capitalism that simply subjugated people in the exact same ways that Black people had already been subjugated for centuries. Ernest wrote, Carter is trying to rationalize in a way that would protect him from those who wish to criticize his lifestyle, because at the end of the day, he feels justified in having pride in his success, in his fortune. He wants to create conditions where he should not have to hide or shrink to make anyone else comfortable, and at the same time, he wants to make it clear that this world of wealth is his to inhabit. He wants to build a dynasty that would transcend generations, and this can only be done if he denies his own humanity.

Tashia turned down the brightness on the screen and tilted it downward so that she could keep reading. She continued to scroll, holding her breath the whole time. She arrived at the recounting of Esi's story. She brought the laptop right under her nose to see the close-up photo of Esi's teenage brother's arm and saw that his injury was not the only one that the Carter Corporation was responsible for. Her conscience was in crisis. This was horrible, and if it was any other corporation, she would want to see everyone on trial. She knew that what Ernest wrote was true, but the way that he had sourced this information was so dishonest, and at her expense. She didn't know what his objective in publishing any of this was, but she also knew that she did not have time to ask. When she had read the whole page, she closed the computer and sat in the dark for a long time.

She looked over at Ernest, who remained asleep, and was hit with a wave of revulsion. He had sat with her tonight and gotten more information about the Carters that he would no doubt add to his page in the near future. He had eavesdropped on her private conversations, used them for his own purposes, and for what? It seemed like he was just building a personal hate blog.

From the time they met, Tashia had appreciated his willingness to open himself up and discuss emotions with her, and she felt between them a growing sense of intimacy that she hoped would become permanent. She now realized that was over. Her feelings about Ernest aside, she knew she had to warn Kennedy. With her phone actually dead now, she packed up the remainder of her things and snuck out of the apartment. She was going to drive up to the Vineyard in daylight. This was something she needed to tell her friend in person.

Her rental car, a silver Toyota Camry, cruised up the Merritt Parkway. When she was halfway through Connecticut, she hit traffic, which was not surprising for a Friday in the summer. She switched her radio from the XM station playing R & B to the traffic news, and that's when she heard the announcer say, "Shelter in place orders have been issued for coastal communities in Massachusetts and Rhode Island. Heavy rain and hurricane-force winds are expected for the next twelve hours. Reports from Martha's Vineyard say that international real estate mogul William Carter Jr. has died."

Tashia briefly swerved off the road but quickly regained control of the car as the vehicles in the next lane and behind her laid on their horns as evidence of their disapproval. What did they mean, *died*? She started hyperventilating and looked at the road signs, searching for the next rest stop. She gripped the wheel tightly and laser focused her eyes on making it the next two miles before pulling off into the gas station parking lot. She shifted the car into park and reached with a shaky hand to retrieve her phone from her purse.

She had been on the road for three hours now and had one missed call and three texts from Ernest, which she ignored. She opened up her recent call log and pressed Kennedy's name. The phone rang six times and then went to voicemail. She called again. No answer. Her heart had still not returned to a normal pace. She tried Kennedy again. Still nothing. She opened a browser on her phone and went to the first news outlet she could think of, and that was the *New York Times*, and there, on the home page, was confirmation of the report that she heard on the radio: William Carter Jr. was dead. She knew she had to get up to Watcha Cove right away.

CHAPTER 31

Kennedy Carter

Watcha Cove, July 2015

Kennedy watched the ringer on her phone go off and silenced it. She saw that Tashia had called her three times in a row, probably because she had seen the news, but she couldn't talk right now. They were still meeting with Jermaine.

Jacqueline was speaking as Kennedy debated whether or not to turn her phone totally off. "If information gets out, bad information, what are the potential consequences?" Jacqueline asked. Kennedy snapped to attention.

"Well, it depends how bad, of course," Jermaine said with a sad smile. "William was a pretty buttoned-up guy, pretty aboveboard on everything. I mean, there might be some unorthodox business practices here and there, but that's run-of-the-mill rich-guy stuff. There's always been people who think they are going to expose or take down the big business interests, but they are mostly internet wackos. Nothing that we aren't already prepared for. We aren't going to uncover anything personally scandalous, I'd imagine, but if anything criminal comes up, specifically, then we are talking about an end to life as you know it."

"What does that mean?" Asher demanded.

"Well, if there was anything illegal, it would lead to an investigation. In the meantime, your assets or any assets acquired with money that was potentially used to commit a crime would be frozen, seized. You'd be . . ."

"We'd be poor?" Asher shouted, voice rising in distress.

"You'd certainly be unable to access your money and your homes, cars, and art. Anything of value acquired with any illegal funds would be repossessed," Jermaine said.

Jacqueline held the bottle of Kentucky bourbon that Asher had requested and reclined in the chair she was sitting in. She smiled a twisted smile that made Kennedy uneasy.

"Someone's been after William," Jacqueline said. Everyone turned back to look at her. "It's been going on for at least a year. Someone's been poking around the business." She took a sip straight from the bottle, but Kennedy was the one who gulped.

"Kennedy, I swear to God," Asher said, shaking his head.

Kennedy was crying now and everyone in the room was uncomfortable. "Mom, it was me," Kennedy said in a whisper.

"Jermaine, can we have a minute? I think the family needs a second," Jacqueline said. The blood was rushing in Kennedy's ears, and everything sounded far away. She was coming to the realization that maybe Asher was right, that her little film project on their father did have something to do with his death. But even worse than that was the thought that her actions had put their entire family and their future at risk. Kennedy raced over to the nearest trash can in the room. She felt the brass cool against her fingers before she threw up, her sobs and the alcohol helping to heave out whatever was left of the junky snacks she had been eating.

"What did you do?" Asher growled at her, feral and accusatory.

"No—nothing," Kennedy stammered, still huddled over the tiny trash can.

"That's vintage, dear," her mother said gently, coming over to wrestle the vessel from her grip. "It's a Fornasetti."

Kennedy released it and leaned against the desk. "It's been me. I was working on that thing you asked me to do, Mom, but I just wanted to make it interesting, to say something real. It was on the company, and Dad, and how he became this incredible success, and I was doing that, but then so many weird things kept coming up. Like, I found this photo of Dad and this man named Kofi, and then I found out that the company had been paying this woman who was a housekeeper a lot of money, like, *a lot* over a lot of years, and I—" Kennedy stammered through her confession, beads of sweat forming at her temple.

"You found Gifty?" her mother interjected incredulously.

"Yeah, I—wait, how did you know? You know about Gifty?" Kennedy asked, dumbstruck.

Jacqueline put a finger to her lips. She crept over to the door, opened it, and stuck her head out to see if anyone was listening. The hallway was empty, but she still motioned for Asher and Kennedy to be quiet.

"Let's take this back upstairs," she said.

Asher and Kennedy dutifully followed, confused but willing. Asher's demeanor was frosty, and Kennedy slunk away from him. It had already been such a weird day.

Jacqueline ushered them, the remaining living Carters, into the primary bathroom, the last place William had been alive. She turned the shower on full blast, and the packed punch of all seventeen jets working together made the sound of a waterfall. She also turned on both sinks and the faucet of the bathtub. She closed the door.

"Go on," she said to Kennedy.

Kennedy and Asher exchanged a puzzled look, but Kennedy pressed on.

"So yeah, Gifty, she's this woman who lives in Ghana, and she's a housekeeper, and Dad, well, the company has paid her, like, millions of dollars since it was founded. Millions. It just seemed so weird. So I called her, and her daughter said she couldn't say much about why, and then she told me to look into Kofi Asare. And so I did, and Kofi was a guy who used to live with Dad, and he died, and something just seemed so weird, and I don't really know what is going on. I was trying to think of how to just explain more about Dad and everything. I didn't think it would get like this." Kennedy rushed all this out, speaking so fast and frantic, like saying it out loud was putting the answer within reach.

"Are you hearing this?" Asher said, looking at his mother for assistance.

Jacqueline was staring back at Kennedy with a look that was a mixture of admiration and disgust. Her eyes seemed to be saying at the same time, *How brilliant, how hideous.*

"And also, there's a lot of evidence that the company does kind of horrible things to people, and I don't know. Are we going to lose everything?" Kennedy finished, sniffling again.

Jacqueline took a breath. "Well, I think that's up to you. First, of course your father found out about the video you were making. He was too busy to stop you, it seems, but he was aware that you were snooping, so to speak. I think that someone else was conducting an investigation of their own, and I don't know who that was. There's something that you should know about your father that you can never repeat to anyone for any reason, ever." Jacqueline, suddenly very sober, looked between her two children for a verbal confirmation, like a flight attendant making sure that the person in an exit row could perform the specific duties. Not that they ever flew commercial, but she'd seen it happen.

Kennedy and Asher both fell quiet, the sound of the rushing water and the hurricane outside competing to make the world's most dramatic ambient noise.

"Your father was paying Gifty. She was blackmailing him, so to speak," Jacqueline said plainly.

Kennedy's breath caught. She was so close to destroying their entire lives. Had she immortalized this in a film, everyone would have seen it.

"What for?" Asher asked shaking his head.

"Well, it's complicated. When your father was in college, he had a roommate, Kofi. Kofi was the one who was responsible for the signature product that the Carter Corporation makes. He was an architecture student from Ghana, and he hoped to make something meaningful in his home country. They were partners, but they disagreed about how to get the company started. One night, your father and Kofi had an argument, and in a terrible accident—yes, I am sure it was an accident—Kofi died. The circumstances around his death would have implicated your father, and so your father faked Kofi's suicide. He's not a killer, but yes, that's still a crime. And Gifty knew, and so your father paid Gifty, which, yes, technically, is also a crime."

"Whoa," Asher responded.

"So now you know," Jacqueline replied.

So that explained the journal, the last entry that detailed that Kofi did not want to partner with Ross Financial. It did make her father look guilty of something. Kennedy didn't know what to say. This was a far worse conclusion than she was expecting, and it might have taken her years to come to it, if she ever did at all. She thought of her father lying several feet outside of this door, unable to speak for himself ever again. She was crying for the millionth time that day. She got up and walked to get herself a tissue.

"I'm so sorry. I never thought—I—" Kennedy started.

"You couldn't have known," her mother said to her. "It took me years to figure out—*years*. And even then, I didn't have all the pieces. I thought Kofi and your father might have been lovers."

Kennedy's eyes bulged.

"They weren't, but that might have been nice for him. Your father wasn't one for romantic love from any source," Jacqueline clarified.

Kennedy felt like she would be crushed by the speed and ferocity of her own thoughts. She was tempted to get into the running shower. So far, the crimes were obstruction of justice, hindering a police investigation, concealing or withholding evidence, bribery, and theft of intellectual property. Kennedy wondered if all of those were bad enough to freeze their assets. She zoned out, imagining a bank vault covered in ice. Even as she imagined this, though, she wondered which was worse: the fear of losing everything or the freedom of having nothing. She considered if she had the strength to survive. She looked at the shower with its multitude of jets and knew that she would be absolutely fine with just one. But then, as she looked at the stricken faces of her mother and brother, she knew that they would not be.

"So we can never tell anyone about this," Asher said, waking her from her daydream. "Ever, Kennedy. And also, while we're being honest, Dad told me how the company runs, and I'm sure it's legal but it's not . . . great, and I don't think we want anyone finding out about that either." He crossed his arms over his chest.

"So what, are we like the Mob now? I mean what is this—organized crime?" Kennedy asked.

"Well, it's not very organized right now," Asher said pointedly.

"We're supposed to be better," she said dejectedly. She thought about the way that she had planned to frame her father for his birthday tribute: a pillar of the community, a person generous with his resources and experience, a humanitarian. But if she had made that video, she would be complicit. This family had made her into a liar.

"No one is better, Kennedy. I thought you knew that by now. No one who lives like this has clean hands," Asher said.

Kennedy suddenly felt like she'd aged ten years. She looked around the bathroom, spotless and stunning. They had everything. It was all so pristine and opulent but now stunk of rot. And was that true? Was everyone terrible? Her father would always say, "You deserve what you have the courage to take." There was a faint feeling that this was still not quite right. The taking was the problem. The fortunes built on weapons and pills and bodies were all tainted. Was there any good version of rich? Exploitation was exploitation, and if there was something criminal about the way that he made his money, weren't the Carters just as culpable? Was it even worse because they were Black? That didn't seem fair either. Why would they have a different moral responsibility because of their Blackness? They had so many more obstacles, and even with money, it was still hard. Kennedy couldn't imagine how hard it would be without money.

She had to get out of the bathroom. She was in danger of passing out. She ran to the door and threw it open. She sprinted past her dead father and down the hall to her own room. She didn't even turn back to look at the faces of her mother and brother. When she was shut inside, she hit play on the video that she had been making and watched the faces of preapproved relatives and friends spew corporate aphorisms about William Carter Jr. He was "the backbone of his company," "an inspiration," "he always did his best . . ." The quips now felt hollow and fraudulent, but on one hand, in one sense of reality, those things were true. He did represent good things to a lot of people, but as it turned out, to others, he was a constant source of pain and torment. He built himself up on the bones of anyone he could subjugate. He had done, more or less, the same thing to his own family.

Kennedy just wanted all this to disappear. The way that the new knowledge she'd just gained made her question her place in the world was uncomfortable. It was difficult and ugly. She wanted to turn away. She grabbed at every spare piece of paper, every note, every scrap of lies that she could find, and clutched the bounty in her arms.

She clicked on the electric fireplace in her room, and within seconds, it roared to life with flames. She began throwing all her papers, index cards, notes, documents, and photocopies into the fire. The inferno reflected in her irises as she torched it all. She felt a twisted relief watching it burn. She could breathe easier knowing that she no longer had to look at the polished simulation of the horrible truth. She grabbed her computer last and walked it back to her parents' suite, where Asher and Jacqueline were gaping at her from the bathroom. She must have looked as undone as she felt. She looked at her father, covered in that white sheet, limp and defenseless.

She wished that he could see her now. "This is for you," she wanted to say. But that wasn't totally true. It wasn't only for him. It was for her mom and her brother and also for her. It was to preserve their lives as they knew it. She wouldn't voluntarily become destitute. She wouldn't bring down what had been built for her. The damage was already done to everyone else—to Kofi, to Gifty, to her father, to the world. Knowing more wasn't going to fix any of that, but doing the right thing with the money might, and she certainly had a lot of it coming her way, so long as she never let anyone else know what she had just discovered. She was sweating now. She took her computer, still open, into the bathroom and dropped it into the full tub. Sparks went flying like a firework spectacular before the screen succumbed to total blackness. Jacqueline and Asher jumped back. They all knew what this meant.

"Thank you," Asher said to her, watching her laptop sink to the bottom of the tub. Kennedy felt her humanity recede. It slipped away beneath the surface like her computer and was replaced by her father's wishes. It gurgled one last struggling breath. She heard a voice that was not her own utter, "It's what Dad would have wanted."

The weight of what she had just buried settled on her.

An urgent buzzing on the intercom broke through the moment. "Miss Carter? Mrs. Carter? A Tashia Carter is here, and she said speaking with you is urgent."

Kennedy heard Tashia in the background, yelling loudly, "Yes, tell them it can't wait."

Kennedy frowned to herself and then looked apologetically at her brother and mother, another disruption, her fault. She quickly walked out of the bathroom and downstairs, where she found Tashia, storm swept and disheveled, sobbing. It registered for Kennedy that something terrible must have happened. Tashia's tears could not have been about her father.

"What happened?" Kennedy asked, rushing to her friend.

"I'm so, so, so sorry," Tashia blubbered. "I think I might have done something really bad."

CHAPTER 32

Asher Bennett Carter

Watcha Cove, July 2015

"By the way," Asher said, now alone with his mother, looking at the watery ruins of Kennedy's laptop sinking to the bottom of the tub. "I know."

"Know what?" Jacqueline asked him, a sense of genuine confusion playing on her soft features.

"I know that I'm not really, you know, *a Carter*," he said, putting air quotes around his own last name.

He watched the shock register on his mother's face, realizing that she was never planning on telling him for as long as he lived that his father wasn't technically his father.

He expected her to offer a groveling apology, but instead, all he got in response was, "How?"

Asher sighed and said, "I heard you and Dad talking a few months ago when I was home. I was a little drunk and a little high, so I thought that I might be confused, but then it kind of made sense. He said something about how I was not really like him."

Asher knew that he was summarizing poorly, but the repeat of what had actually been said was too painful to relive. He watched the color rise in her neck and cheeks, but his mother would never surrender to the indignity of an honest emotion.

Jacqueline looked Asher squarely in the eye. "Well, yes. That's right," she said after a long while. "Do you want to know what happened?"

Asher shrugged. He didn't want to come across as too eager. He was his mother's son, after all. "I'm assuming you had a good reason or whatever," he said.

"Something like that," Jacqueline replied evenly. "I was in my late twenties. I'd made a terrible mistake on a night when I'd received some bad news about an audition that didn't go well. I was desperate because I was getting old and it was seeming like acting was never going to happen for me. I went to a bar after, and I ran into someone who was a friend. We got a little tipsy and . . ."

Asher watched his mother's eyes glaze over dreamily as she broke eye contact and stared out the window. He didn't know where to look either, and so he did the same. They sat like that for a while until Asher made the decision to turn off the shower and tub. The only sound left was the steady drips from the faucets that were no longer running.

"I didn't think I would ever have to tell you," Jacqueline said to him. "Not that it mattered to your father; you were his son."

"So who was he?" Asher asked, uncomfortable at the mention of William Carter Jr., who was lying just in the other room.

Jacqueline pulled at a pill on the surface of the cashmere she was wearing. "Well, that's not important now. What matters is that you are a Carter. You are your father's son, and that's all anyone will ever know."

Asher did have questions, but as a Carter, he also realized this was the most information about it that he was going to get. He rose to his feet and went to leave the room. As he did, he heard his mother start to say something else, so he paused to turn back to her. "I chose the better life for you," she said. He knew that that was the truest thing she had ever said to him, and though he was not as misty-eyed as Kennedy, it touched him because in that act, the love was implied.

"I know," he said and then turned to leave. He went back to his own room, where he hadn't been for several hours, but saw it had been returned to being as clean and immaculate as if he had never been in it all. The staff was making sure that the newest household heads saw their value. The bed was made with tight militaristic precision, and it wrinkled slightly as he sat on it. He leaned his head back and must have fallen asleep, he wasn't sure for how long, but he awoke to an urgent knocking outside his door.

When he opened it, bleary-eyed and lugubrious, he was irritated to see his sister and her friend on the other side. "We need to talk," Kennedy said, pushing past Asher right into his room.

"Uh, hi to you too," he said sarcastically.

He then noticed Tashia's tearstained cheeks and red eyes seemed so out of place, not just in this house but as a reaction to, what, exactly? His father's death? That didn't make any sense.

"So first of all, it wasn't me," Kennedy said, rounding on him once she was inside the room.

"What are you even talking about?" Asher asked, still confused and rubbing the sleep out of his eyes from his nap.

Kennedy looked at Tashia. "Do you want to tell him? Or do you need me to?"

Tashia took a single deep, shaky breath and tugged at one of her burgundy-dyed locs. "I'll do it," she said. "Asher, do you remember someone from Princeton named Ernest Morris?"

Asher reached into the recesses of his mind. He did know exactly who Ernest Morris was, the same way he would know the type of car he first crashed (a Ferrari 458 Spider), but like the car, he had forgotten most details about Ernest as soon as he was ruined. He had recently heard his name when Viraj had run into him, but even then, the memory floated in and quickly receded. Tashia's saying it to him now transported him right back to a cold New Jersey evening when Ernest, flanked by his social justice warrior army, tried to make his personal misfortune Asher's problem.

"Hello?" Tashia said waving her hand slowly back and forth in front of Asher's glazed-over expression.

He shook his head quickly and answered her and Kennedy. "Yes, I know who that is," he said cautiously.

"Well, until yesterday, he was my boyfriend," Tashia said.

Asher fought not to pull a face. He remained neutral with great effort.

"And as it turns out, he was using me to get information on your family fed to me through my friendship with Kennedy, and he was the one conducting investigations that were triggering security alerts for your father," Tashia said quickly, and Kennedy nodded along, vindicated in her innocence.

"Wait, what?" Asher reached into his hair and tugged a little on the curls, trying to give himself a factory reset for his brain. "Why the hell would he be doing that?"

"I don't know for sure, but it seems like he had a kind of vendetta against you maybe, and also really rich people in general. He was, until pretty recently, working at a Carter Corporation–funded school in Ghana, and he said that he saw and heard some pretty fucked-up things."

Asher exchanged a look with Kennedy. He wanted to know what she had told Tashia but could not ask with Tashia in the room. He knew that everything in Ghana was not exactly perfect, but he couldn't imagine what could possibly inspire Ernest Morris to stalk his family. What happened at Princeton wasn't even that big of a deal. Why on earth would he be so obsessed?

"I'm lost," he said, truly confused.

"I came up here as soon as I figured it out. I don't think I was ever supposed to see what he was doing, but he was posting information on message boards anonymously about your father and his business, and he was running a blog with all his findings like some sort of independent reporter. I found the blog and disabled it from being live. He might know by now. I'm not sure. I haven't talked to him since I left his apartment in the middle of the night last night," Tashia said. She let out a tiny sniffle.

"Tell him what the blog said," Kennedy suggested gently in a quiet voice.

"Right. The blog said that your dad is—was—an international thug, basically, that he ran his business off of intimidation and bribery, and that he didn't care who he hurt in the process. He had a story in there about a sixteen-year-old kid who lost his arm working on a project. Also, he had a problem with the founding of the Carter Corporation because it was funded by two white men but fronted by a Black man who then exploited a local population and essentially stole their resources. That's what he said. He said if people wanted real answers, they should follow the money. But the worst part is that because Kennedy had found out about Kofi, he knew about that too. I don't know how much deeper his knowledge is, but I just feel so bad. I didn't know I couldn't trust him."

This certified weirdo had no right to do this, but a new, unfamiliar feeling had begun to replace the immediate rage that Asher felt while learning this information. He recognized it fleetingly as guilt. He had spent months blaming his sister for putting too much time and effort into her birthday video project, for asking too many questions, and this whole time there was an actual interloper attempting to expose, humiliate, and ruin his father. Kennedy was still partially to blame, he rationalized, but not totally, and since they'd both created this mess, they both had to fix it.

Asher cracked his knuckles. He was now finally ready for a physical fight with Ernest. "Where is this guy now?" he asked Tashia.

"What are you going to do?" she asked him back.

"Calm down," Kennedy said, her voice more confident than Asher was used to hearing. "I think we have to handle this ourselves. Mom is dealing with a lot right now, and she doesn't know any of this. I think we need to handle this on our own and . . . quietly."

Asher snorted. "Okay, so what would your plan be?"

Kennedy bit her lip and faltered at a response.

"Yeah, that's what I thought," Asher said. "Okay, listen: this loser obviously has a hard-on for me, so why don't you let me handle it. It sounds like it's me he wants, anyway."

"Well, what are you going to do?" Kennedy asked him.

"I'm going to handle it. What, you don't trust me?" he retorted.

"No!" Kennedy exclaimed.

"Today seems like a great day to start," he said ignoring her protest. Asher turned to Tashia. "I need to know everything that you know. And then, we're going to New York," he said.

Asher felt his posture harden as he listened to Tashia detail the timeline of her relationship with Ernest, and as she kept talking, he felt more and more energized. He began to realize what the source of his newfound personality was. It was power. He had just inherited billions, and with that came the responsibility that he had to protect that at all costs. More than that, he knew that he had to solidify his place in this family, to make himself legitimate even if genetics said that he was not. He finally understood his father in a way that he never had before, and he realized why his father acted the way he did. There were always people trying to come for them, but he had impressively shielded them for most of their lives. He had fortified the family to ensure its continuity, and now Asher had to do the same.

"Tashia, can you take us to him? The element of surprise is on our side. We can take the Gulfstream back," he said, a slight shiver running down his spine that he would not have to ask permission to do this.

Tashia pointed silently, confused, to the window, where the hurricane that had trapped them with his father's dead body in the first place was still raging outside. "Okay, not *now*," Asher conceded. Back in high school he got grounded, literally, for trying to charter the jet to see a camp friend of his out of state, but he liked the idea that he was in charge of when the plane took off and landed now, weather permitting.

"I think you should stay here," Asher said to Kennedy.

"I'm going," she said assertively.

He shrugged. "Suit yourself, but I don't think you have the . . ." He paused and searched for the right word. ". . . *disposition* for what this takes."

Kennedy set her jaw. "I do," she said. "I'm going."

The next morning, on the short flight back to New York, Tashia provided as much additional information as she could on Ernest, on his pressing financial situation—a trifecta of student debt, bad credit, and limited income. For the first time, maybe ever, Asher and Kennedy were seemingly united. They had a singular common enemy and were resolute in their mission that he had to be neutralized.

It was Asher's desire to cause him physical harm, naturally. It was Kennedy's to make sure that Ernest Morris was silenced with tact and discretion. By the time they landed in Teterboro, they had a plan.

This Nondisclosure Agreement (the "Agreement") is entered into between CARTER CORPORATION with its principal offices at 26 WALL STREET, 44TH FLOOR, NEW YORK NY, 10010 ("**Disclosing Party**") and ERNEST MORRIS located at 565 West 175th Street, Unit IA NEW YORK, NY 10033 ("**Receiving Party**") for the purpose of preventing the unauthorized disclosure of Confidential Information as defined below. The parties agree to enter into a confidential relationship with respect to the disclosure of certain proprietary and confidential information ("Confidential Information").

1. **Definition of Confidential Information.** For purposes of this Agreement, "Confidential Information" shall include all information or material that is disparaging, damaging, has or could have commercial value or other utility in the business in which Disclosing Party is engaged. If Confidential Information is in written form, the Disclosing Party shall label or stamp the materials with the word "Confidential" or some similar warning. If Confidential Information is transmitted orally, the Disclosing Party shall promptly provide a writing indicating that such oral communication constituted Confidential Information.

2. **Obligations of Receiving Party.** Receiving Party shall hold and maintain the Confidential Information in strictest confidence for the sole and exclusive benefit of the Disclosing Party. Receiving Party shall carefully restrict access to Confidential Information to employees, con-

tractors, and third parties as is reasonably required and shall require those persons to sign nondisclosure restrictions at least as protective as those in this Agreement. Receiving Party shall not, without the prior written approval of Disclosing Party, use for Receiving Party's own benefit, publish, copy, or otherwise disclose to others, or permit the use by others for their benefit or to the detriment of Disclosing Party, any Confidential Information. Receiving Party shall return to Disclosing Party any and all records, notes, and other written, printed, or tangible materials in its possession pertaining to Confidential Information immediately if Disclosing Party requests it in writing.

3. **Time Periods.** The nondisclosure provisions of this Agreement shall survive the termination of this Agreement and Receiving Party's duty to hold Confidential Information in confidence shall remain in effect in perpetuity.

4. **Relationships.** Nothing contained in this Agreement shall be deemed to constitute either party a partner, joint venturer, or employee of the other party for any purpose.

5. **Severability.** If a court finds any provision of this Agreement invalid or unenforceable, the remainder of this Agreement shall be interpreted so as to best affect the intent of the parties.

6. **Integration.** This Agreement expresses the complete understanding of the parties with respect to the subject matter and supersedes all prior proposals, agreements, representations, and understandings. This Agreement may not be amended except in writing signed by both parties.

7. **Waiver.** The failure to exercise any right provided in this Agreement shall not be a waiver of prior or subsequent rights.

This Agreement and each party's obligations shall be binding on the representatives, assigns, and successors of such party. Each party has signed this Agreement through its authorized representative.

DISCLOSING PARTY

Signature _____

Typed or Printed Name _____ Date: _____

RECEIVING PARTY

Signature _____

Typed or Printed Name Asher Bennett Carter, principal shareholder

Date: 07/31/2015

CHAPTER 33

Kennedy Carter

New York City, July 2015

Asher and Kennedy let Tashia knock on Ernest Morris's door. Since Tashia had come to Watcha Cove to tell her what had transpired between her and Ernest, Kennedy had experienced a strange kind of dissociation. On one hand, the cells in her body felt juiced up, powered by an unseen current of energy, and she felt galvanized in her new mission to protect her family. On the other, she considered that she now knew for sure what her family was responsible for in Ghana, and this was a totally foreign experience for her, making her feel disconnected from whom she thought she was. In a matter of hours, she'd been transformed into someone who was shattered by guilt but then forced to behave like someone with ice in her veins. Was this the truth of what it meant to be a Carter, to preserve their legacy?

That morning before they left, the dew still on the hydrangeas outside, Kennedy crept down to her father's office and used the desk key that she had found to unlock the safe where Kofi's journal sat. She fingered the leather and snuck the book back up to her room. She said a silent prayer of penance while she lit her fireplace for the second time in less than twelve hours and watched the journal burn. She had made her choice yesterday and again this morning, but for some reason, standing outside of Ernest's home with the city heat drumming on her skin, she was having second thoughts.

When Ernest opened the door to his humble basement-floor brownstone studio, she could see the shock on his face. She'd never met him before, but he had an expression that universally translated to "Oh shit." When he had noticed Asher, he visibly puffed up, bringing himself to his full height, squaring his bony shoulders and eventually flattening his thin body against the door to let all three Carters inside. They marched in quietly in a single file line and made a makeshift formation in what Kennedy might have called "a living room" to be polite. They'd achieved the element of surprise, that was for sure, and a certain smugness lingered over Asher as he took in their surroundings.

"So is this a setup?" Ernest asked, immediately on the defensive once everyone had gathered.

Asher barked out a harsh laugh, and Kennedy was startled but quickly regained her composure. "Just so you know, we have security outside and several people know where we are in case you are going to try anything stupid."

Ernest gave his own humorless laugh. "It's three against one, so perhaps I am the one in danger," he said.

Asher smiled at him. "I think by now you probably know that the truth is the story that people will believe, so let's just keep it civil."

Kennedy tried to catch her brother's eye, but he ignored her. He was coming in a bit hot, his attitude not to her liking. But really, should she have been surprised? Since she got no response from Asher, she used the next tense moments where no one spoke to take in the sheets in the windows that doubled as curtains, the mismatched furniture held together with electrical tape and good wishes. And that's when she knew that she and her brother would probably leave here with what they wanted.

It was Tashia who spoke first. "It's not a setup, but how this concludes is entirely up to you. I assume you know who these people are," she said, gesturing to Kennedy and Asher and raising her left eyebrow. "First of all, I know how you used me. I saw your little website. By now you probably saw that I disabled it from being live because we checked on the way here and saw that you reinstated it. Second of all, William Carter Jr. is dead now, so your little stunt is definitely disrespectful. And last, I just want to understand why you did this in the first place." Kennedy watched her friend wrestle to keep her emotions in check. She inched her body closer to Tashia and pressed her arm against hers in a show of support.

Kennedy saw that tiny beads of sweat had begun to form in a curious constellation across Ernest's hairline. She wanted this to be over. She was absorbing some of his nervousness. She wanted to tell him how much pain he had caused her. His actions had misdirected her brother's anger and her father's anxiety, and everyone thought that she was the one who'd done all this. Everything that had transpired in the last few months had been because of him, but even she had thought that she'd done it. And yet, she could admit that he did it for reasons that made sense. He must have thought of himself as a vigilante hero, like Batman perhaps, but Batman's whole thing was that he was wealthy, right?

Ernest smiled a twisted smile and pointed at Asher. "I think he knows why," he said. Tashia and Kennedy turned their attention to Asher, who was pulling out a plastic chair next to a tiny table so that he could sit down.

"Actually, I really don't," he said. "Why don't you tell everyone why so that we can all be on the same page." Asher rested his hands calmly on the table and then used them to brush off some imaginary dirt. Kennedy, not willing to be that petty, simply shifted her weight to stick out one hip and crossed her arms over her chest. She wanted to show solidarity but was weak in the area of intimidation.

"Your dad is," Ernest began, "or *was*, I guess, a criminal. He's not a hero to be celebrated. He's someone who is responsible for a lot of pain and suffering of our people, of people who look like us. Maybe that doesn't matter to you, but I thought that it mattered to you," he said, rounding on Tashia.

Kennedy wrapped her arms around herself. It mattered to her too. She wanted to interject but felt the words stay trapped behind her teeth. No one else had anything to say to this, so Ernest took the floor again. "I spent time in Accra. I saw what the Carter Corporation was responsible for. I talked to families directly affected by the greed of your family. It's a whole system that is designed to keep money flowing one way. People are poor, and they are suffering so that you can be rich, and I just wanted people to be aware of how deep and dark this well was. Trust me, I tried to get other people to care. I tried there. I tried here. I really tried, and your dad had every media outlet afraid, so I decided to handle it myself." Ernest set his chin.

Kennedy felt her heart clench and hold. Her thoughts began to swim, and she felt herself getting dizzy. The scale of this was becoming much bigger than this studio apartment. She wanted to flee, to run outside, get in the car, return to the tarmac, and board the jet to wherever she would not have to deal with this, but her feet remained rooted in place as she considered what Ernest had said. She swayed slightly. Asher gave her a quizzical look and she stared blankly back. The way that she heard this new information delivered so passionately by Ernest felt different. It felt less abstract, less distant. It felt real. She had entered this with the idea that there was something untoward about the way that the Carter Corporation had conducted business abroad, but she was now thinking about how many people must be affected.

"Okay, yes, Ernest. Bravo, you uncovered capitalism," Asher said, clapping his hands slowly. "Let's be real here. My father didn't create these issues. Some people would call that good business sense. It's not criminal."

Kennedy reached behind her brother to pinch his back. A warning. They'd agreed not to provoke Ernest. They came here to reason with him and resolve this matter quietly. She was relieved that with all Ernest was saying, so far he hadn't mentioned Kofi or Gifty, but if Ernest chose to use that information, that would be more difficult to prove.

"So basically," Asher continued, "you have a vendetta. And I think I know why. You're upset with me over some small disagreement we had in college, which is really lame, bro, I gotta say."

"It wasn't some small disagreement!" Ernest exclaimed, suddenly very animated. He stepped forward. Kennedy and Tashia backed up. "It's that you have no principles, no morals. You're ruled by selfishness and greed, and that started with your father."

"And what are you ruled by?" Tashia asked quietly. "Did your perfect morals and selfless behavior allow you to lie to me for months? To use me for this sick revenge project?"

Ernest seemed genuinely ashamed by this. He hung his head and avoided eye contact with Tashia. "It was for the greater good," he mumbled, his eyes still averted.

Tashia's exhale flared through her nostrils, but she just nodded. "So how much good did you do?" she asked.

Ernest let his shoulders sag.

"Okay, look, Ernest, we're just going to cut to the chase. I don't really love the smell in here, so I don't want to stay. What's it going to cost for this to go away?" Asher asked.

Kennedy cringed internally at how rough he was. She thought that someone like Ernest might require more massaging than Asher was willing to offer. Her objective was to deescalate, but she wanted to leave here with Ernest's promise to cease publication on his website, and so she stayed quiet.

"You think you can buy me off?" Ernest spat, staring at Tashia, Kennedy, and Asher all in turn.

"Well, Ernest, we know we can. We would just like to know how much that's going to cost us," Asher said, and for the second time that day, Kennedy recognized her father's voice.

Tashia stole a look at Kennedy. The trio waited patiently for Ernest Morris to name his price. He, of course, did not.

"Ernest," Asher cooed to him, "we know you're in obvious financial trouble. We know about your mother, and the bills, and the loans, and the fact that you work for minimum wage at a coffee shop, so you're basically unemployed. We know. Just tell us a number, and you will never have to hear from us again."

"That's your problem," Ernest said. "You think everything is about money. It's not."

"But it is," Asher said. "Of course it is. Money doesn't really matter when you have a lot of it, but it matters a great deal when you don't have any. We can change your life in this room, so just let us, and then we'll be done with it."

"No. Do whatever you're going to do: send your lawyers, send your goons or whatever. I don't know exactly how you people work, but I have an idea. I don't care. I care about what's right," Ernest said.

Asher rolled his eyes. Kennedy reached out a hand behind Asher's shoulder and gave it a little squeeze, signaling for him to stand down. He shrugged her off.

Ernest shook his head. "I'm not like you. I know you don't get it, but I don't need money."

"Right, you're so much better," Tashia countered. "You're a good person because you don't care about money. Just give it a rest and give them a number. I don't want to be here anymore."

"Do you want to go?" Kennedy whispered only to Tashia. "It's okay if you do."

Tashia nodded slightly, and that was all Kennedy needed to see. She wanted to get out of there too. "Asher, I'll be right back. She needs some air," Kennedy said, guiding Tashia to the door by the elbow.

When they opened the door, Kennedy welcomed the sunshine on her face and questioned the health conditions that might come along with living in a basement.

"Sorry, I guess I just needed a minute," Tashia said before taking deep, hulking breaths.

Kennedy said, "It's okay. Me too. That was a lot. How are you feeling?"

"Confused. Mad. Betrayed. Like I will never trust anyone again," Tashia replied before asking, "How are you feeling?"

"Guilty," Kennedy said. They climbed the stairs to the main brownstone entrance and sat on the stoop. "Can I ask you something?" Kennedy posed to Tashia.

"Sure," Tashia said, inclining her face to the sun and resting her elbows on the stair above her.

"Do you think that covering all of this up makes me a bad person?" Kennedy asked, her eyes searching.

A group of kids across the street ran through the water of a released fire hydrant, its mist making a rainbow and stretching out time while it showered the block. Kennedy reached into her pocket and pulled out a pack of cigarettes. She held one in her teeth while she patted herself down for a lighter. Tashia snatched it from between her lips.

"Okay, yuck. You said you were working on quitting. And for the record, I think that every family has its stuff—secrets, lies, whatever you want to call it. I think that what you've got going on is probably a lot more than most people, but I don't really think it's a very simple answer. If you're asking whether or not I think protecting your parents and brother is a good idea, I would say that a lot of people would make that choice and not hesitate. But I also think when you know better, you have to do better, right?" Tashia said.

Kennedy sighed, a deep one that deflated her abdomen. "My dad smoked, you know. He wasn't great at being secretive about it. Every house we had had to have an outdoor space so he could smoke. He got really sophisticated air filtration systems installed, but he always went outside. I think it was because he was trying to keep it secret, but he did a really bad job. Like, really bad."

Tashia nodded. "That's great and all, and I hate to be the one to point this out to you, but he's not here anymore, so I'm not going to let you suck on these and die. Pick up meditation or something. You, unfortunately, know better, so you have to do better."

"What does doing better look like?" Kennedy asked.

"I mean, I don't know. Don't you have a director of philanthropy or whatever for that kind of thing? I don't know what to do with a billion dollars."

"It's eighteen billion," Kennedy said wistfully. An absurd number. A punch line in and of itself.

Tashia laughed. "Okay. I don't know what to do with eighteen billion dollars either."

"Ernest was right about a lot of things," Kennedy said, getting serious again.

"He can be right about a lot of things and still go about it wrong. That's why all of this is so complicated. It's not like he's squeaky-clean here. I hate that I didn't see it. I'm really sorry this happened to you."

Kennedy waved a dismissive hand. "Please. This isn't your fault at all. There's no way you could have known this would happen. Also, that's kind of how I feel about my dad. I knew that *something* felt weird, but I didn't know what it was, and now that I know, I'm not really sure what to do about it."

"You don't have to do anything right now, you know. He just died. You can give yourself some time," Tashia said.

"Yeah," Kennedy agreed. "But . . ." She let her voice trail off.

Tashia sat up and turned to face Kennedy. Their knees knocked together on the steps. Tashia grabbed Kennedy's hands and squeezed. "It's okay that you don't know how to handle this, you know. This is not a normal problem to have. Inheriting billions and then also finding out the money is tied to exploitation and pain? That's awful, Ken. I used to be so jealous of you. I used to want to go anywhere in the world, and eat fancy food, and have nice dresses, and all of those things that I thought went along with being rich. I used to think 'Wow, her life is just so easy,' and I wanted to know what it felt like. And then the closer we got, the more I got to see what it was like, and the more I noticed that while you had a lot . . . there was also so much that you didn't have. Your dad, both your parents, they withhold and withhold everything. And while I don't have any of that, I'm still perfectly okay, and I'm happy. I'm free. And what's what I want for you. I want you to just be free of all of this if that's what you want. I don't know what to say to make you feel better, but I do know that what went down in Accra or here wasn't your fault."

Kennedy smiled sadly. "It's not my fault, I know, but it's kind of up to me to fix it. Isn't it?"

Tashia looked into her eyes. "Well, you can try."

CHAPTER 34

Asher Bennett Carter

New York City, July 2015

Asher watched Tashia and Kennedy slink out of the apartment. Cowards. He knew that Kennedy didn't really have the stomach for this kind of thing, even if she was trying to prove that she did. It was just as well that she was gone. Now was his chance to finally prove that he was a Carter, once and for all. He stared at Ernest, waiting for a number. Ernest fell quiet again. Asher didn't know if he was thinking of a number or thinking of a way to tell him to get lost. He was prepared to wait.

"Is this what you wanted, Ernest? It's just you and me now," Asher said to fill the silence. Ernest's gaze was empty in return. Asher wondered if that meant he was giving in.

"You know, Ernest, this place you have is pretty shitty, but you know there's a worse place to be, and that's jail. I wasn't going to say anything, but we could put you there for any number of crimes: drug trafficking, illegal possession of firearms, kiddie porn. I mean, if you don't tell me a number, you could always pick an offense instead, and that can be arranged," Asher said slowly, deliberately. He didn't actually know if any of that was true, but it sounded good. Confidence was half the battle. He learned that when he won a regional squash tournament he had no business playing in when he was ten. Even if it wasn't true, he knew Ernest wasn't flush enough to sign up for a litigious conflict that would drag out for years.

"I knew it would come down to threats with you. It always does," Ernest said, shaking his head. He pulled out a mismatched plastic chair and sat across from Asher. They faced off.

"Yeah, well, you threatened us first. Let's just take a wager on who is prepared to make good on their threats, shall we?" Asher asked.

"I never threatened you," Ernest said.

"You threatened our way of life, and that's the same thing," Asher shot back.

Ernest's eyes filled with pity. He frowned.

"Okay, I have to know, what is it?" Asher asked.

"What is what?" Ernest replied.

"What is your obsession with me. Is it a crush? Like what's your *problem*?" Asher broke out the syllables in *problem* for emphasis.

"You think so highly of yourself, it's amazing," Ernest said.

Asher flashed a picture-perfect smile at Ernest. "You say that like it's a bad thing."

Ernest's face fell. He leaned back and crossed his arms over his chest. "You used me. First, I got the Carter Foundation Scholarship, and you and your dad used me as your poor poster boy to feel good about how charitable you are before you went to play some sultan in squash. Then you dismissed me every day that we were at Princeton together. I wanted to get you involved. I wanted your input. You never helped me with anything. It's not even about friendship, but it's about having integrity. You never said anything to your Ivy friends after they kicked my ass for no reason, did you? You never spoke up on my behalf to your squash buddies. You think of me as disposable because my bank account balance is low. And it's not even about that. It's really about how sick it is that all of this allows you to pretend like you're a good person, like you're better than some white billionaire because you guys *care*, or whatever." He was waving his fingers in mock quotation in

Asher's face. "That's pathetic! But then all of a sudden, I show you I am not as weak as you think I am, and here you are."

"So that's it. You wanna be friends, huh? You want access to the inner circle? You want acceptance into a club? Grow up. You're either born into this life or you fucking take it. But I have good news for you. If you want it so bad, it can be yours, right now. You can be in this club, and I have to say, it's pretty great. You won't have to live like this anymore. If that's what you want so bad, I'm telling you right now, you can see what it's like."

Ernest slammed his fist down on the table, and Asher shot to attention. "It's not about that!" he yelled. Asher was admittedly surprised by this outburst, and he decided to let Ernest talk.

"I'm sick to death of how entitled you are. You're a horrible person. Your father was a horrible person. You inflict pain and misery everywhere you go and don't even think twice about it. Have you ever thought about Black folks and how you contribute to inequity and the poverty cycle?" Ernest paused to take a breath, and Asher used that opportunity to swoop in and correct the record.

"I'm going to stop you right there. Of course we do. We volunteer at a food bank every Thanksgiving. Bet you didn't know that. You can't dunk on me over something like that. I do charity work," Asher said calmly, rehearsed, but he actually did believe that made a difference.

"I do know that because you also make sure that there's a camera present every time you do something 'nice' with your time or money. You are an idiot. You don't even deserve to be rich," Ernest said shaking his head, resigned.

"See, that's what *you* don't understand. It's not about being deserving," Asher said. "Everyone knew it wasn't about being deserving. People don't get rich because they deserve to. They get rich because they seize it." Even now, he knew Ernest didn't *deserve* the money, but he needed to get him to see that he should take it. The taking, that's what makes wealth.

"So what now, I agree to your hush money or you make my life a living hell, or worse?" Ernest said, seeming to finally be getting the picture.

"Or better. You take the money, and your life becomes better. You can leave this dump. You can afford to fuck off for a few months. Well, years, probably, looking at how you live. How much good do you think you could personally do with half a million dollars? You could probably get a lot done. Here or anywhere. You could start your own school. You could start your own publication. You could go anywhere you wanted for a while. You could be free. Or you could keep publishing your little blog, and we'll pay everyone involved five thousand dollars to recant their stories, and nothing will ever change." Asher crossed his arms.

Ernest was fixed, his body rigid. He was considering his options, surely, and had to know that a story that every major media outlet had declined to report on and a blog with less than five hundred hits wasn't worth all this trouble. His twisted principles aside, he was still broke, which Asher imagined was very uncomfortable. He dropped the NDA document on the table and waited. For several minutes, Ernest left it where it was and stared at it, but then, with a shaking hand, he reached for it. He leafed through the hefty document, and by the time he was done, large semicircular wet spots had formed on his T-shirt under his arms.

"I want eight hundred thousand," he said at last.

Asher fought the urge to smile. He respected him more for not accepting the first offer.

"Great, we can swing that," Asher said, not even bothering to counter. "Sign."

Ernest retreated the four steps to his kitchenette and pulled open a drawer to retrieve a pen. Asher noticed two mousetraps on the counter and immediately looked elsewhere. He needed to get out of there as soon as possible. Ernest signed and initialed all required pages. He handed over his laptop and all other material associated with any information that he found on the Carter Corporation. When Asher exited

Ernest's apartment, he ran into Kennedy and Tashia on the steps above. He was triumphantly clutching the laptop and signed NDA.

"What happened?" Kennedy asked him.

"He signed it. I think that's all you really need to know," Asher said.

They rose and followed Asher to the waiting black Escalade.

William Carter Jr.'s funeral was held the following week in New York. It was just as well attended as his birthday party would have been, probably even better. Asher and Kennedy flanked their mother, and both spoke about their father, only touching on the version of the man that everyone knew. They were recommitted to maintaining the mystique.

After the funeral, Asher briefly returned to Massachusetts for a meeting on the Harvard Business School campus. He'd requested bereavement leave to avoid sitting for any final exams, gave a generous nine-figure donation to the school in William Carter Jr.'s name, and suddenly he had a diploma. "It's what Dad would have wanted," he said to Kennedy on the phone a few weeks after it was official, parroting what she had said a few weeks prior. He didn't know which part of it their dad would have wanted more: the Harvard Business School diploma or the way he didn't have to get it like everyone else.

He had, in fact, taught them a lot in life. He might not have taught them how to ride a bike, or how to drive, or how to swim. He taught them things that were far more useful for their station, and Asher seemed to finally understand what it was all for. He'd taught them how to be rich.

Cast Biographies

Jacqueline Bennett Carter plays Lady Macbeth to make her triumphant return to theater after dedicating her life to raising her children, one currently enrolled at USC and the other a Harvard Business School graduate. Jacqueline hails from Elkin, Kentucky, but has called New York City home for over three decades. She was a former pageant queen and worked as an actress before she had her children. She received her degree from Columbia in theater arts. She rediscovered her love for acting after her husband's sudden death. She says her family is her inspiration.

CHAPTER 35

Jacqueline Bennett Carter

New York City, December 2015

After the funeral was over with, numbness set in for Jacqueline. Her children had evolved into very independent beings, which they confirmed to her when they recounted the way that an ex-classmate of Asher's had been responsible for the stress that William Carter Jr. was facing and how they had handled it on their own, without her. She was uninterested in the details. She now found herself with increasing amounts of spare time. Not that she was that closely involved with wifely and parenting duties to begin with, but certainly there was less to do now. Asher had graduated from Harvard Business School, and Kennedy was taking some time off from school and had moved back in with Jacqueline.

Jacqueline busied herself in the expected ways. She decorated and redecorated their homes. The main residence on Fifth Avenue was starting to look like a museum, overstuffed with priceless antiques, populated by useless artifacts that were more William's style anyway. In a major real estate coup years before, the Carters had secured a unit at 834 Fifth Avenue. The property was home to only twenty-five units, a blend of triplexes and duplexes that all had their own design signature, so no two apartments were alike. This in itself was a statement.

Jacqueline had worked closely with a design team customizing the space when they had first moved in, but now it was time to make it her own, and she was far less concerned about having to impress William's colleagues. Her tastes had developed considerably over the years, and she was proud, and so she took her time creating a new decor, selecting the art that she liked, the furniture that she thought was comfortable, and the color schemes that appealed most to her.

With William gone, Jacqueline found herself rethinking her relationships, including the strategic friendships he'd encouraged her to make with women and men who were better suited to advancing his business interests. Sure, they ended up enriching her life as well in some ways, but did they really have any common interests outside of their lust for status? And then there were the obligatory relationships she'd maintained for the sake of her children's lives, children who were now adults. Jacqueline was slowly realizing that it was time for her to call the shots on who she would associate with during her second-act years because now . . . well, she was free.

Kennedy was staying with Jacqueline in the Fifth Avenue apartment, and she had also spent time remaking her room into something more becoming of a woman in her twenties. Occasionally, they would have dinner together, which both of them genuinely wanted to do, the two women chattering away for hours about this movie, or that TV show, and which actor was at the top of their game, and which director was making interesting cinematic choices. Jacqueline was slightly inclined to try to connect with Asher as well, though she had to admit that she wouldn't be heartbroken if her son chose to live in a faraway place like London or Hong Kong. Jacqueline was not interested in becoming lost in a maternal fantasy. She saw so much greed and selfishness in her son, and after all her years with William and seeing how he'd died, such obsessions mattered increasingly little to her.

Some days after the funeral, Jacqueline sat in her home theater, complete with eight plush recliner chairs trained at a projector screen, watching Diana Ross in *Mahogany*. Jacqueline had felt Kennedy's presence before she saw her, and sure enough, Kennedy was hovering meekly in the doorway, just like when she was a girl. "Well, you might as well come in," Jacqueline called to her. Kennedy answered by tiptoeing into the room and taking the chair next to her mother. They watched the rest of the film in silence, each taking in the glamorous narrative about how much a Black woman must often give up to reach her dreams. When the film was over, Jacqueline used another remote to brighten the dimmed lights in the room. Kennedy squinted at the change.

Jacqueline stretched her arms over her head. Kennedy did the same. They laughed at their own accidental synchronicity.

"I love that movie," Kennedy said. "Good memories. You always used to watch it when I was a kid."

"You remember that?" Jacqueline said, touched and surprised.

Kennedy smiled. "Yeah, Mom. I remember."

They both fell quiet. It wasn't exactly a comfortable silence, but it wasn't painful either. That's how most things were in their home. Jacqueline regarded her daughter, the only real Carter heir, and tried to see if she could find William in there. Ironically, he was more present in Asher than anyone else.

"What are you looking at me like that for?" Kennedy asked with a nervous laugh.

They had been trying to talk more, to bond. Jacqueline smiled. "I'm looking for your dad, actually," she said.

Kennedy perked up. "What about him?" she asked.

"I'm just looking for signs of him. What of him you got. That's all," she said.

"I'm not really sure I got any parts," Kennedy said, looking at the credits rolling on the screen.

"Oh, you definitely did," Jacqueline replied. "The thing about your dad was that he worked so hard. He was so smart and driven, and nothing could stop him. That's you, though your tenacity serves your art." With that, Jacqueline gestured to the home theater screen.

Kennedy nodded. This much she must have known.

"But at the same time, I think he really struggled," Jacqueline continued. "It was hard for him to have his own father working at his fancy boarding school. I told you that. All those kids always being little shits. I think he felt really embarrassed and judged. You know how it is to be a young kid."

"I know," Kennedy said.

"And I think that embarrassment made him sad. I think he wanted to never have you feel that. He didn't want to feel that anymore himself, and he just—he ran from it his whole life. It's funny, he didn't want to become his father, but from what I learned about your grandfather, maybe that wasn't such a bad thing to be."

"I didn't want to be like Dad either," Kennedy said in a small voice.

Jacqueline did a double take. She raised her eyebrows. "Oh?" she asked, waiting for Kennedy to elaborate.

"I tried to make things right. I know I can't fix everything, but I couldn't stop thinking about what Ernest had said to us about the business in Ghana. I made the request to explore a suspension of the insurance policies in the Accra residences, and I went back to visit Ernest after that meeting with Asher and gave him money to provide funds to families harmed by accidents in the Carter Corporation's history. We made our money; there's no need to continue gouging people who have nothing. But I'm sure Dad would have considered that weak."

"That's not weak, Kennedy. It's very generous. I think maybe it's time we all start thinking more about what we want now that our boss is permanently retired," Jacqueline said, reaching out to pat her daughter's knee. "The way your father did things does not have to be the way that you do things. His ways were very old-school, and perhaps it's best they die with him."

Kennedy nodded, taking a deep breath as tears filled her eyes. She seemed satisfied with her confession, and it inspired Jacqueline to make a confession of her own.

"You know, I think I'm going to start acting again," she said to her daughter. "I've signed up to do community theater work in the East Village."

"You should!" Kennedy said, looking at her mother with a humongous smile. "Oh Mom, you'll be awesome. You've gotta let me film you."

Jacqueline nodded, and feeling especially generous toward her daughter, she said, "I made the mistake of not talking—I mean, really talking—to your father for a very long time. I let there be too many secrets between us, and I didn't allow you and Asher to have the freedom to choose who you wanted to be and what relationship you wanted to have with the Carter legacy. You need to be able to do what you want."

Kennedy's face registered surprise, and Jacqueline felt a nakedness that she had felt only when performing a role for the first time, when all the rehearsals and table reads and costume fittings were done, and all that was left was a trust that muscle memory would activate and everything would go according to plan. She felt a similar way letting go with Kennedy, and she wasn't apologizing for the past but was laying more groundwork for honesty. She granted her daughter the privilege of seeing her as she was, a flawed woman. She watched Kennedy shift from shock to understanding. It seemed like she was finally on her own path. She had a steely look in her eyes, decisive, a look Jacqueline had rarely seen in her too-sensitive daughter. A new type of Kennedy. William's tenacity indeed, finally expressed in his only biological child.

"I'm glad you're being honest with me," Kennedy finally said. "And I want to be honest with you too. I don't know how much of this 'job' I can do."

Only the right corner of Jacqueline's mouth lifted. She knew this already. She'd heard from Jermaine that in addition to trying to help Ernest, Kennedy was also forming a special in-house corporate unit to initiate far-reaching reforms in Carter Corporation policies, but she did not want day-to-day duties at the company. Jacqueline suspected that the family business MO of profit at all costs was about to change, that Kennedy would be far more concerned with making sure employees and tenants were treated as humanely as possible than securing another billion. Time would tell.

"So don't," Jacqueline said affirmatively.

"It's just that—" Kennedy paused. "Well, I'm not sure Asher is the best person to do it either. I mean, he's maybe more like Dad than me, and maybe that's not the best . . ." Kennedy's voice trailed off as she looked down, embarrassed.

"Well, since we are doing this truth thing, I won't lie to you," Jacqueline said. "I imagine that your brother will put up a huge fight if he sees that any of these new policies are going to affect the company's bottom line, and I mean this: I don't want you both headed for a nasty showdown. I want to stay out of it, but between you and me, that company could never make another dime and all of us would still be fine, maybe even better off." Jacqueline said this knowing that she would hold on to her newly found peace and freedom at all costs.

Kennedy smiled, and her eyes crinkled. "Wow, Mom, are you sure you want to do this acting thing for real? Can I hire you as a consultant instead?"

Jacqueline chuckled. "Ah, no thank you, darling. I am far too expensive, but I will give you something on the house: I'll keep an eye on Asher for you."

"Deal," Kennedy said gratefully and stuck out her hand for a shake.

Jacqueline didn't know what kind of leader Asher would turn out to be, and as hands-off as she wanted to remain, she also wanted to prevent the absolute corruption of what was left of her son. If Asher stepped too far out of line, she would most certainly bring up the matter of his genealogy and how that might be the last thing he'd want out there if he wanted to remain a public Carter. Jacqueline was sitting on the nuclear codes and was prepared to use them if she felt it might save him. She could play the game as well. William would be proud.

As she looked at Kennedy, she smiled, suddenly feeling energized. She had planned to turn in but instead cocked her head toward the screen. No time like the present to start something new, indeed.

"You know, I'm in the mood for another movie. Will you join me? Pick a genre," she said, handing her daughter the remote. "Really, whatever you want, Kennedy. You can choose."

ACKNOWLEDGMENTS

I can't thank everyone in my life enough for tolerating me during the excruciating process of writing this book. It was the hardest thing I have ever had to do, and I look forward to torturing you all when I write the next one *and* treating you to a lovely vacation when I get something made into a show.

Thank you to my agent, Jessica, who has really shown me what agenting is with this project. Thank you for your tireless work on my behalf.

Thank you to my editor, Laura, for believing in this book just as much as *Token Black Girl*. Thank you for talking me off a ledge more than once during this process. I appreciate everything you have done for me.

Thank you to Clarence for all your hard work on this book. Thank you for your guidance and help with distilling the story and keeping me focused and honest.

Thank you to Angela, Emma, Nicole, Rachel, and Robin for your very careful editing work and thoughtful suggestions. And I especially appreciate you doing math for me.

Thank you to Gabby, who had to hear about this book every week for the last two years. Thank you for your patience, ideas, and input. Thank you in advance for bringing this book to Andy Cohen in the Bravo Clubhouse.

Thank you to Mommy and Daddy, please note that this is a work of fiction and these characters are in no way, shape, or form based upon you. I hope you enjoy traveling with me for the book tour!

Thank you to Sue for being my art consultant and confidant. I am so inspired by your creativity and if you hate this cover, it is not my fault.

Thank you to Mercedes, the fastest reader I know. Thank you for manifesting with me, for all your good energy, and for your many years of friendship.

Thank you to Preetma, my official Tiger consultant. I will keep the rest of what you told me in the vault.

Thank you to Mateo. I could not have done this book without you. I know I made you my unofficial publishing mentor, but I am so grateful for your help and support. I look up to you in all aspects, and I can't thank you enough for how much you've helped me.

Thank you to all my New Orleans friends for allowing me to be antisocial, to blow off plans, and to be late because I was hearing dialogue from these characters while biking to dinner over the last year. I am very thankful for your support and understanding.

Thank you to Ryan, who did not dump me while I was writing this when he probably should have. Thank you for seeing me through the worst of this. Thank you for the love, the snacks, the flowers, the encouragement, and the cheese curds. I don't want to lure you into a false sense of completion, lest you think there won't be a repeat of this experience. The good news is, we only have to do this about fifteen more times.

ABOUT THE AUTHOR

Photo © 2021 Scarlet Raven

Danielle Prescod is the author of *Token Black Girl*, a fifteen-year veteran of the beauty and fashion industry, and a graduate of NYU's Gallatin School of Individualized Study. A lifelong fashion obsessive, she was most recently the style director of BET.com. With Chrissy Rutherford, Danielle cofounded 2BG Consulting, which aids fashion and beauty brands and influencers on their anti-racism journeys. She dedicates her time to researching how feminism and social justice intersect with pop culture. Recently, her work has appeared in *Porter* magazine, *Harper's BAZAAR*, *ELLE*, and *Marie Claire*. An avid reader and writer, Danielle also loves TikTok, the arts, staying active, and especially horseback riding. For more information, visit www.danielleprescod.com.